"When's the last time someone whispered love words to you, Ami?"

She stared at him. "We aren't talking about me."

"I am. When?" Jeff straightened against the desk and, arms folded, watched her through narrowed eyes.

She returned his gaze, her eyes going to his mouth. The wayward tingling she remembered each time she thought of him returned, and she swallowed hard.

"Well?" he asked. She shook her head.

He moved, covering the steps between them in seconds, and his hands spanned her slim waist. He pulled her against him, placing his mouth over hers. None too gently, he forced her lips apart, pressed her head back, playing havoc with her breath. He raised his head enough to look into her wide, shocked eyes, unaware of the feelings he aroused in her....

ABOUT THE AUTHOR

Zelma Orr had a most interesting career before
turning to writing full-time. She was a U.S.
Customs Officer for the Treasury Department
in her home state of Texas. Zelma loves to
travel, and keeps a diary of the places she has
been to use for story ideas in future books.

Books by Zelma Orr

HARLEQUIN AMERICAN ROMANCES
  7—MIRACLES TAKE LONGER
18—IN THE EYES OF LOVE
55—LOVE IS A FAIRY TALE

Love Is a Fairy Tale

ZELMA ORR

Harlequin Books

TORONTO • NEW YORK • LONDON
AMSTERDAM • PARIS • SYDNEY • HAMBURG
STOCKHOLM • ATHENS • TOKYO • MILAN

Published May 1984

First printing March 1984

ISBN 0-373-16055-0

Printed in Canada

Chapter One

She couldn't see the flaming rays of the setting sun behind the Franklin Mountains, but Ami knew it was there. It reflected in the tiny windows of the old adobe building across the street from her animal clinic, and she stared at the crimson-lined clouds lying on top of the dark rocks, the end of the Rocky Mountain chain in Texas. To her, it was a restful view and, tired as she was, she sat still, relaxing her body and mind at the same time. It was after normal office hours, and she had just finished operating on a small Yorkshire terrier, wanting to wait awhile to see how he came through the anesthesia before she went home. Wearily she pulled her stained smock off and threw it into the hamper.

"Tell them we're closed, Rio," she called when she heard the bell at the front of the clinic.

A moment later her young charge stood in the doorway. "Mr. Hilton wants to talk to you, Ami."

She looked around, startled, seeing the two men behind Rio. The man in front grinned. "I'm Steve Hilton, Miss Whitelake. This is Jeff Wagner, owner of Wagner Ranch."

Ami took the outstretched hand, looking into light blue eyes topped by sun-bleached blond hair. He was a bit over six feet tall for her to have to look up at him from her five feet eight inches of height.

"We should have called, since it's so late," he apologized.

"That's quite all right," she said, taking the hand extended by Jeff Wagner. He was taller than Steve Hilton, his dark gray eyes set in a deeply tanned face, and he had dark brown—almost black—hair. He smiled politely, showing even white teeth.

She walked behind her small metal desk and motioned them to the remaining two folding chairs that made up the furniture in her office. It had been several weeks since she answered an advertisement in the *Veterinarian's Association Gazette* for the position as veterinarian at Wagner Ranch in southeastern Arizona. In the Christmas rush she had forgotten about it until last week, when Steve Hilton, the foreman from Wagner's, called to see if she was still interested in the position. She had assured him she was, and he had promised to call later to arrange a time he could come to see her to discuss it.

Instead of calling, he showed up in person, bringing the owner of the ranch with him.

The foreman looked around the room and back at Ami. "Miss Whitelake," he began, "Jeff has been out of town a lot lately, and since he was home, we took the opportunity to come out to talk to you. I hope we haven't caught you at a bad time."

"I understand," she said, glancing at Jeff Wagner, who studied her with an almost angry expression on his face. She stiffened, and a nerve in her temple quivered as an unfamiliar wariness filled her, wondering if he blamed her for being called away from whatever duties he was bound to.

Steve Hilton went on. "Wagner Ranch is about seventy-five thousand acres, with several breed of cattle: Hereford, Brahma, Charolais; horses, of course, and a few sheep. Our vet covers all territories, and in all fairness, it's a big and lonely job, since you spend most of your time in the line camps, which, I must say, are not modern motels.'' He smiled at Ami and sent a look at Jeff before he looked back at her. "It will be rough on a woman.''

Ami expected hesitation over hiring a female for such a job as veterinarian at a big ranch would be, and was surprised they had gone this far. She had no intention of arguing the male point of view, but he wasn't going to get away with pushing her out of the picture before she had her say. He was going to have to tell her bluntly that he didn't think she was qualified before she would accept it.

"Any veterinary job is hard, whether it's filled by a male or a female, Mr. Hilton.'' Her voice was quietly determined. "If you prefer to have a man on this job, why are you here?''

Steve Hilton's eyes widened at her unexpected question, and Jeff Wagner straightened in his chair, which seemed too small for him. It was he who answered her, his voice just this side of cool.

"Your qualifications are as good as we've seen, Miss Whitelake. We merely want you to know the situation before you decide anything.''

Ami nodded and waited. Steve leaned forward. "We'd really like you to see the ranch, and then let's discuss it some more. We can determine from that if you'd be satisfied, and I believe seeing you in those surroundings would help our decision, too.''

It had to be some operation to warrant such precaution, Ami thought. "I think that would be a good idea,'' she said and stood up. "Have you had dinner?''

Steve answered. "Well, no, we were trying to catch you before you left work.''

"I've had a long day and I'm hungry.'' She grinned without apology, the dimple in her left cheek showing briefly. "I'm not much of a cook, but there are some excellent restaurants on this side of town. Give me a few minutes to change, and we'll check out one of them."

A few minutes later she emerged from another room at the back of the clinic, in clean jeans and shirt, and called Rio, introducing him to the two men. "You want anything to eat?" she asked him.

"A hamburger," he said.

Her smile at the young man was indulgent at the typical teenaged request for food. "We won't be long," she told him.

Over dinner Ami asked quesitons about the ranch. "What happened to your vet?"

"Hammett is still with us, but he'd like to retire. He has arthritis in his legs and isn't able to ride as much as he needs to. He'll be there to help out when there's too much for one person. We also have an excellent school in Tucson that we call on when we're short."

Ami was conscious of Jeff Wagner's dark eyes on her each time she asked or answered a question, as if judging her. She met his gaze without flinching, but her heart did a swift upturn for no accountable reason as his eyes went from hers to her mouth as she touched it with her napkin.

With difficulty she turned her mind away from the odd feeling and asked, "How long will you be in El Paso?"

We plan to head back tomorrow. The ranch is about six hours drive from here, and we want to stop in Las Cruces." Steve Hilton did most of the talking, but his boss was taking in all the conversation, his gray eyes seeming to bore deep into Ami's private thoughts. Strange stirrings began again in her chest, and she was unsure if they came from the man's constant attention or from her own failure to recognize the feelings.

Keeping her voice carefully level, she said, "Before you leave, I'd like you to meet Dr. North. I bought the clinic from him about two years ago, and he can advise you on my working habits and the operation I have here. It's very small compared to what you've described at the ranch."

"We'd like that." Steve glanced at his watch. "Are there motels nearby?"

"Yes. Right on the interstate."

When they left the restaurant, Ami pointed out two of the nicer ones to them. She told them good night as they dropped her at the office, and gave Rio his hamburger and french fries before going on to her apartment. She prowled restlessly. If they made the trip that far, perhaps she was being considered for the job, although it could be only a token visit so they could report to labor organizations and equal rights advocates that they had looked for a female but found her unqualified. She thought about it a few more minutes, shrugged, and went to bed.

Dr. North was puttering in his workshop behind his home when Wagner and Hilton paid an early morning visit to him. He eyed his visitors and grumbled. "I get somebody who knows how to handle my animals, and she goes looking for another job." The faded eyes twinkled at Ami, then he turned to the two men.

"Ami has one fault, gentlemen. Or maybe it isn't a fault. She has a much stronger preference for animals than for humans, possibly justified." He looked at Ami, leaning against the doorframe, her long body relaxed, a half-smile tilting her upper lip. "She'll make you a good employee; outstanding, as a matter of fact. I prefer to have her here, but—" He let the sentence dangle. They had discussed the job at Wagner's before she applied for it, and Dr. North encouraged her to answer the advertisement. As much as she loved animals and enjoyed working with them, he was sure she'd be an asset to the ranch owners.

Ami couldn't resist her next statement. "Doc, they

seem to have some doubts about hiring a female. Did you ever have any qualms about working with a woman veterinarian?''

Bushy white brows quirked upward for a quick glance at the two men, then his eyes went back to Ami. ''Certainly did.'' He shook his head and laughed out loud. ''I was scared to death, but my pioneering spirit won out and I've never been sorry.''

They talked about the widespread rabies on the border and the mild El Paso weather, then took their leave of Dr. North and returned to the clinic. Rio had already fed the animals and gone to school, leaving Ami's office door open to the bright sunlight.

''Do you have any family that would object to moving from El Paso to the Arizona wilderness, Ami?'' Steve asked. ''It's very different from living in the city.''

She smiled. ''No. Rio and Remus are all I have. I'm Rio's legal guardian, and Remus is an old rebuilt mongrel, not worth much, but all mine.'' She added, ''Both of them.''

Steve studied the tall girl in front of him. ''When could you come out to look over the ranch?''

Ami looked from Steve to Jeff Wagner, meeting a dark, almost unfriendly gaze that gave her a thorough once-over. Butterflies fluttered in her stomach, and she stiffened under his scrutiny as she turned back to the foreman.

''Anytime, really. I could be there early on any Monday and back here by Tuesday night, so I wouldn't have to be closed more than a couple of days. Dr. North will keep an eye on the office and Rio for me.''

Steve watched her for a moment, a thoughtful look in his eyes. Jeff's eyes narrowed as he listened to the exchange. ''How about next Monday? We'll have someone pick you up at the airport.''

She nodded her agreement. ''I'll call to let you know

the flight schedules before I leave.'' Good-byes said, the two men left her, and Ami watched the car as it turned the corner at the end of the next block, grinning to herself.

I'd love to be a fly on the roof of the car and listen to their conversation between here and their ranch, she thought. She shook her head. Or maybe she wouldn't, she amended, thinking of Jeff Wagner's distant expression and obvious misgivings about her ability to cope as a veterinarian on a big ranch. He talked very little, and perhaps that caused her curiosity about him. It had been a long time since she had been exposed to the strong silent type, or any type of male, for that matter.

Ami went about the chores that always needed doing at an animal clinic, her thoughts moving in a wide-ranging circle as she kept busy. Her mind was full of Jeff Wagner and Steve Hilton, and her thoughts scurried from past to present and back again.

There wasn't really anything to keep her in El Paso, should she get the job at Wagner's. She enjoyed the clinic, and Rio was happy in his school and with the friends he had made here in the lower valley on El Paso's east side. But they could adjust to living elsewhere. Dr. North urged her to move on to bigger and better things if she could, telling her she could always come back to El Paso if she wanted to.

"Any diversified experience will be to your benefit, Ami," he told her when they discussed her application to Wagner's. "I'll miss you and Rio, but you can come visit me anytime." Dr. North smiled at her, and she hugged him affectionately.

Two years ago, just out of graduate school for veterinarian training and running from a broken marriage, Ami had arrived in El Paso, looking for a suitable location for a small animal clinic. All she had left behind her was the man she thought would be her husband till the end of time. Losing him through no fault of her own, she had determined to pick up the pieces of her life, and in order to do that, she had left Laramie, Wyoming, where she had finished college, married and settled down, turning to a strange place where she could start over alone. From childhood she had been a loner, and that never bothered her.

Lon and Roma Whitelake were the only parents she had ever known, adopting her after she was abandoned by her birth mother in an alley back of a bar in Cody. Before she died the young unmarried woman managed to put the small girl in the alley where people passed at all hours, and lucky for Ami, it was Lon and Roma who passed first. They didn't stay on a reservation but lived with and worked for a rancher who helped them cut through red tape to adopt the tiny baby and keep her as their own, even though they were already old.

Roma was deaf, and she and Lon had developed their own system of sign language. Before she could speak any words of the English language, Ami could communicate with her adoptive mother through lightning-quick hand signs learned from the two people she loved dearly. Her playmates were the animals in the forests and high desert, and she sang in tune with the birds that flocked to the fields to feed. She was five when old Lon made her a guitar and taught her how to play it.

The old Indian couple loved her, raised her to enjoy life, and taught her to survive in an alien world few Indians near them cared to know. It wasn't easy for them, she realized in later years, and she knew she was a curiosity to her schoolmates, with her odd turquoise-colored eyes in a smoothly tanned face, capped by hair the color of wild hickory nuts she gathered from the forests she roamed as a child.

Ami was in her first year of college when a flu epidemic hit, and Lon and Roma died within days of each other. Hurt and lonely, Ami still knew they would never have had it any other way, neither wanting to

survive without the other. During her senior year she
met and dated Tim Stanton, transferring all her love to
him, and they were married after she was graduated.
Tim was already a successful coach with two Olympic
hopefuls on his track team. Deliriously happy and in
love with him, she settled down to make him happy,
not even following the vocation she had set her sights
on all the past years.

"Let's start our family now, honey," Tim said one
night as he held her. "Have at least two children before
we get too old to enjoy them."

Happily, she agreed, and when after a reasonable period of time she failed to get pregnant, she went to her
doctor. She still shivered at Tim's reaction to the doctor's verdict that she would never have children. He
couldn't visualize a healthy young female body failing
to produce the children he wanted, and her pleas for
adoption fell on deaf ears. Tim wanted his own flesh
and blood, not someone else's. After weeks of silent,
cold hostility, they were separated, and she was left
alone again to live with her failure as a wife. With nothing to settle in a divorce court, she gave him back his
name and took back the one given her by the old Indian couple she had loved as her own parents. In the
wild loneliness that followed the divorce she grieved
anew for the only family she had ever had.

Running from the hurt, she reached El Paso, looking
for a job or a small clinic she could manage on her own.
Dr. Joe North was the first veterinarian she visited.

He had eyed the girl sitting in front of him, tall with
odd-colored eyes, a few freckles scattered across the
tilted nose, lips turned up in a half-smile that never
seemed to leave her mouth, becoming a quick grin at
regular intervals, showing a small dimple in her left
cheek. Her shining dark hair, sun-streaked, was cut
short to frame her face.

"I'll tell you, Ami, I'm thinking about retiring. If

you'd care to work here with me, let me make up my mind, then if I decide to retire, you can have the clinic. If not, you'll have some experience behind you and can look around."

It was an unexpected offer, and she accepted unhesitatingly. A while later a near-fatal heart attack made Dr. North's decision for him, and she acquired the clinic as her own. The hard work helped heal the hurt inside of her, and as time passed she was able to think of Tim without pain, and she knew she was on the road to recovery that she had thought she'd never find.

The slam of the side door brought her back to the present, and she heard Rio talking to the animals as he made his way through the pens, knowing he would find her in the small office at the back of the clinic.

Ami smiled at him as he stopped in the doorway. The black eyes met hers squarely, and she knew he had been thinking about the new job all during the day.

When she had first applied for the veterinary job at the Wagner Ranch, Rio hadn't said much, perhaps because her own attitude had been one of only mild interest, believing as she did that there would be many applicants for the job a lot more qualified than she was—and men, at that.

"Are you going to take the job?" Rio's question interrupted her musings.

She took a deep breath, watching him as she spoke carefully. "I'll go out to Wagner's and see how the ranch is run, but I imagine they have several more people to see. I didn't ask, but a vet for a big outfit like theirs is never selected just from one interview. Besides that, I want to see for myself what goes on." When he didn't say any more, she continued. "Dr. North will look out for you and Remus for a couple of days while I'm gone."

"And if they decide to hire you, what then?" he persisted.

"Rio, I have about as much chance of getting that job as being elected president. Women are not encouraged to look for jobs that big in a man's world. Too bad you're not qualified—you'd have an excellent chance."

He eyed her uncertainly. "You're good. Why wouldn't they hire you?"

Rio was still innocent in the ways of the world, but he would have to learn that things didn't always happen as they should—or the way he had them figured out. In two years he had forgotten how it felt to be abandoned with little hope for the future; Ami had helped him forget.

"Women are supposed to stay at home and raise kids, Rio." Her statement uncovered a bad memory, and she hurried on. "Or go out and work at some low-paying job a man wouldn't have, then go home and take care of everything and everybody." She stopped, not interested in showing any bitterness to Rio. The world was confusing enough without her adding to it, she decided.

Rio dropped into the chair in front of her desk, staring out the window over her shoulder. He had matured in the two years they had been together, and a smile softened her features as she remembered their first encounter as though it had happened yesterday.

She had worked late that night and locked the door of the clinic behind her, careful to leave a night-light on for the animals.

She was hungry, and as she turned the corner to the area where the dusty Subaru Brat truck sat, she paused, listening. Distinct sounds came from the darkened spot. Her heart thumped as she made out a shadow bending near the wheel of the truck.

"What are you doing?" she asked.

The figure whirled. Ami saw a dark face, straight black hair over startled dark eyes, before the boy bolted. She went after him, her long legs covering

ground in a hurry. She gained on him, and the two
bodies hit the ground, rolling over and over with Ami
coming out on top, one knee in the boy's chest, the
other pinning his arm. He had hit harder than she had
and, breathless for a moment, didn't fight her.

"All right, amigo. Before I call the cops, what were
you doing?"

Sullen defiance answered her. She shoved her knee
into his chest. "I asked you a question. Answer me."

"I wanted the wheel covers."

"What for?"

"Vende."

She pressed her knee downward. "Speak English."

"I sell."

"How much would you get for them?"

The dark eyes closed as he waited a second to
answer.

"How much?" she demanded.

"Dollar. Dollar and a half."

The boy suddenly found himself free of the knee
pinning him as Ami looked down at him. "Get up."

He sat up but made no effort to stand.

"What's your name?"

"Rio."

"Rio what?"

He shrugged.

"You hungry?"

No answer.

"Come on and let's find something to eat. I'm
starved."

The look on Rio's face was as though she looked into
a mirror: scared, hungry, and lost—the way she had
been enough times to recognize desperation. Dr. North
would chew her out royally for what she was doing, but
she smiled, turning back toward the deli.

"Come on, Rio. I haven't got all night." She looked
back at him as he got up to follow.

She kept him. A check with local police and immigration officials disclosed only that he was a native-born United States citizen. A faded card he carried in a ragged wallet gave his name as Rio Lawson. Lawson? An odd name for a Mexican-American, but there the trail ended. She was informed by disinterested officials that there were many cases of lost children close to the southwestern borders, and her best bet was to turn him over to the welfare agencies experienced in dealing with that type of problem.

Dr. North thought she was out of her mind, but he helped her clear through all the red tape and legal jargon to have her appointed as Rio's legal guardian.

"You have to go to school and you have to work," Ami told him.

She was twenty-seven and he was fifteen, and sometimes he resented being told what to do by someone just enough older than he was to assert authority. They worked out their problems, and Ami considered him an outstanding investment, finding to her delight that he was intelligent with no problems, once they placed him in a grade with children of his age.

Her apartment was too small for both of them, so they redecorated a small room at the back of the clinic and furnished it in simple furniture he chose himself. That way he could be independent and still close enough for Ami to keep an eye on him.

Not long after Ami acquired Rio as her legal ward, they found an old dog near the clinic who had been hit by a car and left for dead. They dragged the animal into her small operating room and spent two hours rebuilding the bones.

"Will he live?" Rio asked, his big dark eyes wide with fright.

She shook her head. "Maybe not, but we tried." They nursed him back to health and they became an odd trio familiar to the neighborhood. She named him

Remus from her memory of Brer Rabbit and Brer Fox fairy-tale books, and Rio laughingly adopted him as his guard dog to share his room at the animal clinic.

"I'm hungry. Can we eat at Leo's?" Rio's voice startled her back into the present, and she smiled at the normal growing boy's request.

"Sure," she agreed. "Let's go." For the moment the question of the new job could rest.

Chapter Two

As the orange-and-silver Continental 727 circled over Tucson, Ami watched the desert coming up to meet them. Flying was a convenience she could well do without, she decided, never having reconciled herself to being seven miles above the earth with only space to support her. It seemed ridiculous to put people on the moon when she had a great desire to keep her feet on solid ground. Over one hundred people shared her flight, and she felt less uneasy as she looked at other passengers calmly waiting for the huge machine to land. It touched down on the runway with only a slight bump, and she breathed easily again.

It was early, the airport uncrowded. As she entered the long hallway from the plane exit, an announcement came over the loudspeaker: "Miss Whitelake, meet your party at the information booth."

Curious, she made her way to the counter, where several people were gathered.

"Miss Whitelake?" At the sound of her name, Ami turned to face a tall suntanned cowboy, Stetson in hand, silvery strands mixed in dark hair cut above the collar of a denim shirt. Levi jeans completed the well-recognized uniform of the working southwesterner.

"Yes."

"I'm Jasper Clayton from Wagner's." He grinned, white teeth slashing the darkness of his skin.

She smiled back at him. "How did you recognize me?"

"Steve told me you were young and tall, and I was gambling you were pretty. I won."

"I tried to tell Mr. Hilton I'd rent a car, but he wouldn't hear of it."

Jasper shook his head. "Takes too much time to drive that distance. This is easier on everybody." He led her to the baggage claim area and picked up the small overnight bag she indicated on the conveyor.

Feeling a slight uneasiness, Ami asked, "We're not driving?"

"No. Wagner's has its own plane, and I'm part-time pilot, part-time cowboy." He eyed her. "You afraid of flying?"

She shook her head. "Not exactly afraid, Mr. Clayton, but I'd rather keep my feet on solid ground. Or at least no higher than a eighteen-hand-span horse."

"Call me Jasper." His smile was sympathetic. "I'll try not to scare you."

The plane they approached was a sleek silver-and-green four-passenger Convair. He strapped her in, climbed into the pilot's seat, and talked into the radio. In moments they were taxiing to a takeoff position.

Ami closed her eyes, her head braced against the back of the seat. Almost before she let out her breath he was saying, "About twenty minutes now.

"That's Wagner's below," he said after a short time, pointing to his right.

The razorbacks of the rocky mountains below them rose in splendor, protecting the desert and valleys between. The perfect geometric design of the earth from the air surprised her, like a blueprint with perfectly lined squares and rectangles. She swallowed over the dryness in her throat as the plane began to drop, watching the ground rushing toward them. The wheels hit, and they bounced once, rolling smoothly to a stop.

"That wasn't too bad, eh?" Jasper reached for her and swung her to the ground.

Ami let her breath go. "Now that we're down safely, I must agree it's better than hours of driving."

Jasper's truck was parked near a small building at the end of the private landing strip, and as they drove toward the houses in the distance, Ami took in the passing landscape. Elevation at this point was almost a mile high, but mountains rose thousands of feet over them, many miles distant. As far as she could see was cultivated grazing land, a scattered herd of several breed of cattle much in evidence. She stared at strange-looking cattle she recognized as the Charolais, a breed without horns that she had read about but had never seen up close.

"Those cattle are experimental, aren't they?" she asked.

The man beside her nodded. "Jeff's had some a few years, and they've done well here. He's planning to start breeding them soon."

"Are they strong?"

"Exceptionally so." He grinned. "And expensive."

Ami studied Jasper's profile as he drove, thoroughly relaxed behind the wheel of the truck as he had been at the controls of the small plane. He didn't talk like the usual cowboy with a western drawl, but sounded more like a schoolteacher. He was quite good-looking, too. Her lips curved. *One of these days that characteristic might interest me,* she thought, *but then, he's probably married. I guess they're all married,* she amended her thoughts, and felt a small unidentified thrill as she thought of Jeff's dark gray eyes boring into her. She looked away from Jasper. Of course, they all had families.

They turned from the gravel road onto a lane that led toward a grove of cottonwood trees. As they got closer Ami saw the low building of adobe and cedar logs sprawled across the end of the lane and rambling back some distance. She fell in love with the simple architecture blending into the desert landscaping, with the purple mountains, miles away, forming a perfect backdrop for the setting.

She drew in her breath. "Beautiful."

Jasper followed her gaze and agreed. "Yes, it is." He pointed to her left. "The foreman's home is there. You remember Steve? And his wife, Janie. The veterinarian's house is just the other side. The bunkhouses are behind the big house, and the home corrals are beyond them."

He stopped the truck and climbed out to come around to her side. She was standing on the ground when he got there and found that, even with her lanky height, he was still six inches taller. Ami had always been self-conscious of her height because extra-tall men were not easy to find. Already she had met three men from Wagner's taller than she.

"I'll take you to meet the household first. You met Jeff, the boss. He has his daughter, Amanda, in Baltimore for tests." Jasper stood for a moment, gazing away from her. "She's six years old." He took a deep breath as if making a decision and looked down at her. "She's deaf." His eyes narrowed as though against pain.

Ami swung around to face him as the statement sunk in. She waited, but he didn't say anything more. "Is she completely deaf?" she asked finally.

He nodded. "Accident when she was two. Jeff has had her to every clinic and expert that he thought would help. Nothing. I think this is his last hope." He took a deep breath and added, "They'll be gone another week or two."

Ami was right about Jeff's being married, then, and in addition to the errant thoughts she had entertained about him, she felt sympathy for the family, remembering Roma. Roma had never asked for sympathy and managed without problems with her own set of hand languages, but a six-year-old child had a long way to go in a different world than Roma and Lon lived in.

There were more questions she would have liked to ask, but Jasper was walking toward a door on the long side porch. He opened the screen and stood aside as she entered. It was the kitchen—a huge sunny area that had to be the biggest working kitchen she had ever seen. Near the double sinks stood a dark-skinned woman of ample size who smiled at Ami, looking her over at the same time.

"Ami, this is Lily, our chief food ambassador. Her husband, Harris, is her assistant. They do the almost impossible job of feeding our hungry crew when they're in the local area. Lots of hungry mouths at Wagner's."

"How are you, Lily?" she asked.

"Fine, Miss Whitelake. You're too pretty to be a cow doctor."

Ami's eyes flashed to Jasper. "Your chief cook might become my favorite person."

Jasper laughed with her and led her on through the big house. "Hazel is Lily's daughter, and she looks after Amanda most of the time and, of course, helps with all the jobs that have to be done."

The house was simply furnished with heavy oak pieces, elegantly male. You could tell who the boss was here, Ami thought. Where was Mrs. Wagner's female individuality?

The image of Jeff's face came to her, and she felt again the tremulous flutter under her ribs. *Watch it, Ami. You're thinking about your boss, who just happens to be married.*

Then they were outside, walking a quarter mile toward the attractive rock-and-log house that belonged to Steve and Janie Hilton.

Jasper knocked lightly, and a friendly, gamine face appeared. "Jasper, come on in." Janie leaned a little toward overweight, but her pleasant, outgoing personality drew Ami to her.

"Hello, Ami," she said, hand outstretched. "Steve, Jasper and Ami are here."

Steve ambled in. He and Janie looked enough alike to be brother and sister, features and coloring the same, except Steve was lean and almost as tall as Jasper.

"Good to see you again, Ami."

The four of them sat down, and as they drank coffee Janie had poured, Steve went into detail about the ranch, and Ami asked more questions. "It's even bigger than I imagined," she told Steve.

He nodded. "It's a lot of territory," he agreed. "Let's go take a look around," he said, and Jasper walked with them to the corral. She noted the sturdy workhorses, the clean roomy stables. Near a gate was a miniature gray burro, nuzzling a small goat, pushing it to the fence with playful nudges.

Ami laughed delightedly. "What's that?"

"That's Charlie, Amanda's burro. Janie and I found him in the mountains. He aggravates everything and everyone within miles, especially when Amanda's gone and can't pet him every day."

"He's adorable." Ami watched the antics of the tiny animal and could picture a six-year-old leading him around. She sobered, realizing Amanda could not hear him make his peculiar noise that was so like a laugh.

Jasper, standing near her, said, "I'd better get on to my work. See you all later." He strode away from them, whistling a lively rendition of "Cotton-Eyed Joe."

Steve watched him go, then said to her, "Jasper is also the family lawyer and looks after all of us to see we don't get into too much trouble."

"Family? Are all of you related?"

Steve laughed. "Well, not really. Jeff, Jasper, and I were all in the same outfit in Vietnam. We swore if we came out of it alive, we'd stick together. We made it, so Jeff brought me and Jasper back here and gave us jobs. Jasper and Jeff were pilots; I was their navigator."

Ami was thoughtful, seeing the three of them plotting to get themselves out of the hell of Vietnam and back to really living.

"Are you all from this area?" she asked.

Steve shook his head. "I'm from Washington state, originally. I worked for Boeing Aircraft before the war. Jasper is from Colorado. He was just starting out as a lawyer when he was drafted."

A straight-backed figure limped toward them from one of the stables. "Ami, this is Claude Hammett, our retiring vet. Claude, Ami Whitelake."

"Ami," the gravelly voice acknowledged. His faded blue eyes meeting hers held a wealth of knowledge that deteriorating health couldn't take away. The rough hand that grasped hers was firm, and she wondered if he had trouble holding instruments a vet needed. She smiled as she met his speculative glance, taking in his possible replacement. Jeff probably told him the lady in question would never be able to fill his shoes. *But I'll try, given the chance,* she decided as she walked on with Steve.

Next in their line of the tour was the house reserved for the veterinarian. As they started in she said, "I really don't want to intrude in Mr. Hammett's home."

"He hasn't lived here in six months. When his wife died last year, it got to be too big for him and he moved into the bunkhouse, where he has lots of company."

It was a lovely house, almost as big as Janie and Steve's, furnished the same with very simple heavy oak furniture. Ami, impressed by the people she had met, could see successful business in capital letters.

"I've never handled anything anywhere as big as this," she told Steve.

"You run a clinic."

"Yes, a small one," she admitted.

"Basically they're run the same, Ami. As I said before, Hammett still helps out around the home corral, and the school in Tucson is very dependable." He studied her face as she gazed around.

The blue of the late afternoon sky darkened as it lay across the ragged mountain peaks that stretched as far as the eye could see. The desert, as much an enemy as armed troops unless you respected it, lay in its own splendor across the thousands of acres between the ranch house and the mountains. Ami couldn't decide which of the two scenes she loved the most, for both had been her world as long as she could remember.

They ate the big evening meal in Lily's kitchen, and Ami, usually a light eater, was miserable. Her cooking efforts left much to be desired, and she took full advantage of Lily's expertise. Pork chops, cabbage that tasted fresh from a garden, corn on the cob, mixed salad, fresh baked rolls, and corn bread. She should have left the huge helping of apple cobbler alone.

"How can you eat like this and stay so slim?" she said, groaning.

"Isn't easy, as you can see," Janie said, looking at her not-too-slender figure.

Back in Janie and Steve's house, they sat, talking about weather comparisons. "It's dry in El Paso, Ami, but we have the same climate here. It's high desert, low humidity," Steve said.

She nodded, looking around the comfortable living room. Two walls were paneled in light oak and one wall was covered with a pale yellow flowered wallpaper. The fourth wall was solid bookcases. Unexpectedly Ami yawned, and then blushed as she apologized.

Janie laughed. "It's getting late, and you've been on the go all day. Let's get some sleep."

In the large airy bedroom she stood at the window, looking toward the rugged mountain ranges she could see only as distant shadows. She liked the people she had met today, and the ranch was like nothing she had ever seen in its vast dimensions. The slight uneasiness she felt when she thought of Jeff Wagner was the only question she didn't get answered to her satisfaction. Undressing, she slid between cool sheets, drifting easily into sleep.

Ami was up early the next morning, out at the corral as the sun peeped over the eastern mountain range. Old Hammett was there, feeding, brushing, and fussing at Charlie.

"Little pest," he said, his voice gentle.

As they talked Ami asked more questions. "Good job here, good people to work for," he said. "If you don't miss city ways." He eyed Ami's slim figure, her ringless fingers. "Not much social activity out here."

She grinned. "Cowboys must have entertainment, Mr. Hammett. How about grange dances?"

"You dance?"

"Well, I used to, but it's been awhile. You mean square dances?" The laughing eyes showed interest. "Do you have good callers?"

"Yes, they have a monthly dance in Tucson, and there's one every week at the grange hall in Tombstone. Jeff's a regular caller. Good, too."

"Jeff?"

"He'll be your boss if you take the job," he said.

She nodded, picturing again the silent, stern-faced Mr. Wagner. "Do you know what my competition is for the job? I haven't asked how many others are being considered."

Hammett snorted inelegantly. "There've been several people out here, but Steve's mighty hard to please." He went on after a moment. "He's pretty particular about who he selects because of our isolation. You have to be able to get along with everyone and you spend a lot of time alone, too."

Recalling Steve's remarks about the loneliness, Ami said, "I can see that. It's such a modern ranch, though. I wouldn't call it isolated, except geographically. All those windmills must make you pretty self-sufficient as far as water and power, right?"

"Yes, Jeff's grandfather was way ahead of his time when he built this place. Chet, Jeff's dad, followed in his footsteps, and Jeff is just as smart and as hard a worker."

At that moment Steve joined them. "Sleep okay, Ami?"

"Oh, yes, thanks."

"Let's get some breakfast, then ride around, and I'll show you some of the stock."

She waved good-bye to Hammett and, after one more look around the corral, followed Steve.

Hours later they stopped at Camp 20 near the ragged line of the Dragoon Mountains, where she met Carue, the chief camp boss. Carue was mostly Indian, Ami guessed, and he looked at her with dark-eyed suspicion as Steve introduced her.

"Rough job for a girl," he grumbled.

Ami's eyes danced at the echo of Steve's remarks earlier. It was the first word spoken against her as a female since her arrival and even to her it seemed a halfhearted protest, as if they had already been warned. "Why more rough on a girl than a boy?" she asked.

He looked her over. "No modern conveniences in the line shacks and camps. No mirrors to see how purty you look."

Steve watched and listened to the exchange with a grin on his face, recalling Ami's quick retort when he had mentioned it being a hard job for a woman. He also knew Carue disapproved of a woman in this very much male-dominated domain.

"Mr. Carue, you should see where I was brought up. Your camp looks like Radio City by comparison." Ami grinned, then stepped closer to him and whispered, "Don't worry, I don't have the job yet." As she walked away with Steve she was conscious of Carue's gaze following them.

Steve continued to explain the layout of the ranch. "We have several camps that we work from, and they're numbered for reporting purposes. There're a lot of isolated places, so we have a radio system for reporting in at regular intervals. That way, if you have to be out of range, we know about where you are and how long you'll be there. If someone should get hurt, or in trouble of any kind, he won't be missing long before someone goes looking for him."

Ami nodded in approval. As they drove back to the big house Steve asked, "What time's your plane leave, Ami?"

"Eight forty-five."

"I'll alert Jasper. You'd better leave here about six thirty."

They rode in silence, Ami's eyes busy with the scenes around her, interested particularly in the huge portable irrigation systems, looking like monstrous granddaddy longlegs. Silos and windmills dotted the rolling acres of land.

"It's beautiful," she said.

Steve glanced at her, taking in the curving mouth, wide eyes, strange-colored and searching, beneath the tousled cap of dark hair. He grinned, appreciating anyone who could see beauty in the wild, untamed desert. "I'd like you to take the job, Ami."

Her heart jumped and she caught her breath, unable to answer him for a moment.

At her silence Steve asked, "Any doubts? I'll have

to tell you in all fairness that I'm not kidding when I say it's a lonely job and you'll be on your own and working alone most of the time. Sometimes we go a couple of weeks without seeing Jasper or Jeff." He smiled at her. "Janie's hoping you'll take the job; she'd love having you around."

Ami swallowed hard. "Rio and Remus? Can I bring them with me?"

"Of course. There's plenty of room. How old is the boy?"

"Seventeen. He graduates from high school in May. I've had him for two years." She met his gaze directly. "I'm quite bad about picking up strays, Steve. I'd better warn you now."

He laughed. "We're all strays of a sort, I guess."

"What about Mr. and Mrs. Wagner? Do you just hire, or do they have to approve?"

"There's only Jeff," Steve told her. "Myra died when Amanda was two."

Shock kept Ami silent as he went on. "Jeff leaves the hiring to me. Would you rather call me after you've thought it over?"

She smiled. "Give me till we get to the house. I can make up my mind by then." Her mind was having a hard time realizing Jeff Wagner was a widower; a young, good-looking widower. How very sad.

Steve agreed as he again took in the tall boyish figure, the odd-colored eyes, the long slender fingers.

They had almost reached the house when Ami asked, "Can Amanda talk?"

"No. She's good at using sign language, and most of us can understand her. Jeff and Hazel are both excellent in the language, and Amanda doesn't let it slow her down at all."

"What happened to her mother? She must have been awfully young."

"Yes. She was twenty-six. It was one of those freak

car accidents. About twenty miles west of here." He was silent, thinking back. "We thought Jeff would go crazy. Wife killed and child badly injured. It was doubly hard once he found out that Amanda was deaf."

Ami was quiet. Tragedy strikes indiscriminately and is always impossible to understand. When she realized the truck had stopped, she sighed, opened the door, and slid to the ground. Her eyes took in the house once more, the clean, well-kept area as far as the eye could see. She thought of Rio. It would be a good life if he would accept it.

Maybe that was a selfish slant, she thought as she turned to Steve. "I'll take the job."

"Great." Steve put out his hand, and she took it.

Jeff was a widower. That was her first solidly conscious thought as her flight lifted into the darkening sky. At least he had Amanda, she thought, and remembered the dark gaze, almost angry, as he had listened to her discussions with Steve, saying little. Her curiosity where he was concerned was strictly boss and employee, she told herself not too convincingly. Jeff Wagner was good-looking, and the magnetic pull she felt caused her to move restlessly in the seat.

But Steve said she wouldn't see any of them often, and it would be to her benefit to stay away from Mr. Wagner.

Chapter Three

Settling into her new home was a pleasant job, with Janie, Steve, and Jasper there to help. Janie, delighted to have another young female in a heretofore practically all-male kingdom, was an instant friend. Jasper, of all things, was a bachelor and evidently enjoyed that status with no mind to change things, according to Janie.

On Friday, after arriving at Wagner's, Ami accepted Janie's invitation for dinner, along with Jasper. She sat, feet curled under her on the couch, satisfyingly full of good food, half listening to Steve and Jasper reminiscing about their Vietnam experiences with Jeff. Some of their tales were comical, but she shivered at the close calls they remembered and the utter disregard for human life they had faced.

A light knock sounded at the door, and Steve went to answer it. "Jeff," he said. "Come on in."

Ami got to her feet. Jeff had stayed on the east coast with Mandy longer than he had planned, and this was the first time she had seen him after her arrival at Wagner's. As she faced him the tremor under her ribs that she had ignored for weeks was back, and she bit her lip, silently telling her body to behave.

"Jeff, you remember Ami."

Jeff extended his hand, and Ami smiled up at him as she took it. "Of course. Are you settled all right,

Ami?" he asked, dark gray eyes looking her over thoroughly. Perhaps he thought she might have changed after becoming his veterinarian. Her hand tingled as he continued to look at her without releasing his hold.

"Yes, thank you." He let go of her fingers, and she put her hands behind her to hide their shaking.

"Any answers, Jeff?" Janie asked.

He shook his head. "Nothing." Disappointment showing, he explained about the tests. "I'm not surprised, of course, but—" Here he shrugged.

"And Amanda?" Jasper asked.

"She's tired. Hazel's putting her to bed." He grinned a little. "She's better off than I am."

After a few minutes, Ami took her leave. "Thanks for dinner, Janie. It's a good thing I won't be around here very much. Between you and Lily, I'd soon waddle instead of walk."

She said good-bye and left, but not before promising to meet them in Tucson at the motel Janie named on Saturday afternoon. They had enthusiastically invited her to the monthly grange dance, and she found herself looking forward to going.

"No jeans," Steve told her.

She smiled to herself, wondering where she'd come up with anything other than jeans. Maybe in the old trunk, she thought.

For long moments she stood looking at the midnight blue of the sky, with the stars sparkling white, seeming near enough to touch. A cool desert wind carried the fragrance of sagebrush and mesquite bushes, and the friendly animal sounds were familiar music to her. Humming an old western tune, she walked the quarter mile to her cottage, thinking of Jeff and his disappointment over Amanda's hearing tests.

Maybe she should talk to him about Linda and Dave, she thought. She and Linda had graduated from the University of Wyoming the same year, and Linda and her husband had gone on to study medicine, specializing in hearing problems. She would trust their opinion above any other expert on ear troubles.

The trunk didn't yield much in the way of square dance clothing, but memories crowded their way in, try as she would to keep them out. She had only a few items left from her college days and two-year marriage, and the picture she found at the bottom was the last one she had. They were on bicycles, laughing, on a picnic in Laramie; young, carefree, and in love. She and Tim had shared a happy two years, the dark ending a shock to both their systems. Her fingers moved over the glossy surface of the snapshot. Tim was handsome; a healthy specimen who would make some woman happy if she could reciprocate by bearing his children.

Ami knew she should have thrown that picture away, but she didn't.

Pushing the sudden emptiness away, she reached into the trunk and pulled a black skirt from underneath everything else, frowning as she tried to remember what she had worn with it. The red print top would have to do.

She had to do something about her clothes, she thought. Anything would be an improvement. She had never been much for dressy clothes and, since Tim, she had gone from bad to impossible. After repacking the odd lot of items into the trunk, she went to bed.

Ami met Amanda the next morning as she stood watching Hammett and Remus herding a stubborn calf into the corral. The little girl came flying around the corner of the stables, colliding against her.

"Whoa!" Ami said, holding the slight figure steady. She looked into clear gray eyes, wide spaced in a thin suntanned face. The puzzled look in the gray depths caused Ami to remember the child's deafness. Setting her on her feet, she stepped back and, using the sign language learned years ago, she said, "You must be Amanda. My name is Ami."

Serious eyes regarded her steadily, and a grin crossed

the face, wrinkling the small nose. Tiny fingers moved in answer.

"Hey, you're good." Stooping so that she was on a level with Amanda, she asked, "Where did you get Charlie?"

Amy understood by Amanda's signing that Steve and Janie had found him in the mountains. "He's a year old," Amanda signed. The intense gray eyes sparkled. "I'm six."

Ami took her hand and led her back to the corral, where she found Charlie loping back and forth between Hammett and Remus, trying to get their attention. She and Mandy sat on the fence, laughing at the antics of the tiny burro and conversing like old friends. As she left them, Ami signed to Mandy, "Come to see me at my house, okay?"

Amanda grinned her agreement and turned back to the animals. Ami headed toward the cottage, anger stirring in her chest at doctors who would give up on the tiny girl and say there was no hope at all.

I'd certainly argue with them if she were mine, she vowed.

At six o'clock Saturday morning Ami called Linda in New Jersey. "Hello, Dr. Monroe."

"Ami. Where are you?"

She smiled as she heard the familiar voice. "In the wilds of Arizona. How's everything in the east?"

"Fine. Dave's already at the clinic, and I was on my way out. When are you visiting us again?"

"I need a favor, Linda." She told the story briefly and got the answer she wanted.

"You know we'll try, Ami. Talk Mr. Wagner into letting us have a look at Amanda and call me back."

As the connection was broken Ami sat back in relief and felt confidence in Linda and Dave that she would have to transmit to Jeff...Somehow. Mandy must have another chance to hear.

Perhaps Jeff was right; perhaps all the experts were

right in thinking there was no chance that Mandy would ever hear again. When she heard it from Linda, she would believe it.

Ami's thoughts went back to when Linda was only a speaking acquaintance at the University of Wyoming in Laramie, where Linda was in premed and Ami was taking the animal husbandry courses, preparing for her veterinary career. She had started across the street as a car careened around the corner, hitting the curb and coming straight at her, and the other girl had just stepped into the crosswalk. Even as she stared, horrified, she had made a flying tackle, taking the girl with her, rolling into the street and from under the car. The damage had amounted to Linda's broken arm, multiple scratches and bruises on both of them, and the shock suffered by the driver of the car when his brakes failed. She and Linda had become the best of friends and remained as such through the years.

Feeling satisfied that she was right in initiating a campaign to give Amanda at least another fighting chance to hear, Ami went about her work, making sure all the chores around the home corral were finished up for the weekend. It would be a lot easier for her when Rio was graduated from school and came out to join her.

Upon her decision to take the job at Wagner's, Dr. North had agreed to let Rio stay with him till his graduation from high school in May, not too many weeks away. The new owners of the clinic were glad to have him help them with the animals for the remaining few weeks.

It was early in the afternoon when she left the ranch to drive into Tucson alone and checked into the motel, reserving an adjoining room for Janie and Steve. On the front seat of the truck beside her was her old Giannini guitar she had lugged around with her for years. In the years since old Lon made her first guitar from pine, she had never been without one, entertaining herself as well as her classmates when they cared to listen.

Downtown, she found new jeans and a T-shirt and a set of strings for the Giannini, ate a sandwich at the drugstore, and went back to the motel. She finished restringing the guitar and let her fingers slide over the new strings. Softly, she murmured the words of a current love ballad.

Her hands grew still. Almost two years, and some of the hurt left over from losing Tim was still there. Not often, not deep, but there. Unbidden, Jeff Wagner's face came between her and the guitar, dark gray eyes probing into her thoughts. Shaking her head, she stretched on the bed and was instantly asleep.

She woke suddenly, wondering where she was. A loud knock startled her. Sluggish, she sat up, looking at the door of her room.

"Ami, it's us. Are you there?" It was Janie.

"Yep, just a minute." She glanced at her watch as she moved to the door. Five o'clock. She had slept a long time.

"Where've you been?" Ami asked as she opened the door.

"We waited for Jeff. He wanted to ride with us." She smiled as Jeff stepped into sight behind Steve.

"Were you asleep?" Janie asked as she flopped across the bed.

"I sure was. Now I'm ready for tonight."

They chatted awhile, and Janie said, "We'd better get going. Are our rooms next door?"

"Yes, but I only got one." She looked at Jeff.

"No problem," he assured her. "The owner's an old friend. He'll find something for me." His eyes told her, "You don't have to worry about me." She turned away from him.

A few minutes later Janie called to her, and Ami joined the group to pile into Steve's six-passenger, long-bed truck for the short drive to the grange hall.

It was a good group: the band was excellent and the square dance callers were in great form. Jeff called two dances, and Ami liked his voice, clear and easy to follow. She saw Steve near the band, talking animatedly with his hand going full time, and she remembered Janie saying he loved country-and-western music and all the instruments the band used.

"Going with me, Janie?" she asked, heading for the rest-rooms she had seen earlier.

"I'll wait here for Jeff. I think he's through calling."

Returning on the opposite side of the stage, Ami saw Steve, guitar in hand, talking to the piano player. Picking up the Giannini resembling her own, she stood beside Steve, letting her long fingers slide across the strings. Surprise showed in Steve's eyes as he watched her, leaning relaxed against the piano.

He grinned. "Can you play that thing?"

"A little," she admitted.

"You wouldn't, by any remote chance, sing, too?"

The turquoise eyes smiled. "Some."

"How up-to-date is El Paso on country-and western standings?" Steve's eyes showed increased interest.

"Very much so."

"Ever hear 'Old Flames'? Joe Sun has a great recording of it."

Ami fingered the strings, blending with Steve's key, and she heard the piano player join them. On the second chorus her husky voice picked up the words, and as she sang she forgot she had an audience.

Steve nodded as the song was finished, and they went on into "Even Cowgirls Get the Blues." They kept up their playing and singing till the regular band came back from their break. The audience, quiet until now, gave them a spontaneous round of applause.

On the way back to the table Ami wiped her sweaty palms on the folds of her skirt. "I was scared."

Jeff was standing by her chair. "You didn't look scared," he said. "Ever sing professionally?"

She shook her head. "Not me. I don't have any training and not enough nerve."

Gray eyes dark and unsmiling watched her. "You could do it."

"No, thanks. I like my job at Wagner's."

Tom Pardue from Kingston's Ranch, on the other side of the mountain from Wagner's, had wangled an introduction to Ami earlier, and now he came to claim her for the next dance. She went from his to several pairs of arms, then found herself dancing with Jeff.

"Trust these cowboys to find a pretty new girl around." He swung her expertly across the floor.

Ami smiled up at him. "This is one time that being a minority is definitely in my favor." She didn't add that his arms around her felt just the way they should and was glad he couldn't tell her heart had sped up at the touch of his hands. She found herself suddenly wondering if he had a girlfriend and, if not, why not. He had to be among the top eligibles in their corner of Arizona.

As they left the dance Jeff said, "I'm hungry. Is that little café with the good Mexican food still open, Steve? The one near the old airport road?"

"Yes. Shall we try it?"

Everyone agreed, although Ami would rather have waited for breakfast. The food was good as promised, and she enjoyed it, but riding back to the motel, sharing the backseat of Steve's truck with Jeff, she groaned, "I ate too much."

A muffled chorus answered her. Jeff said, "You don't look like you ever eat too much."

"Frequently," she said, turning her head to smile at him. "I run it off, chasing erring cattle."

"The usual question: Why a veterinarian?"

"I ran wild with the animals up near Cody while I

was growing up, always patching up the hurt ones and crying over the ones I couldn't help.'' She smiled, remembering. "I still do.''

"Still patch them up?''

"And cry over the ones I can't.''

Jeff looked at her, but her eyes were closed, a smile turning up the corners of her mouth, with the short upper lip accentuating the fullness of the lower one. She was unaware of his gaze lingering on her mouth. They separated at the motel, agreeing to meet for breakfast before starting home the next day.

Ami slept fitfully and she blamed it on the late-night meal. At five thirty she got up, took a barely warm shower, then turned the water to stinging cold. As she stepped from the shower and reached for a towel, she thought of Jeff and met her own startled eyes in the mirror, letting the towel drop, and looked at the reflection of her long slim body. It had been a long time since a man had held her, and she felt Jeff's touch again as she dressed.

That would never do, she decided, shaking her head resolutely, and headed for the coffee shop, hoping it was open. It was. An older couple sat in one of the booths and a young couple with two bright-eyed boys were at a table. Ami headed for a booth and slid across the red Leatherette seat.

"Good morning.''

Her head came up at the familiar voice. "Good morning.'' Jeff looked fresh and wide awake as he joined her. He, in turn, noticed the faint lavender tint of shadow beneath her odd-colored eyes.

"Would you like a menu?'' The young waitress flashed a fresh smile at them, but her gaze lingered on Jeff. Ami took a long look at her boss and silently agreed that he was worth looking at.

"Coffee for me,'' Ami told her. Jeff, too, refused breakfast in favor of coffee.

When the coffees came, Ami said, "I'm still full from our midnight feast—or one o'clock, or whenever."

"So am I. Our friends still asleep?"

"Anyone with any sense at all would be," Ami said.

"Thanks." Jeff grinned.

She smiled back at him, wondering briefly where he had slept, but had better sense than to ask. "Amanda gets her eyes from you. Other than that she must favor her mother." No one had mentioned Myra's name around Jeff, and she wasn't sure he would talk about her, but he answered easily.

"Yes, she's small like her mother and has her turned-up nose and blond hair."

Ami leaned forward, elbows on the table. "You weren't able to get anyone to offer you any hope at all of her ever hearing?"

His lips tightened and he hunched his shoulders as if against an attack. "No."

"Jeff, listen, I know you've been to the best-known doctors and—"

He broke in. "And the last one. No more tests. The same rhetoric over and over."

"I was in college with a girl who went on to be a pediatrician. She and her husband specialize in hearing problems. Let me call them and ask about Mandy."

"No. Thanks, anyway."

"They might—"

"No." He looked at her, his eyes hard and uncompromising. They finished their coffees without speaking.

Ami broke the awkward silence. "I think I'll go on home. Steve and Janie may sleep all day."

"Mind if I ride with you?"

A bit startled at the question, she said, "Of course not. My things are in the truck. All I need do is check out."

"Be with you in ten minutes. I'll leave a note on their door."

The sun was coming up as Ami pulled the little Subaru Brat out onto Interstate 10. Jeff was quiet, and she made no effort to speak.

"What's the name of that song?" His question broke in on her thoughts, and she glanced at him, wondering. "You've been humming the same one off and on for miles."

She thought a moment, and the words came to her. "'Years,'" she said. She had been thinking of the words of a song about years of hanging on to dreams that were gone. But she had stopped hanging on to her dreams, although they had died hard. At least she had let them go.

Ami drew in a deep breath. "It's a beautiful day," she said and heard the man beside her murmur his agreement.

Chapter Four

An early morning breeze kicked tumbleweeds down the narrow street of the small desert town as Ami leaned her long body against a post outside the café where she and Rio had breakfasted. From her stance she could see the low horizon running south from Douglas and over into old Mexico, to her right the route she would soon follow to the Wagner Ranch. She could see the long jagged outline of the end of the Dragoon Mountain chain, looking deceptively near, but long acquaintance with desert distortions told her they were many miles in the distance.

Leaving El Paso after Rio's graduation from high school, they took the long way to the ranch, dropping south of I-10 below Lordsburg, New Mexico, through the sparsely settled corner of the state of Arizona, coming out just east of Douglas. She wanted Rio to get an idea of the type of isolation they would be living in.

A movement down the street caught her eye and, turning, she took in the scene some fifty yards away from her. Three cowboys, dressed in dusty jeans and sweat-stained shirts, blocked the sidewalk. Rio was the center of their attention. Separated just enough, they formed a barrier designed to keep him from passing.

"Ah, amigo," the taller of the three addressed him. "Why the hurry?"

Rio stepped aside with a murmured good morning,

but the second man stood in his way, grinning down at him. It was plain the boy wanted no part of the three and equally plain they were bent on harassment.

Ami's eyes took in the scene and, before it was completely engraved as an image, she straightened away from the post, moving before she gained her full height. In seconds she stopped outside the circle of men.

"Everything okay, Rio?" The question was directed at him, but her eyes watched the closest bearded cowboy.

"*Sí, señora.*"

"Hey, look, Hank, he belongs to the pretty lady." The cowboy, enjoying his role, grinned to show a tobacco-stained, broken tooth behind thin lips. Pale blue eyes shifted from Rio to Ami, lingering on her figure.

The man addressed as Hank turned to look at Ami, taking in the oddly smiling eyes, curving lips, and tousled head almost even with his own.

"I'm ready to leave, if you are, Rio." Her eyes never left the group as she spoke.

Hank grinned. "How about that, Luke? She's taking Rio with her, not even polite enough to introduce herself."

As he finished the sentence his arm snaked out and caught the slim figure around the waist, sweeping her against him. Ami looked into the grinning face, dark eyes close to her own, smelling tobacco and sour sweat.

The curving lips tilted a little more, the eyes darkened a trifle, and suddenly she relaxed against the imprisoning arm, forcing Hank to shift his weight to hold her. As he did Ami brought the heel of her right boot to his instep and, as he yelped and partially released her, she slammed her left knee into his groin. With a grunt of pain he let her go, only to catch her elbow just above his ear. She was free as he staggered and sat hard on the concrete. She stepped away from him and, as the other two started toward her, hooked her thumbs in her belt and said in a soft voice, "Touch me and I'll yell rape so loud, they'll hear me in Tucson."

The men hesitated, glancing from her strange eyes to their fallen companion.

"Let's go, Rio." Rio glanced at the three, turned, and followed her. The incident had taken only a few minutes, and no one appeared to have noticed the altercation.

A few parking places down the street Ami and Rio stopped at the dusty pickup, where Remus waited in the front seat, wagging his tail in a hearty welcome. Ami patted the huge head as she swung up behind the wheel, and Rio, entering from the passenger side, added his touch of affection. Neither of them looked back nor spoke as she started the truck, heading toward U.S. 80, which would put them near their destination.

In the back of the pickup, covered with tarpaulins, were all of Rio's belongings and a few she had left behind on her first move. There were still boxes of her medical and animal care books, and Rio's books on painting and charcoal drawing, his hobby at which he was quite good.

Ami was thoughtful as the little truck gained speed outside the city limits. Already enjoying her new job in the isolated Arizona desert, she was hoping Rio would adjust to the loneliness and hard work, a world away from the small animal clinic and neighborhoods he was used to.

They couldn't have asked for a more perfect end-of-May day for traveling. The desert unfolded around them as the miles added to the speedometer, and it was still morning as she turned down the gravel lane leading to the big ranch house.

Rio stared with wide eyes at his surroundings. "Where's your house?"

"Ours," she corrected. "Unless you want to stay in the bunkhouse."

He turned to her. "Would you mind?"

She grinned. "You'll soon be eighteen, Rio. It's your choice. Let's look."

There was no one in sight as they walked to the corral, where they found Hammett polishing a leather saddle. As Ami introduced Rio, Charlie came loping with his sideways gait from around the stable.

Rio laughed, remembering Ami's description of the small animal. "This must be Charlie. Is Amanda around, too?"

"No. She and Hazel are in Tucson with Jeff. They'll be back in a couple of days." Hammett put the saddle aside as Ami explained that Rio was interested in the bunkhouses. "Come on, Rio, and I'll show you some of the quarters." As they started away he looked at Ami and said, "We missed you, girl."

Ami stared after him in surprise, and a warm glow flushed her cheeks. She liked the old man, but he wasn't one to show much outward feeling, and pleasure brought a big grin to her face. He had accepted her as veterinarian, replacing him in a job he had held for many years, and never showed any resentment toward her.

They were back in a short while with Rio enthused about moving into the bunkhouse, and they set about unloading the truck. The books were the hardest but, packed in sturdy boxes, they could be unpacked as needed.

Her worry over Rio adapting to the new life was unfounded, and they fitted themselves into a hardworking routine for the hot, dry summer. In the line shacks and camps more than at the ranch, the trio, including Remus, of course, who accompanied Ami on every trip, was a closely knit family. Rio loved the wild desert and mountains as she did, missing only the hamburgers from their daily fare. They took their books with them, studying some each day, sometimes by the oil lamp late in the evening.

It was on one of these evenings that Ami mentioned more schooling to Rio. "It's too late to get you into any of the colleges for the fall semester, but what do you think of starting some classes for the spring term?"

Rio looked up from the book he was reading. "I want to be a veterinarian."

"Is that right?" she asked, feeling a thrill of pleasure.

He put the book down. "Yes." His voice was firm, and he sounded sure of himself as he talked. "I know it will cost a lot of money, but I'll work and pay you back." He smiled at her.

Her mind went back to the evening they had met, and her features softened, remembering the past years, their good times and bad times. "That's a good choice, Rio, but it's a lot of studying and hard work."

"I know," he said simply, "but it's what I want if you think we can manage."

"We'll manage," she told him and made a mental note to send off for catalogs they could look through. And she did, in her spare moments, though they were few with all the work to be done on the ranch.

The young heifers and spindly leg newborn colts were a full-time job for weeks, getting them shots and marked, the system she liked better than branding, since clips in the ear were faster and not painful to the animals. At the end of the month they headed back to the home corral, where paperwork had to be taken care of and supplies ordered. Ami had the entertainment of the grange dances to enjoy with Janie and Steve, sometimes Jasper and Jeff, but Rio spent most of his spare time with the Sandovals, the family of the big chief foreman. There were six children, one of whom was Nada, a lovely seventeen-year-old with liquid brown eyes, black hair to her waist, and a shy smile that fascinated Rio.

Wagner's held their annual barbecue around Labor Day, a big, well-celebrated holiday for all employees. The affair had been postponed until mid-September because of trips taking Jeff and Jasper away from the ranch.

Ami, working alone far away from the ranch house, was late getting back on Friday afternoon, and the shindig was well underway as she stopped her truck behind the house. She eyed the colorful crowd, listened for a moment to the laughter and voices calling above the noise, then turned and went inside.

A shower first, she thought, wrinkling her nose. She smelled like cows.

Feeling better with a definite improvement in emanations, she pulled on jeans and a sleeveless red terry cloth T-shirt. Outside again, she looked at the crowd and shook her head, directing her steps toward the kitchen. Rio would be with the Sandovals, who seemed to have more or less adopted him, and she no longer worried about his being lonesome. Life after many months on the ranch was great as far as they were both concerned.

Lily turned, frowning, as Ami opened the screen door. "It's time you—" she started, then saw Ami.

"Oh, honey, I thought you were that no-good Harris. I guess he's in the beer barrel, and I need some climbing."

Ami laughed. "Let him enjoy his beer, Lily. Tell me what you need."

A moment later she had the step stool in the huge pantry and was climbing through the trapdoor to the giant storage loft. She found the items Lily named and started down.

"What the hell are you doing up there?"

Ami looked down into Jeff's upturned face, and the

small dimple flashed in her cheek. "I may get hungry sometime and I was checking out the goodies."

"Where's Harris? That's his job."

"Mr. Jeff," Lily broke in. "Ami offered to help. You know where Harris is."

It was Jeff's turn to laugh. "Yes, I do, Lily. But you could have yelled for help. Ami should be at the barbecue, eating, since you're the one who's always trying to fatten her up." He stopped and looked back at Ami. "Pass those things to me."

A few minutes later she turned and backed down the ladder, only to be caught by the waist and swung to the floor. Big hands held her a moment longer, and she was forced to look straight at him. Quizzical gray eyes searched her face, then he let her go.

Ami was aware of an odd sensation in her stomach as she turned away. "Anything else, Lily?"

"No, thanks, Ami. Go enjoy the party before Mr. Jeff has a fit."

As they walked side by side through the hallway, Ami turned to Jeff. "Can I talk to you a minute?"

"Sure. In here." Jeff turned into his study, and she followed him. He walked to the huge desk, sat on it with one leg swinging, and motioned her to a chair. She shook her head. She looked around the big room she had never been in, hesitating to voice her question now that she was alone with him.

"Any problems with your job?" he asked.

"No. Everything's going very well." She drew in a deep breath and plunged. "Jeff, I'd like you to reconsider talking to Linda and Dave about Mandy. They're the friends I mentioned, doctors who specialize in diseases of the ears."

"No." It was a flat, uncompromising statement.

Even though she had expected that reaction, her heart sank. She wet her lips. "Can you really pass up the chance that they may be able to help her?"

"If there was a chance, but there isn't. I've told you, Amanda has been through enough tests, and the best medical sources say she'll never hear." He sounded as though he were gritting his teeth. "Why does it matter to you, Ami? Do you get a percentage out of recruiting patients for your friends?"

She refused to be baited, and persisted. "Mandy is an adorable, intelligent child, and I know she can manage the deafness and not being able to talk, but she should have the chance, slim though you think it is, to hear someone say I love you and be able to say that aloud to someone she loves." She took another deep breath. "Are you satisfied with her saying I love you this way?" Her fingers went to her lips, to her chest, then extended toward Jeff in the sign language she knew so well. With her hands out to him, she suddenly forgot she was talking about Mandy and her I love you wasn't repeated with feelings a small girl would have.

He regarded her intently. "When's the last time someone whispered love words to you, Ami?"

She stared at him. "We aren't talking about me."

"I am. When?" He straightened against the desk and, with arms folded, watched her through narrowed eyes.

She returned his gaze, her eyes going to his mouth. The wayward tingling she remembered each time she thought of him returned, and she swallowed hard.

"Well?" he asked. She shook her head.

He moved, covering the steps between them in seconds, his hands spanning her slim waist. He pulled her up against him, placing his mouth over hers. None too gently he forced her lips apart, pressed her head back into his shoulder, playing havoc with her breath. He raised his head enough to look into her wide shocked eyes, unaware of the feelings he roused in her.

"Kiss me back, Ami," he demanded, his mouth still touching hers.

She tried to shake her head. "No, please."

"Yes, or we'll stay right here until someone comes looking for us." She could see her reflection in his eyes. "That could be awhile."

Sensing danger to her peace of mind, she tried to think of a way out, but he held her tightly. She stood on tiptoe and her hands went to his shoulders and, tilting her head back, she found his smiling mouth with hers. A warning light flashed somewhere as a sharp thrill shot all the way to her toes and his mouth took possession of hers once more. She slid one hand behind his head while the kiss held, taking her breath and sending a warm glow through her body. She pulled back a little to look at him through half-closed lids. Their lips were a whisper apart when, suddenly, the tip of her tongue seared a path across his mouth and, as she felt him draw a sharp breath, her hand brought his head down, crushing her lips against his. The surprised response of his body to the unexpected byplay was immediate as his hand moved flat over her hips, his metal belt buckle pressing hard into her middle. Ami stood on tiptoe, stretched to his tall slimness, the thoroughness of the kiss sending electric waves shimmering through her.

She waited for him to make the first move and, as he lifted his head, she reluctantly stepped away, staring up at him, one hand touching her throbbing mouth. Her voice was soft, almost a whisper, as she said, "I don't remember the last time someone said I love you but that's the first kiss in a long time."

She turned blindly to the door. With one hand on the knob she looked back at him, standing where she had left him, his arms again folded, gray eyes unreadable.

"Please call Linda and talk to her and Dave."

"You never give up, do you?" he asked. "After that outstanding performance, you think you can get your way."

"You started it; I just responded." She shrugged, a

casual move far from what she was feeling. "Rather a natural reaction, don't you think?"

"Touché," he said, smiling a little.

"Will you call?" she persisted.

"No, Ami."

She returned his steady gaze a moment, opened the door, and walked out. *I sure didn't win that battle,* she thought, her emotions trying to sort themselves out and failing.

Making her way around the outskirts of the crowd, she called responses to greetings and waved to others as she moved. The band was a real cowboy band, all right. They were in the middle of a square dance, and she stopped to watch the dancers whirling on the improvised board floor.

Across from her, she saw Eileen McKane, Jeff's girl-friend of long standing. Her white peasant-necked blouse, tucked into a billowing green checked skirt, set off the smooth honey-tanned skin and upswept blond hair to utmost perfection. The McKanes and Wagners had been neighbors for a lifetime, and rumor had it that Eileen would be the next mistress of Wagner's.

She hadn't known about Eileen when she wondered about Jeff's girlfriends, but wasn't at all surprised to find he had a very special one. For a long moment she allowed herself to remember Jeff's hard kiss, which had made her forget all her sensible warnings to her own heart. The best thing to do was beat a fast retreat out of the line of fire if she didn't want to get burned again.

"How about a song?" It was Steve beside her.

"Why not? A real captive audience." She grinned and took the guitar one of the men in the band handed her.

A couple of ballads later she asked Steve, "Heard that new one 'Old Habits'?"

"No. How's it go?"

"Give me a straight E, and we'll have it," she told him.

Games of horseshoe went on around them, but most of the crowd turned to listen as Ami sang. She got to the last verse, conscious of the crowd's attention, when she turned her head to meet Jeff's gaze. Impudently she kept her eyes on him as she sang.

It wasn't at all hard to sing to him, she realized as, finally, she put the guitar down, waved to Steve, and made her way through the group in the opposite direction from where Jeff stood. She spotted Rio with the Sandovals, being attentive to Nada. She smiled; Rio was growing up.

Rounding the corner of the fence around the corral, she came upon a group of the children jumping rope. Mandy was with them, blond pigtails bouncing, gray eyes sparkling. She saw Ami, broke away from the others, and ran to meet her. Ami stooped to hug the little girl.

"Having a good time, Mandy?"

Mandy signed "yes", then she took Ami's hand, pulling her to the jump rope, and they ran in, jumping easily together.

Finally out of breath, Ami waved good-bye and walked toward her cottage. She still hadn't eaten, but it didn't matter. Her disappointment at not being able to convince Jeff he should take Mandy to see Linda and Dave rankled deep. She couldn't really blame him for his doubt, because of so many negative reports and disappointments, but surely Mandy deserved one more chance, and Ami had confidence that if anyone could help, it would be Linda and Dave.

Mandy took her up on her first invitation to visit, and they had got to know each other. She enjoyed the small girl's silent company—silent, but friendly and outgoing with her. They understood each others' sign language most of the time, and she grinned, remembering once when they didn't.

They had been drinking lemonade in Ami's kitchen one hot August afternoon when Mandy asked a question Ami didn't understand. Impatiently Mandy left her chair and came around to her side of the table. She reached up to place tiny fingers over Ami's eyes and withdrew them to repeat her question, making her signs slowly and distinctly as she might to a dim-witted individual.

Ami laughed aloud as she understood. Mandy had asked, "Where did you get your funny-colored eyes?"

"I don't know what my parents looked like, Mandy," she told her. "But the color of my eyes probably came from one of them. Yours are like your dad's, so maybe my dad had funny-colored eyes and I look like him." The answer had satisfied Mandy, and she went back to drink her lemonade.

Rounding the corner of her house near the back door, Ami looked off to the western ridge of mountains. Clouds bumped over the jagged outline, drifting toward Tombstone. The usual September rainy season had not reached Wagner property, and unless the winds changed, the clouds she was watching would be too far south to help them.

Sounds of merriment from the barbecue activity came faintly as she sat on the step, enjoying the cooler air as the sun lowered behind the mountains. It hung on a golden thread for a moment and disappeared beind a purple curtain, putting on a spectacular display for her.

Remus rounded the corner of the house, stopped to wag his tail, and came to sit beside her. She patted the big head, hair divided in places where she had stitched him back together. Aside from his scars he seemed totally healthy again.

She looked up as Jeff came across the yard, carrying

Mandy. His tanned face looked even darker than usual against the sun-streaked blond head on his shoulder.

He sat beside her as she made room, and Mandy gave her a sleepy grin. Jeff looked her over and said, "Don't you like celebrations?" She wondered if it was her imagination that his eyes lingered a bit on her mouth as he spoke.

"I like the short workday and long weekend that goes with this one," she said, conscious of her own feelings as she remembered his hard kiss. In spite of trying to control it, her heart accelerated its beat.

"Do you need some time off?" he asked.

"No. I needed a chance to bring our supplies up to date, and Rio needed to catch up on hamburgers."

Jeff looked down at the quiet child on the step near him and said, "I want you to hear how Amanda feels about more tests." He looked back at Ami, eyes narrowed. "She's the one who has to endure all the shots, tubes, poking, and questions."

Ami stiffened. "I would never do anything to hurt her. Linda and Dave are—"

"Doctors," he said. "And doctors don't think much beyond the guinea pig status of their patients they don't know what to do about."

"It's not true," she protested. "They've done some wonderful things with children who could hear no better than Mandy." He had no right to put her on the defensive, and she felt anger building inside.

Ignoring her, he turned to Amanda, and she read the question he asked. "Ami knows a doctor who might help you hear, Amanda. She can get an appointment for us if you'll go talk to him."

In the gathering dusk Amanda stared at Jeff, turning questioning eyes to Ami, who smiled, hiding the uneasiness she felt inside. To her dismay tears filled Mandy's dark gray eyes and her lip trembled.

Ami made a move toward her, but Amanda stood up

and took a step forward. She looked at Jeff, and her tiny hands moved. "Can Ami go with me?"

"You want to go?" Jeff asked Amanda.

The pigtails swung in a negative movement. "No, but if Ami goes, I'll go."

Her heart hammered as she met Jeff's dark gaze across Mandy's head. His mouth tightened. "You have your answer," he said. "If you want her to go, you'll have to go, too."

"I can't do that," Ami told him, surprised at the turn of events.

"I thought you had such great faith in your friends." He stood, picking up a yawning Amanda.

"Yes, but—"

"But not enough to be bothered going through tests with her, is that it?" He shifted Mandy so her head rested on his shoulder. "In that case, we won't bother." He strode away from her.

"Wait," she said, running to catch him. "Can we talk after Mandy's in bed?"

He gave her a brief glance, nodded, and said, "I'll be back in half an hour."

In her bedroom she searched briefly for the packet of clippings in a flat folder and pulled them out to look, the first time in months. It showed a small graduating class on a stage with an inset picture of a pretty blond girl smiling shyly at the camera. Attached to the picture was a clipping headed "University of Wyoming graduate cited for work in hearing defects." It went on to say: "Linda Garson Monroe was given a prestigious scientific award for her extended research into hearing defects, which has resulted in the revolutionary use of the patient's own body material to repair damaged tissues and nerves." It gave Linda's year of graduation and the doctorates she had received since that time. "Dr. Monroe and her husband, David, also a hearing specialist, have recently opened their own clinic in Newark, New

Jersey, specializing in diseases of the eyes, ears, nose, and throat.''

Smoothing the clipping with her fingers, she smiled at the pretty girl, remembering how close they had become after the accident and how Linda and Dave had taken her under their wings when her marriage to Tim broke up. She had gone, blindly, not knowing where else to turn, and they had been there when she needed them and applauded when she finally decided she could survive without Tim. For a long time she had been doubtful that she could.

A brief knock brought her back to the present, and she went through the short hallway to the already-opened front door.

"Come in, Jeff," she invited, and as he walked past her, he gave her a hard look. She motioned him to a chair and she sat opposite him on a big hassock, the clippings beside her.

She wet her lips as he continued to look at her and felt again his kiss from the afternoon. "I—it's an unusual request for me to go with Mandy," she began. "Perhaps Miss McKane would prefer to go with her, since—since—" She stopped.

He looked slightly amused. "Since what, Ami?"

She linked her hands together over her knees and said, "She might not appreciate having me travel alone with you." *I wouldn't hear of it if I were in her place,* her thoughts continued silently.

"Is that your only objection to going?" he asked.

"It's a busy time here."

He nodded. "I know, but Hammett and Rio can handle it. Any serious problems, and they can call the school," he said.

She remained quiet, searching for words to use to explain that he and Mandy should go alone. In truth, she was afraid to go with Jeff Wagner, and for the life of her, she couldn't decide why. She had never been afraid of anything that she could recall, except facing life without Tim, and she had managed that, too, after all. Surely one kiss could be forgotten without any trouble. It didn't seem to affect Jeff, still...

Ami picked up the clippings, handing them to Jeff. "This might make you feel a little easier about trusting Linda and Dave," she said and sat still as he read through the articles.

He gave them back to her. "I'll take her because she's willing to go and she'll go only if you go with her. It's up to you." His mouth was a straight line, but she could feel the curve of it over her own.

This is ridiculous, she thought. *You'd think I'd never been kissed before.* "Suppose I call Linda tomorrow and see how soon we can get an appointment?"

"You'll go, then?" he asked.

She nodded. "They'll want to do complete tests before they decide if an operation will help. It could take a week."

"We have a week," he said and stood up to leave. "Let me know what Linda says." He smiled briefly, said "Good night," and went out.

Jeff well knew how long tests would take; he had been through enough of them with his tiny daughter in the past four and a half years. She winced at the idea that she had reminded him how often he had gone with high hopes for examinations and tests.

Uneasy dreams about Mandy's tear-filled eyes disturbed her sleep, and Ami awoke early, placing her call to Linda at six o'clock, eight o'clock on the east coast.

On the third ring Linda spoke into the phone. "Dr. Monroe."

"Linda, it's Ami."

"Ami. I didn't really expect to hear from you so soon. Did you convince Mr. Wagner?"

"Well, he wanted me to set up a date with you for

the tests when you have an opening." She looked down at her crossed fingers.

"How about next Thursday? If he can check Mandy in real early, we can start on her right away." Linda hesitated. "We'd like her to come prepared to stay a week while we check tissue compatibility."

"Yes, I'm sure that will be all right. And, Linda, I'll be with them."

"Oh, Ami, that's just great. It's been so long." Linda's laugh was delighted. "You can stay with us."

"I'd better stay near the clinic. Mandy's going because I'm going with her, so I can't disappoint her."

"I'm disappointed, but just so we can see you. Dave will be happy about it, too." Linda took a deep breath. "I'll reserve rooms for you at the motel close to the clinic for Wednesday evening, and if you have a change of plans, call me."

"Thanks, Linda. I'll see you on Thursday morning." She hung up the phone, conscious of trembling fingers. With lots of luck, Dave and Linda's sure hands, Mandy would have a good chance to hear the night calls of her beloved desert.

Jeff's Bronco Jeep was gone when she went outside, and she reasoned he'd be at the regular Saturday night grange dance; plenty of time to tell him about the appointment. She took her list of supplies to Lily, leaving them for Harris to collect when he came in.

It was late afternoon when she whistled for Remus and watched him come loping toward her. He still favored the leg she had rebuilt, causing him to roll a little to the right. It didn't bother him as he jumped into the front seat after she opened the door for him.

Ami pulled into the parking lot at the grange hall minutes ahead of Steve and Janie. "Okay, Remus. Take care of everything. Blow the horn if you need me." She rolled the window down a bit and locked the truck. The dog watched her leave, then settled down to wait. She swung into step with Steve and Janie, waving at some of the regular crowd that called greetings to them.

"Hey, look who's with Jeff." Ami turned at Steve's comment to see Jeff talking with the Howards from a neighboring ranch. Next to him stood Eileen McKane, blond head only to Jeff's shoulder. The dress she wore would cost two months of Ami's salary. The palest of lavenders, caught at the tiny waist with a cummerbund of matching print, it hugged Eileen's petite shape at just the right places. Very much self-assured, she didn't look overly enthused to be in the hall. Brown eyes swept the crowd with studied indifference.

"Eileen, as I live and breathe," Janie said. "How did he accomplish that miracle?"

"I saw a dress like that while I was shopping in Tucson. I was afraid they'd charge me just for looking." Ami's voice held grudging admiration.

"Yes, and doesn't she wish she was anywhere but here!" Janie smiled.

"Why?"

"Well, now, this here is for cowboys and such, not enough uptown for her ladyship," Janie drawled.

"Isn't she a ranch owner?"

"You said it right—owner. Not to be confused with worker, as such."

"Oh." Ami wasn't sure she understood that at all.

"Jeff usually leaves her at home when he comes here, but guess she figured if he wouldn't stay with her, she'd bless us with her presence. I'm impressed." Steve looked anything but impressed, his grin wide and devilish. "Let's dance, Janie, my sweet." He turned to Ami. "I'll be back for you. Fight off any predators who might venture around."

Ami laughed and looked around. All the usual grange crowd was there.

."Hello, Ami." She looked up.

"Hello, Jeff."

"You know Eileen?" he asked.

Ami smiled at the woman by his side. "I saw her at the barbecue yesterday."

Eileen gave her a small smile. "Yes, of course, the new veterinarian." She made it sound equal to being employed to shovel manure.

"Yes, I work at Wagner's. Nice place." Her eyebrows went up as she eyed the woman's insolent expression. What did Jeff see in her, she wondered, aside from the fact that she was gorgeous and owned half of Arizona?

Jeff pulled a chair out for Eileen and settled into the one opposite Ami. "Were you able to contact Linda?"

Ami leaned forward. "Yes. You have an appointment Thursday morning at nine. Linda will take care of motel reservations for you." She glanced at Eileen to see her sit up with a jerk, eyes narrowed.

Jeff, too, looked at Eileen and back at Ami as he recalled her hesitation about the other woman's reception of the idea that Ami accompany them to Newark. "Did she indicate how long we'd be there?" he asked.

"She'd like you to come prepared to stay a week. Something about different parts of the body having different tissue compatibility." Jeff nodded. He had heard all that before.

"What are you talking about?" Eileen demanded to know.

Jeff explained. "Ami has friends who are doctors specializing in hearing problems, especially children."

She interrupted. "I thought you were through wasting time on those quacks. Hasn't Amanda been through enough? Why don't you admit she'll never be normal and put her in that special school in Tucson, where she can learn as others like her do?"

Ami stiffened, lips parted to lash out at her, but Jeff

spoke first, his voice quiet. "I'm not ready to give up completely, Eileen. Perhaps—"

She broke in. "Always one more chance, throwing money away." She was furious, her full lips pouting, her eyes shooting sparks at Ami.

Angry at the woman's unthinking remarks and uncomfortable at the exchange between her and Jeff, Ami wished she were anywhere but witnessing the quarrel, and was glad to see Janie and Steve return to the table. They talked ranch talk with Jeff while Eileen sat in stiff silence.

"Come on, Ami," Steve said, "it's our turn." He pulled her through the crowd, and she heard Eileen say, "Must we stay for this?"

"Are we 'this'?" she asked Steve.

"Afraid so. Miss Eileen isn't a country-and-western fan." Steve wasn't disturbed at all by that knowledge.

"Is she a fan of anything?"

"Well, she likes Jeff. Doesn't care to share him, however."

I don't think I would, either, Ami thought, remembering a strange kiss that turned her knees to water. She was still shaken by the outraged anger in Eileen. Whatever her private feelings, she should support Jeff in his search for relief for Mandy. They must be close to marriage if he allowed her to express opinions like that.

They were at the stage. The band had already deserted except for Ben Caskey, the piano player. They talked for a minute, and Ben said, "Hey, Ami, sing 'Broken Down in Tiny Pieces' for me."

"Sure thing."

Closing her eyes to the crowd and her mind to the words of the song, she picked up a guitar and blended her key with Steve's.

The author of the words she sang decreed that if you analyzed the value of love, broke it into pieces to really

look at it, you wasted your time. As she sang the philo-
sophical words of the ballad, Ami realized more than
ever that time had nothing whatsoever to do with
love's worth.

From that, they swung into a lively, lilting tune designed to lift everyone out of the dumps, and the crowd
joined in. Even with Eileen around, it still turned out to
be an enjoyable evening.

Driving back to the ranch alone, she was aware that
it didn't hurt anymore to sing the love songs. Tim was
in her past and, bittersweet as the memories were, she
no longer wished things were different.

*I hope you're happy, wherever you are. May you have
ten kids; five for each of us.* Feeling an emptiness for a
moment, she shrugged the feeling away. *No way I can
change; maybe I can finally accept it.* Her thoughts went
to Mandy, left without a mother; and Jeff, losing his
love so young. She felt a new impatience with Eileen
and her adamant refusal to realize possibilities existed
to help Mandy gain at least partial hearing.

"No one ever told us life would be all roses and
moonlight, huh, Remus?" The old dog snored softly
beside her.

The following morning she left word with Hammett
for Rio to join her at Camp 20 on Monday and took
Remus along with her on the ten-mile trip, stopping by
to have coffee with Carue and Ed Sparks, one of his
crew of cowhands in the isolated camp. Carue, after his
first outburst against a woman veterinarian, had taken
her under his wing, and anyone would have thought
she was his own private acquisition.

Jasper and Rio found her at the line camp on Monday, and she shared a cup of camp coffee with Jasper
before he went back to the ranch house. "We'll be in
late tomorrow, Jasper," she told him. "And Rio will
be helping Hammett while we're in Newark with
Mandy."

Rio echoed her own thoughts. "Will Mandy be all right?"

"I hope so. It would be wonderful if she could hear, wouldn't it?"

"*Sí,*" he said, and she smiled at the soft sound of the Spanish word.

Chapter Five

Wednesday morning she packed her suitcase, trying to remember what late September was like in New Jersey. No matter. Ami had little beside jeans, but as she rummaged through the closet she discovered a mauve-colored pantsuit she couldn't remember wearing. She pulled it from the hanger and surveyed it with critical eyes. It would do.

The phone rang, and she put the pantsuit on the bed to answer it. "Ami here."

"It's Jeff." As though she wouldn't recognize the deep voice. Surprised, she stared at the goose bumps on her arm. "Jasper will fly us into Tucson. We should leave about noon."

"All right."

When he knocked on the door a few minutes before twelve she was ready. She opened the door to see Mandy smiling up at her. Dressed in yellow overalls and a long-sleeved yellow shirt, she looked like a gray-eyed buttercup. Ami smiled at Jeff and stooped to hug Mandy.

Jeff drove the Bronco to the airstrip, where Jasper waited to transfer their luggage, and strap Mandy in the seat behind his.

"I wish I had a tranquilizer to last till we get to Newark," Ami told him as they readied for takeoff.

He laughed at her. "Don't you trust me yet, Ami?"

"You more than the big ones, Jasper. Jeff would kill you if anything happened to his plane." She relaxed a little as both men laughed.

Mandy peeked around her seat and grinned. She had no fear of flying and trusted Jasper anywhere.

They didn't have long to wait in Tucson, and the big airliner took off right on schedule, landing in Newark at eight o'clock, Newark time. It was already dark.

As they waited for their luggage Ami took out the paper with the name of the motel on it. Linda had called Jeff to confirm the reservations for him while Ami was still out at the camp.

Mandy nodded as they rode in the taxi to the motel, and Ami pulled her close, turning to look out the window as they moved along. In the dim streetlights she gazed at the full-leaved trees, thick and dark. It was too early for the leaves to have fallen, and even in darkness she could feel the differences from their Arizona climate in the damp air. The taxi slowed and turned into the driveway of a dimly lighted motel. The driver took their bags, and Ami waited as Jeff got their keys to the adjoining rooms, then picked up the sleeping child from her side.

"Let Mandy stay with me," she said as he unlocked the door.

He gave her a long look and nodded, placing the little girl on one of the twin beds. "Do you want me to put her pajamas on?"

She shook her head. "I'll do it."

Jeff brought in their bags and opened Mandy's, and after saying good night went into his room. The child yawned and smiled as Ami wiggled her out of her overalls and into the pyjamas. Ami picked her up and took her to the bathroom, kneeling beside her to let the little girl lean on her shoulder. She tucked her in bed, undressed, and slipped beneath the sheets in the other bed. She stretched, trying to relax, and her thoughts went to Jeff next door.

Eileen was crazy, she decided. Ami wouldn't let Jeff out of her sight, especially with another woman. She smiled to herself. Eileen was so sure of herself, she assumed there was nothing to worry about, which was probably true.

She called Linda at six thirty the next morning. "I was afraid I might wake someone," she said.

Linda laughed. "We've been up for ages. Dave is already in surgery. We'll meet you at the office at nine. Will that be all right?"

"Yes, of course." Jeff had already gone to rent a car, and Ami was expecting him back at any time. Mandy was at the window, watching for his return.

"Oh, Ami. I can hardly wait to see you and talk to you." Linda sounded the same as always. "It'll be so good."

"Yes, it will. See you about nine."

By the time Jeff returned with the rented car, they were dressed and hungry. They had breakfast at the motel restaurant, with Mandy bright-eyed and signing away, giving no indication that she was worried. Ami was conscious of the attention they received from other diners. The tall man, slender woman, and small girl all using sign language, so that there was no indication who was deaf until Jeff turned to speak to the waitress and then to Ami in a normal voice.

Linda had furnished directions the short distance to the clinic, and Jeff drove down Winters Avenue, turning at Langtry, and immediately pulled into a parking lot behind a low brick building. A sign at the side heralded the Monroe Clinic.

Mandy stood by Ami, holding tightly to her hand, as Jeff locked the car and took her other hand. He looked down at the child and, as she met his glance, he smiled and winked at her. Mandy skipped between them as they crossed the parking lot to the entrance. A sign said: DO NOT KNOCK. PLEASE ENTER.

Jeff pushed the door open and waited for Mandy and Ami to walk inside.

"Ami," a voice called, and she looked up to see Linda hurrying toward them.

"Hello, Linda." Ami was caught tightly, and after a moment, Linda held her away. Linda looked up, searching the smoothly tanned features.

"You look wonderful," she said and turned to face Jeff.

"Jeff, Dr. Monroe," Ami said, and to Linda, "This is Amanda," and signed for the child. "This is Dr. Monroe."

Linda shook hands with Jeff, then stooped to Amanda's level. "Hello, Amanda," she signed.

Solemn gray eyes looked Dr. Monroe over. Mandy looked at Jeff, who nodded, and she smiled, dipping her head a little as she did so.

Linda took her hand and led them into the inner office. "Dave will be here shortly. The operation took longer than expected, which happens frequently." She sighed. "We don't care how long it takes, just so it works." She pulled a chart to the center of her desk. "Let me get this filled out before we start any discussions."

The next several minutes were spent with Jeff answering questions and Linda recording the information. Ami played a game with Mandy, asking her the questions, and Mandy gave her own version of the answers, giggling when Ami called her a smarty-pants. Linda didn't miss the exchange between the two and smiled at them several times as she wrote on the chart.

"I'd like Amanda to stay in the hospital during the tests. Except Sunday, when we want all of you out for dinner." Jeff translated for Mandy this time, and Ami saw a look of doubt come into the child's eyes. Ami reached for her hand and squeezed it and was rewarded with an uncertain smile. She forced herself not to give in to the urge to pick her up to reassure her.

After checking Mandy in, Linda led them down the hallway to double doors that stood open. It was a big room with four beds, each by a window. Three of the beds were occupied, and a young nurse came by and smiled at Amanda, walking ahead of them to turn back the bright yellow spread from the pillows.

She turned and, with sign language, said, "I'm Ellen. You must be Amanda."

Mandy nodded and lifted her arms to Ellen to be helped onto the bed. Ami bit her lip, realizing Mandy knew what was coming and was reconciled to it. She looked at Jeff, wishing she could apologize for being pushy, accusing him of not wanting to give Mandy another chance to hear. He looked at her as if aware of her thoughts and, suddenly, he smiled as though he knew what she was thinking and accepted her apology.

A hand on her arm turned her to face Dave, who laughed and said, "My favorite vet, as lovely as ever." He bent a little to kiss her cheek and held a hand out to Jeff. The men exchanged pleasantries, and Dave explained in depth the steps they would take to determine what they could do for Mandy.

Hours later Jeff drove them back to the motel. "You must be starved," he said.

"I am hungry," she admitted with a smile.

They ate in the motel restaurant, both quiet as they thought of the day behind them and all the ones to come. She looked up to find Jeff watching her and smiled at him.

"You're very quiet," he said.

Ami was glad he couldn't read her mind, because she was remembering the feel of his mouth on hers.

"Hospitals aren't my favorite places to visit," she told him.

"Nor mine." He reached and touched her fingers lightly. "I'm glad you came. Amanda has been much easier to deal with this time."

"I'm glad, too, although I do feel guilty leaving Rio and Hammett alone."

Jeff leaned forward. "They'll manage." He continued to look at her, his eyes going over her face until they rested on her lips, and she wet them with a flick of her tongue. When he looked up to meet her own gaze, his eyes darkened before he smiled and went back to eating.

It was nine o'clock before they stood in front of her room. Jeff opened the door and turned to her, blocking her entrance into the room. His hand came out to lift her chin so that she was forced to look up at him and watch as he leaned to place his mouth on hers. She stood still, hoping the tremors throughout her body didn't show. As his lips lingered on hers, hers parted involuntarily as the pressure increased.

He lifted his head, his hand still under her chin, and said softly, "Good night, Ami," standing aside to allow her to enter the room. She went inside without answering him and leaned against the door as he closed it behind her.

"This will never do," she murmured aloud to the empty room, and had a feeling she was in for a lot of talking common sense to herself.

Friday and Saturday till noon were spent in much the same way, tests and talks but no decisions. On Monday Mandy was scheduled for tissue to be removed from her inner ear for biopsy examination, but they had the weekend ahead of them. It was one o'clock Saturday afternoon when they checked her out of the clinic with an overnight pass.

"Would you like to see the water, Ami? The upper bay comes between New Jersey and New York about an hour's drive from us," Jeff said as they left the parking lot.

She turned to Mandy sitting between them, asking her the question, receiving an enthusiastic yes.

The day was warm and sticky with a breeze coming directly off the water. They passed an amusement park, shuttered and locked, with a sign indicating CLOSED TILL SUMMER.

"It's different," Ami observed, enjoying the heavy leaves of the trees along the sidewalk, just beginning to show a touch of autumn gold.

The last time she was in Newark it was different, she remembered, when Tim divorced her and she ran to Linda and Dave in their small apartment, licking her wounds and pulling herself back together. They had been her support, helping her to find her way back to living again. She shivered. No one should be allowed to hurt that way.

The car stopped, and she realized they had reached the water. "Too bad it's foggy. We could probably see ships coming up the water," Jeff said.

Strain as she would, Ami couldn't see past the thin gray curtain of fog over the water. She turned to Mandy, who was sitting forward, staring at more water than she had ever seen in Arizona. Jeff stopped the car at a lookout point, and they got out to go stand by the rock wall. The mournful sound of a ship's blast of warning echoed through the mist, and they saw it coming toward them in the middle of the river.

Jeff stooped and lifted Amanda to the top of the wall, and Ami smiled at her as the child's eyes widened.

"It's a freighter," she told her. "A ship that carries things from one country to another."

Mandy nodded and continued to watch the progress

of the ship. As it passed by them, Jeff put her down, and held between them, she skipped on the sand. Ami looked down as Mandy pulled her hand away and looked up at Jeff.

"I'm hungry. Can I have a hot dog?" the child signed.

He laughed. "It's dinner time. Let's find a place and all of us can eat."

Back in the car, Jeff headed toward their motel. Ami and Mandy watched the neat rows of homes pass and occasionally smiled at each other. Ami looked around when the car stopped to see they had reached the restaurant that Linda and Dave had recommended. Mandy was able to get her hot dog.

It was dark when they finally left the restaurant, and Ami gathered Mandy to her as she leaned against her in the car. By the time they reached the motel, she was asleep.

Jeff came around to open her door and said, "Wait till I unlock the room, and I'll come back for her." He came back and bent to take the sleeping child from her, and his hair brushed her cheek as he straightened. He still smelled of the outdoors. Ami locked the car door and followed him into the room, conscious of a fluttering in her stomach. *Well,* she argued to herself, *he's an attractive man, and it's been a long time since I've been this close to one. And it had better be as close as I get,* she concluded, thinking of the fire in Eileen's brown eyes.

Jeff placed the sleeping Mandy on the bed she had slept in on Wednesday night and removed her slippers. With movements learned from long practice, he undressed her and took the gown Ami handed him, slipping it over the blond pigtails. He turned the covers back and lifted Mandy to place her on the pillow. The little girl sighed and slept on. Jeff stood a moment looking down at her and moved away. Ami was watching his every move and was surprised at the tightness of his mouth, realizing again the worry he was going through alone as he had so many times before. She touched his arm, and he turned to look at her and reached to pull her into his arms, holding her tightly against him for a moment before he pushed her away.

"Good night, Ami," he said and walked through the connecting door to his room.

She undressed slowly, getting ready for bed, glancing at the tiny girl, who didn't stir. When she turned out the lights, she went to look out the window at the thick shadows all around. It had been a long four days for her; what must it seem like to Jeff and Mandy? Her sympathy was with Mandy; the feeling for Jeff was more than that, and she was filled with uncertainty.

They had breakfast late and took out the map Dave had drawn for them to use to locate the house. It was easy, only a mile from the clinic, and near the small apartment they had lived in before buying the larger town house.

The house was like Linda: organized and lovely. The sour beef and dumplings were done to perfection, as was the homemade strawberry shortcake. Dave and Jeff retired to the patio, and Mandy went to sleep with no urging. Ami leaned against the sink, watching Linda put everything in its place.

She asked the question uppermost in her mind. "Does Mandy have a good chance?"

"Excellent, as a matter of fact. Think success, Ami. When have you let insurmountable odds bother you?"

"The odds were never for Mandy before."

Linda stopped what she was doing and turned to face her. "How about Tim, Ami? Are you over him?"

Ami considered the question. "After two years, I think it's time, don't you."

Linda nodded. "But I asked if you are, not if you should be."

"Yes." And, suddenly, she knew it was true.

"Hooray for you." Linda hugged her. "Now, what about Jeff?"

Startled, Ami asked, "What about Jeff?"

"Are you in love with him?"

She stared at her friend. "Are you crazy? Eileen has a capital claim staked there. You don't think I'd be foolish enough to get into competition with her? I only tangle with domesticated animals—not wildcats." Even as she denied loving Jeff, she couldn't help but wonder at the odd feelings about him, and the kisses she couldn't treat as casual touches.

"Well, I don't know Eileen, but I do know you, and you've got her beat all the way."

Ami laughed. "You're prejudiced."

"No prejudice allowed here." It was Dave. "Who is, in this day and age?"

"Your wife, sir. You should talk to her." Ami was still laughing. Inside, a weight had lifted. She was free of Tim. How wonderful, she thought, feeling exhilaration building. She never thought it would happen. She turned to find Jeff towering in the doorway with Mandy smiling sleepily in his arms.

"As much as I hate to eat and run, we promised to have Amanda back before eight. We'll see you in the morning."

In the car Mandy, still cuddly from her nap, sat in Ami's lap. She allowed them to check her into the clinic with no fuss, but Ami felt her throat constrict as they left her.

"Let's stop for a drink. Our last chance to relax for a while."

"All right." Ami watched his profile as he drove. His lips were drawn tight, matching the guarded look in his eyes.

The small bar where they stopped was almost empty. Possibly it was early, or people were off enjoying the last of the good weather before the onset of a long, cold winter.

"You'd better tell me what you want. I've never seen you drink."

"A piña colada sounds good."

Jeff grinned as he gave their order. "Sounds terrible."

Neither of them attempted to make conversation, but their silence was shared companionship without having to talk. As he left her at her room he bent to kiss her as naturally as he would if it were an everyday occurrence, and left her with her thoughts tangling around the feelings he brought to the surface.

Ami shook her head as she undressed, pushing her unruly thoughts into the back of her mind as she slid between the cool sheets. Tomorrow promised to be a very long day.

Chapter Six

They sat in the audio room of the clinic with Dave, Linda, and two other doctors who were consulting on the case.

Dave spoke first. "We've isolated Amanda's problem, Jeff, and Dr. Herbert, here, agrees with us that it's one that we can be confident of a great deal of success in if we operate. Dr. Herbert is from Boston, where they've done extensive research in traumatic hearing impairment. Since you were at Johns Hopkins with Amanda, you probably recognize Dr. Maldin as a prominent surgeon in the same field."

Jeff nodded, leaning forward. "What was your final evaluation?" His voice was tense as he asked the question.

It was Tuesday afternoon. Monday had been a gruelling battery of more tests, more talks, more waiting, and Ami was feeling uncertain about the entire procedure, fully realizing now Jeff's reluctance to put Amanda through all of this. She wanted to touch him, let him know she was there, but she sat still, listening.

"We'd like to operate. We wouldn't be using her as a guinea pig, Jeff," Linda said, her soft voice intense as she tried to convince him of the possible results of the operation. "We've done this type of operation with great success. It's usually on older people, but Amanda has a very good chance of hearing. Not as good as you or I, but as well as a lot of people who aren't even aware they have a hearing problem.''

Jeff stared from one face to the other, his glance finally resting on Ami. She looked back, hoping he couldn't see how her heart reacted. He stood up and walked to a table where a coffee pot had been set up for them, but he didn't touch the cups there. Instead, he turned and looked at the faces watching him.

"All right. If you think she has a fighting chance, go ahead.''

The operation took place early Wednesday, and Mandy was back in her room at one o'clock. Ami left to get them a sandwich and coffee. She bit her lip to keep the tears back, thinking of the tiny, still figure, her blond hair shaved two inches above each ear.

They took turns sitting with her until ten that night. Mandy was awake and fretful when the night nurse came by.

"I'll give her something for the pain, and she'll sleep. You should go home. I'll stay with her.''

Groggy from worry and exhaustion, they accepted the offer. They didn't talk on the way to the motel, and Jeff left her immediately with a quiet "Thanks, and good night.''

Thursday morning it was raining; a slow, chilling rain that caused Ami to shiver as she looked outside. End of Indian summer, she thought.

While Jeff went to see Mandy, Ami stayed with Linda, sympathetic but confident. "I know you think you're neglecting your job, Ami, and I understand your wanting to get back. Amanda is on the way to healing very well, and all we need is a week, maybe ten days, to see that the grafts take and there'll be no infection. I'll call you Saturday morning after we run the first hearing tests on Mandy.''

Ami had decided to return to the ranch on Friday,

since Mandy was doing so well. Jeff had agreed with
her decision, knowing she was reluctant to leave
Mandy.

Linda looked around at her. "It's been so good having you here." She hesitated, then asked, "Wonder
why he had you come rather than Eileen?"

Ami laughed. "Stop thinking, Linda. It was Mandy,
not Jeff, who wanted me to come with her."

"All right. Wonder why Mandy asked for you, not
Eileen?"

"The way I understand it, Eileen not only thinks
children shouldn't be seen or heard, but any illness dis-
turbs her. She refers to Mandy's not hearing as an af-
fliction."

"And Jeff lets her?" Linda was furious.

"I'm sure he's never heard that reference, or he
might wash her mouth out with soap." Ami's voice
was dry.

A few minutes later Linda dropped Ami at the motel, promising again to call her on Saturday.

It was twelve thirty, and Jeff was still at the clinic,
telling her to rest while he stayed with Mandy. They
were going to dress the operation to examine it, and
Mandy would be sedated.

She undressed, folded the mauve-colored suit carefully, put it in her bag, dragged out her faithful jeans
and plain white shirt, then headed for the shower, trailing the pale yellow terry robe behind her. She stayed a
long time, shampooing her hair and letting the warm
water soothe the tension from her neck and shoulders.
It had been a hard week for her, but what about Jeff?
He must be tied in knots.

Belting the robe around her, Ami went to stand by
the window. The sky was a smooth dark gray, rain
pouring steadily, and streetlamps were already on, even
though it was just a few minutes past one o'clock. She
shivered and pulled her robe tighter when a knock
sounded on the door. She brushed her damp hair from

her face as the knock was repeated, and Jeff called, "Ami, are you home?"

Smiling, she opened the door, forgetting she wore only the yellow robe. Jeff's hair was even darker with the rain on it. He shook his head. "The monsoons have arrived." He glanced at the robe, the still-damp hair. "I thought we could both use a drink and picked up some brandy. Will that be all right?"

"A small drink, Jeff. I guess it's going to be a long, long evening. Were they satisfied with the way the healing was progressing?"

"Yes, it looks good." He poured brandy in their water glasses, handing the smaller drink to her. "They're optimistic, and I'd like to be, but I can't help but remember all the other times it looked good." He stretched out in the armchair and sighed. He lifted his glass toward her. "Here's hoping this is the miracle we've been searching for."

She lifted hers back and sat in the chair opposite him.

"No real boyfriends, Ami?" The question out of the silence was unexpected.

She smiled at his emphasis on *real*. "No. No real ones."

"Why not?" Jeff sipped the brandy. "And why is a lovely girl like you stuck out in the desert with a raggedy dog and an orphaned Mexican?"

"I'm a vet. Remember?"

"You could have brought a husband or a boyfriend with you."

"I just told you, I don't have one."

"And I just asked why not?"

She could stop this type of fencing right now. Bluntly she said, "I'm getting over a broken marriage."

That stopped him for a moment, and he studied her over his glass. "What happened?"

Ami shrugged. "The divorce papers said incompatibility."

Your fault or his?" He was still watching her.

"Mine," she told him.

"You assume the blame mighty quick."

She sipped the brandy but didn't answer. The drink was warm down to her stomach. This was the most conversation they had managed in private the entire week. The subject was disturbing, and the direct questioning more than she needed.

"Where is he now?" Jeff had his head back against the chair, eyeing her through half-closed lids.

"I don't know."

"How long since the divorce?"

"Two years."

"You still love him?"

The inquisition was getting out of hand. Ami got up and walked to the window. Trees were bending with the heavy rain and wind, and as she watched, orange and blue lightning flashed, outlining the trees in silhouette. A heavy rumble of thunder followed.

"I wonder if Mandy will like thunderstorms when she can hear all the noise."

"Do you?" he asked.

"Yes, especially our southwestern storms. They're wild and beautiful, even if we don't get much rain with them. Here they seem sad and lonely."

They were silent, listening to the pouring rain. "You didn't answer me. Do you still love him?"

"No." She turned away from the window. "Do you need another drink?"

Jeff looked at his glass, drained the little left in it, and handed it to her. She filled it, adding a little to her own. Passing his chair, she handed him the glass and kept walking to the window and pulled the draperies closed, turned the lamp on, and returned to her chair.

"Did you have lunch?" Jeff asked.

She thought about it. "No, we had rolls and coffee. Linda was due in surgery. You?"

He grinned. "I ate some of Amanda's." He stretched.

"Maybe the rain will let up and we'll go out. I don't much want motel food, do you?"

"No, but I'm not hungry."

"By the time we get out, you may be starved."

They were quiet, and she was beginning to think he had gone to sleep when he groaned and sat up.

"What's wrong?"

"What will I do if this doesn't work?" His voice was uncertain, and he gave her a hard look. "I think I'll hate you."

She was beside him, kneeling by the chair. "She'll be able to hear. I know she will, so she can hear Charlie laugh."

He shook his head. "You told her Charlie laughs?"

"Yes."

"Of course. That's why she loves you so much. You see the world through her eyes."

Bright turquoise eyes laughed up at him. "It's prettier than through mine." She was still kneeling beside him, her face almost level with his. The dark gray eyes, clouded with worry, widened as he searched her features, and it required only a slight move on his part to cover her mouth with his, fingers beneath her chin to keep her there. In her unsteady position her body swayed, and he reached, pulling her into the chair with him. One arm held her close; the other hand slid beneath the folds of her robe. He drew in his breath as his hand touched the warm bare flesh.

I'd better move before this goes any further, she thought, but she didn't, watching as his face lowered to hers. There was an instant's hesitation before his mouth touched hers and, with a sigh, she relaxed against his shoulder. Her hands slid up his arms, pulling him closer, and his arms tightened, crushing her to him. Her head slipped back and her mouth shaped to his kiss, answering the need she felt in him. Lips parted, she felt his teeth against hers as warm, forgotten feelings stirred inside her. How long it lasted she didn't know, till he lifted his head, watching her through black lashes. Lightly his lips brushed her cheek, then found her parted lips again. His kiss was gentle this time, tracing the full lower lip, the curve of her cheek, then back to her waiting mouth. They sighed in unison, and she felt him slide forward in the chair, one arm beneath her legs as he lifted her. The bed gave with their combined weight, his hands pushed the robe from her shoulders, and his lips brushed against the rushing pulse in her throat.

"Jeff." It was only a whisper. She heard the sound of a word, not knowing if he had said anything. "We can't—" she started, but he silenced her as he found her mouth again. His hands beneath her brought her fully into his embrace, and she stretched her long legs against the hard length of him. Suddenly she was a woman, too long denied the demands of her young, healthy body, with no wish to stop their headlong move toward the fulfillment they both wanted. Her hand touched his cheek, his firm lips. Her eyes, searching the rugged features, found his looking straight at her.

"Move your hand, Ami," he whispered. "Undress me."

She did, unbuttoning his shirt and unfastening his belt as he twisted to slide his pants from his hips. His hand went down her body, slowly over the contour of her hips to her thighs to push her backward, caressing across her flat stomach, curving over her small high breasts. Hungry desire caught at him as she responded with slow movements against him. His lips parted over hers as he moaned deep in his throat, taking her with his powerful thighs, bringing a shattering, explosive breath from both of them. His mouth grew gentle on hers as he cradled her to him until both were breathing evenly again.

Time was lost as they lay close together, then she felt

his hands move over her, touching her breasts, trailing fingers across her flat stomach. She heard him whisper "Ami?"

It was a question she answered by turning, outlining her body to his, moving her head back so that he found her lips. They moved together until he took her breath with a soaring sweetness, his arms imprisoning her willing body. She was vaguely aware of the storm still raging outside, no less than the one inside the room.

When she awakened, the lights were still on and, for a moment, she wasn't sure where she was. Realization came as she turned her head to see Jeff asleep beside her. Black lashes against the tanned cheek didn't hide the shadows under his eyes. It had been a rough week for him, and she felt a rush of tenderness for him, compassion for Mandy, who was going through so much she didn't understand. Then it dawned on her what had happened as she studied Jeff's face. Knowledge that she was in love with him hit her, constricting her throat, bringing tears to her eyes, with not a chance in the world that it was returned.

Jeff's eyes opened and widened as they took in the face so near his. His glance moved over her face to her lips, back to her rumpled hair. Their eyes met. His hand moved to follow the curve of her hip, teasingly across her stomach to cup her breast. She drew in her breath, and Jeff's eyes darkened as he raised himself on one elbow, leaning to touch her lips. Her eyes were wide, and he saw the sparkle of tears.

"Why?" was all he said as his kiss closed her lids.

"Why what?" Her throat hurt.

"You're crying. Did I hurt you?"

"No."

"Then why?" His lips moved away and he was watching her. She shook her head, not knowing how to answer him.

His arms cradled her to him as his lips, warm and searching, moved across her face to her throat. He pulled the lobe of her ear between his teeth, nibbling gently, and went back to her mouth. He pushed her back against the pillow and propped himself up on one arm, looking down at her. His finger traced the lips like warm rose satin, the curve of her cheek, the tilted nose with five freckles he counted one by one. He followed the line of her jaw to the hollow of her throat, down to the cleft between the small breasts. A gentle caress across her breast hardened the brown tip, and he lowered his head to tease it with his lips. Warmth spread through her body as he moved to the other breast, rubbing the mound with his lips, his tongue closing over the hard nipple. Her breath came quick and warm, then stopped completely as her explosive feelings threatened, waiting to be released by his movements.

Both her hands went behind his head, holding him to her, relinquishing her hold only to allow his mouth to return to hers, where he whispered "Darling Ami" as he took possession of her once more. His measured movements were gentle, his hunger not as demanding as before.

He came out of the shower, saw her still stretched full length on the bed, her nude body clearly outlined by the thin sheet. He stood over her. "I can come back to bed."

She smiled. "I'm hungry." Then, as she realized he was fully dressed, she said, "You aren't going out, are you? It's too nasty."

Jeff sat beside her, not touching her, concentrating on her body beneath the cover. "There's a Chinese restaurant a couple of blocks away. I called, while you were sleeping and it's ready to be picked up." He smiled. "You do like Chinese food?"

She laughed. "I wouldn't dare not to after that, would I?"

He bent to kiss the laughing mouth. "No." He stood up. "I'll be back shortly."

Ami lay still after he had gone, realizing her life was in for some changes. Hurt lay just a kiss away. And she thought she was doing so well. She left the bed they had shared, took a shower, and dressed. When she heard his key in the door, she crossed to open it for him.

"Whew, you're right, it's nasty out there. Hope the food's worth it." His eyes went over her jeans and shirt, and her freshly brushed sun-streaked hair. "I like the other outfit better," he said, watching the color flare in her cheeks.

They were hungry and ate in companionable silence. "Your plane leaves at ten forty-five in the morning, so, if you want to, you can see Amanda before you go."

"Yes, you know I do." She leaned back, looking at her watch. It was ten thirty, almost ten hours since they had the first drink. She was cooking up years of heartache, she thought, feeling lonely. Eileen would never give up her possession. Not that Jeff would want her to; he had needed someone, and Ami was available.

"A penny?" he asked.

"Not worth it." She smiled at him, and rubbed her stomach. "I'll have to diet after this, or I can stay at the shack a couple of weeks on C rations."

Jeff was silent a moment. "I wasn't thinking, Ami." She waited as he hesitated. "I wouldn't want to be responsible for your being pregnant."

She stiffened and stared at him. He couldn't be expected to know he had nothing to worry about. "Would it help if I said don't worry?"

He looked at her sitting with her long legs across the chair arms. The gray eyes changed, and his voice was withdrawn as he said, "Yes, I should have known you could take care of yourself."

The intonation hurt for an instant, then Ami remembered her willing response in his arms, not blaming him for his suspicions. She said nothing.

He got up and walked to the window, opening the drapes she had closed hours ago. It was pitch dark and the sound of wind and rain seemed louder than before. "Turn the light out and come here."

Ami did as she was told, walking slowly in the darkness to stand beside him.

"More rain than we see in a year." She could hear the smile in his voice.

"I love the rain, but nothing beats our climate."

"Not everyone feels that way, you know."

"I guess not."

He pulled her closer, and with the same thought, they sat on the floor, leaning against the low windowsill. "Tell me how you came to be good friends with Linda." His tone was conversational.

"I met her when we were both in graduate school; she was in med and I was in animal husbandry training."

"All of it. Dave only told me a little about it. You saved her life, didn't you?" His glance covered her face, the strange-colored eyes, dark tumbled hair. "Dave would do anything for you. That's why I was able to get Amanda into the clinic so quickly."

"I was there when the car skidded and headed for Linda. I tackled her and broke her arm. A surgeon's arm." She laughed. "Some rescue."

"Arms heal; necks usually don't." Jeff was nuzzling against her throat, and she could feel the rough beard scraping her cheek. She wanted to run, hide from the heartache she could see coming. Too late, a voice reminded her. Much too late.

"Who are you, Ami? No one owns you. You're free

as the desert breeze." His lips traced her palm and he folded her fingers around his kiss. "Oddest eyes I've ever seen." His arms tightened. "There were tears before. Why? You said I didn't hurt you."

She turned her face so that her mouth was against his. She whispered, "No, you didn't hurt me." That would come later, she was certain.

Their lips caught and held, and, slowly, he turned her until they lay side by side on the carpeted floor. She made no objection as he unbuttoned her shirt. Her hands moved over the rough hair of his chest, holding him, and long moments later she lay close to him as he slept in her arms. It was a long time before she, too, slept.

Sometime during the early morning hours Jeff moved in her arms and left, returning with a blanket to cover her. She watched him go through the connecting door, and the memory of what happened came to haunt her.

What a mess. She lay still, eyes closed, refusing to believe she could be so gullible. *That's what I get for thinking I'm immune to loving anyone.* Dread of what was to come filled her.

Mind and body protested every move as she got up and dressed. Six thirty; four hours till plane time. A quiet knock brought her abruptly to the time she had to face Jeff. She was not ready. She opened the door.

Dark gray eyes smiled at her. "Let's get some coffee." It was as though he had never touched her. He didn't mention the hours spent in her arms, nor did she. Let it be said she could take a cue when offered, she thought. So be it.

Mandy was subdued when they got to her, still under sedation. Ami hugged her. "I have to go back to work, Mandy," she said. "See you in a couple of weeks." The gray eyes, so like Jeff's, were hazy, but the smile was Mandy's. She nodded.

Then they were in the car and on their way to the

airport. Ami kept her hands clenched into fists in her
lap as Jeff concentrated on driving through heavy traffic. She felt as desolate as the wet streets looked and
fought the heaviness inside her as they pulled into the
airport parking area.

"Ami?" She turned to face him. "I know what happened shouldn't have, but I can't really say I'm sorry."
When she didn't answer him, Jeff tipped her chin so
that she had to look at him. As their eyes met, his darkened. "Can we live with it?" he asked.

Ami said what he wanted her to say. "Yes." Not for
one moment was she sure.

"Thanks for being here with Mandy. It made it
much easier for me." He bent his head and kissed her
and, for a moment, he held her close. At the gate he
pulled her to him again as though reluctant to let her
go, then she was on the plane, and Newark was a pat-
terned, misty picture below her.

She didn't remember much of the flights but was
glad when Jasper deposited her at her door. He listened
with delight as she recounted the days with Mandy,
shaking his head at the mere thought that she might
hear. Jeff had already called and talked to everyone,
and Ami had only to add her detailed account.

Talking to Janie, she sensed the jubilation in everyone, expecting the best for Mandy.

*And I should be happy, but I feel like I lost someone—
someone I never had.* She sighed, turning her mind away
from Jeff and Mandy and concentrating on the job at
hand.

Chapter Seven

Linda called her at six Saturday morning. "Ami, I hate to call so early, but I have surgery at nine. Best news, my friend. Mandy has at least fifty percent of her hearing, and that will improve." Linda's voice was ecstatic.

At the sound of Linda's voice, Ami froze. The silence went on till Linda said, "Ami, are you there?"

She swallowed over the dryness in her throat. "Linda, did anyone ever call you an angel?"

Linda's laugh sparkled. "Among other things."

"Linda, what about speech? She has so much catching up to do."

"Dr. Mathers and Dr. Preston are our best audio therapy specialists for children, and they'll work with Mandy while she's here the next ten days or so. They'll contact their counterparts in Tucson and get Mandy enrolled in their programs. It will take a little while, Ami, but Mandy learns very quickly, and in no time she'll be talking away. Trust us."

"Oh, I do, Linda. If there's ever anything I can do for you and Dave—" She stopped.

"I'm alive, Ami, thanks to you. Visit us again soon?"

"Yes. Yes, I will. Thanks again." She sat silent as the connection was broken. Mandy could hear, at least some. Who said the age of miracles was over? Hugging herself, she did a whirling dance step across the floor

and was confronted by Remus, who grinned at her as if
to say "Ain't it a blast?"

She went outside, breathing in the first dawn breezes,
looking toward Janie's. There was a light on, and she
started on the run, detouring by the corral, where Hammett was already busy.

She skidded to a halt in front of the startled old man,
then, with a whoop, wrapped her arms around him and
danced a jig.

"She can hear, Hammett. Mandy can hear."

He stared. "Are you sure?"

"Linda just called."

Tears clouded the bright blue eyes. "Lord have
mercy."

The old man eyed her, shaking his head. "I never
dared dream. I just never dreamed."

"What's all the fuss?" Rio asked from behind her.

Ami went over the news, seeing Rio's face brighten,
the dark eyes flash in disbelief. Then he was hugging
her, swinging her around as though she weren't as big
as he.

When they calmed down a little, she said, "I have to
talk to Janie and Steve. See you two at breakfast."

The door swung inward as Ami raised her hand to
knock, and Janie stood there, tawny brown eyes dark
with shock. "Jeff's on the phone. Mandy can hear." It
was like Christmas bells heard around the world.

Janie pulled her inside, and they stood arm in arm,
listening to Steve's half of the conversation. Steve said,
"Ami, Jeff wants to talk to you." He handed the phone
to her and reached for Janie.

Her hand clenched around the receiver as she heard
Jeff's voice. "Ami, how are you?" He sounded tired.

"Wonderful. And you?"

"No way to explain it, Ami. No words." There was a
brief silence. "Ami, I want to thank you for everything, although that sounds bland for what I'm feel-

ing.'' She stiffened at the polite words. He went on. ''Mandy was better off for your being with her, and she already wants to come home.''

''We can't wait to see her,'' Ami finally managed over the choking in her throat.

''We'll see all of you in about ten days, I guess.'' He was gone.

Ami took a deep breath and turned to face Janie and Steve. With one movement they were all hugging.

When they settled down a bit, Janie said, ''Now, tell us what they did.''

Ami shook her head. ''I wish I could. Dave explained some of the techniques, but it's over my head. I know they replaced some part of her inner ears with her own body material from her wrist. She only has a tiny scar on the inside of her arm, and Linda says that will fade in time. Lord, I love those two.'' The other love was one she didn't mention.

Ami's heart was light as she took Rio and Remus and headed for the line camps early Monday morning, knowing there was plenty of work to do before the late fall rains came. The cattle in the flash flood areas had to be moved to higher ground, and they went with them, checking the water and feed troughs. As they moved Ami's eyes were alert for deep scratches or bloody spots that might be an injury that needed tending or for infected insect bites. The long hard hours sent them to bed at night tired, but content with their life.

Days turned into weeks, with Ami and Rio learning from their daily adventures and experiences. She worked her way through the crisis of cattle injuries and viruses, going to Hammett occasionally for advice. The old man was a good sounding board for ideas and, more often than not, he agreed with her, adding only some point she hadn't yet thought about. He was one of many good friends they had made at Wagner's.

Jeff followed Dave's advice and put Mandy in the special school for speech in Tucson. Ami's heart went out to the tiny girl, alone all week with strangers, learning a strange language. She came home weekends, and the times Ami was at the ranch, Mandy came to see her.

One Saturday afternoon they sat on the back steps, concentrating on the work Ami held in her hand. She touched Mandy's shoulder and, using a mixture of sound and sign language, she told her, "This is patchwork. You put the design on this square of material and stitch around it." She handed her the needle and a square of white with a cutout of material shaped like the head of a longhorn steer. The little fingers were clumsy as she attempted to draw a thread through, so Ami put her arms around the slight shoulders and took the needle from her, showing her how to make the tiny stitches through both pieces of material. Concentrating, they both started as Jeff spoke.

"Homework?" he asked.

Ami laughed. "No. Patchwork. Mandy couldn't understand what I was doing, so I was showing her."

He reached for Mandy, who went into his arms, holding around his neck. "We're going to Eileen's for dinner, and Hazel needs to bathe you."

Mandy shook her head vigorously. "I'll stay with Ami."

Jeff smiled. "She's having hot dogs especially for you."

"I'll stay with Ami," she repeated, looking straight at him.

Ami stood up. "I'd love to keep her, Jeff. She's no trouble."

He hesitated. "I'll be late getting home, but you can take her to Hazel about seven."

Ami turned to the little girl. "Want to stay all night with me?"

Mandy nodded, wiggling down from Jeff's arms, going back to the square they had been working on.

Ami smiled at Jeff as he stood there, his eyes going over her slim figure in the long-sleeved denim shirt and jeans. He had held her and made love to her not many weeks ago, and now it was as though it never happened. To him, perhaps. She remembered every day.

He bent to kiss Mandy's cheek, and she gave him a smile, waving as he turned to make his way across the yard toward the big ranch house. Pushing her feelings to the back of her mind as she always did, Ami sat back down with Mandy, watching the little girl tackle the patchwork in her hand.

There was no doubt the school was helping Mandy. The words she spoke were easily understood. Sometimes she squinted, trying to think of the right sound to go with a word, and would revert back to sign language to make herself understood. At these times they laughed together and figured out the words she wanted.

Ami fixed hot dogs for their supper and, when Mandy yawned, put the pajamas on that Hazel brought her and lay down with her until she went to sleep. After a short while, Ami got up and went to sit in the living room, staring into space. When Jeff and Eileen married, what would happen to Mandy? Mandy never mentioned Eileen, but she didn't stay around when Eileen came to see Jeff at the ranch, staying at the corral with Charlie and Hammett, unless Ami was at home, then she chose to stay with her. After she became mistress of Wagner's, Eileen would probably insist that Mandy go to school in Tucson full time to keep her out of the way, where there would be no competition for Jeff's attention.

The thought hurt her and she went to stand outside. The sky was full of stars, the cold air clear and scented with desert smells. Jeff would do what was best for

Mandy; it wasn't Ami's problem. She winced at the realization that she wished she did have a say in what happened to the little girl.

Time moved along, and Ami marked off the calendar, watching the holidays approach, wondering how to avoid staying around the home corral when she knew Jeff encouraged shorter hours for everyone. Through Janie and Steve, and sometimes a visit from Jasper in the camps, she kept up with Mandy's progress.

"She's something to watch these days, Ami," Jasper told her on one of his visits, laughing as he described Mandy's sudden awareness that she could hear and understand most of what was said in a normal conversation. "You should come in more often on the weekends when she's home. She misses you."

Ami answered him very carefully. "This is a busy time for us, Jasper. Maybe things will slow down after the holidays and the rainy season are behind us." She couldn't tell him it would be dangerous for her to be too near Mandy, since it would mean being close to Jeff, where she had no business to be.

Sometimes during the long nights, unable to sleep, Ami's thoughts were full of Jeff. His personal life was strictly apart from her, as it should be, and the fact that it included Eileen by the same token excluded her. The short hours in his arms left her with memories that haunted her, wanting more, knowing what he had taken from her was more than repaid. She needed him as much as he needed her, but falling in love was a side effect she hadn't counted on.

If you loved once, she thought with some bitterness, thereafter you should have immunity from the disease.

The quiet of the vast canyon she had driven into prompted her to get out of her truck and walk with Remus trotting nearby. Breathing in the clean air, she could feel the approach of colder weather definite in

the late fall temperatures. The toe of her boot hit a
clump of dried mesquite, and her arms flailed outward
to balance herself. She gave a half glance at the offend-
ing stubble and stopped. An unfamiliar pattern in the
hard soil was out of place, somehow, as though a giant
armadillo had slept, then ambled toward the runoff
gulch near the foot of the mountain. She had seen
something similar last month over by Camp 19 when
she had been looking for the cattle tagged in the spring.
Sure that she had left a good number of the young Charolais in that area, she nevertheless couldn't locate
them.

Her gaze followed the marks a few hundred feet
where they disappeared into a wash. Whatever tracks
went in the wash were wiped out by the water coming
out of the higher elevations after the rains of a week
ago. No rain had fallen here, so the odd impressions
remained.

But there were high winds, she mused to herself. She
would ask Steve about it. She looked upward over the
six-thousand-foot mountain range that separated Wagner's and the O'Toole property, which had been up for
sale a long time, since the old man died a couple of
years back. She went back to the truck, puzzling over
the indentations, turning toward the ranch again.

Wagner's celebrated all holidays by letting as many
hands off as they could. She was caught up on her
work, cattle and horses well taken care of for the time
being, and she'd be able to do some paperwork. Over
the long weekend she'd talk to Steve and Jasper about
the unusual markings she found.

When the Sandovals invited Rio for Thanksgiving
dinner, she accepted Janie's invitation to eat with
them. Jasper was there, too.

"I don't think I could take two hours of listening to
Eileen," Jasper said with a malicious grin.

Janie laughed. "Now, Jasper, most men would be

able to be around Eileen and never hear a word she
said, enjoying the scenery.''

"My hearing's too sensitive, I guess,'' he told her
and added, ''Oh, she's nice, but not my type.''

Steve put in his two cents worth. ''What you're saying is, 'What in the world will we do when Jeff marries
the girl?'—isn't it?''

Jasper glanced at Ami before he answered, and she
felt her cheeks grow hot. Jasper wasn't stupid by any
means; nor were Steve and Janie. ''She isn't anything
like Myra, that's for sure,'' he said.

Ami waited for a break in the conversation before
she mentioned the missing cattle to Steve and the odd
marks in the soil.

''Remember, Ami, Jasper and Scully moved some
to the holding area. Probably that group if you're missing so many.''

Jasper thought about it for a minute. ''Yes, we did
take some with us the last drive up there, but I don't
think we had more than two dozen of the Charolais.''

''Did you notice any tracks or marks that you didn't
recognize?'' She described the odd figures in the soil
near the canyon.

''No, but the wind was really high and it makes
tracks like that coming down those canyons at eighty
miles per hour.''

''You may be right,'' she admitted.

Janie changed the subject. ''Did you know Amanda
is going to school full time in Tucson after Christmas?''

''For how long?'' There was a sudden misgiving inside her as she waited for Janie's answer.

''She'll be there for a semester and won't be home
before June. Just in time for the big wedding.''

Ami went still, feeling her face drain of color.
Somehow she had known. She swallowed. ''I thought
they would have a tutor come here for Mandy once

she had been through the elementary steps of the therapy.''

"Eileen wants her to have the best care, you know. That includes getting her away from the lowly influence of the ranch hands." Janie was watching her. Ami was sure her friend guessed some of what happened in Newark, although it was never mentioned.

Ami stood up. "Is Jeff at home today?"

"Yes. They're all having dinner at the house."

"Thanks for the lovely dinner, Janie. I'll see you all later." Ami's long strides took her the quarter mile to the ranch house in a few minutes. She contained the anger inside her as she detoured through the kitchen.

"Lily, how are you?"

"Ami, why didn't you eat with us? It's been a long time." Lily's face beamed at her favorite veterinarian.

"Business before your fattening dinners, Lily. Rio was at Sandoval's, and I ate with Steve and Janie." After a moment, she asked, "Is the boss through eating?"

"Yes. He and Miss McKane are in the living room."

"See you, Lily." Ami found her way through the long hall to the living room. Through the open door she could see Jeff standing near the mantel, and she stared, taking in the tall slimness, remembering things she tried hard to forget. Eileen lounged on the couch, a drink in her hand, very much at home. For a moment she considered turning around and leaving, protecting herself from the hurt she was courting just by talking to Jeff.

Ami's anger disappeared. She knocked, and when Jeff glanced up, she smiled. "Can I see you a moment, Jeff?"

"Come in, Ami. Can I get you a drink?" The dark gray eyes swept her figure and came back to her face. She felt heat in her cheeks, remembering his statement: *"I wouldn't want to be responsible for your being pregnant."* Had it been long enough for him to put his mind at ease? If anything, she was more slender than ever, always losing a pound or two when she was working the camps.

"No, thanks. I wanted to ask about Mandy."

"Sure." His eyes on her were disquieting. Since the night Mandy stayed with her she had seen him only once at a dance and, after that, she didn't go to any more when she thought he would be attending. It hurt, and she wasn't tough enough to face him as though nothing had happened between them. He might be able to ignore it, but she couldn't.

After a glance at Eileen, who regarded her with ill-concealed annoyance, she asked, "Why did you decide to send Mandy to school full time in Tucson? Why not a tutor here? The school will help you find a good one."

Jeff's hands went still on the glass. "The doctors think she's ready to advance to a full-time schedule, and, for that, they prefer her to stay there."

"I disagree." She faced him, realizing he could tell her outright it was none of her business. But it was. "You know she'll be better off here with you."

"And you?" Eileen's laugh was silky. The pale green velveteen dress, worth a small fortune, pointed out the delicate beauty in the tiny face, fitted over her rounded hips, accentuating the small waist. Ami felt big and awkward, not at all dressed to face the boss in her jeans and long-sleeved white shirt.

She turned resolutely back to Jeff, but before she could say anything, Eileen went on. "She'll be better off at school with people just like her and away from your spoiling."

Fury at her careless "people just like her" brought words to Ami's mouth she didn't dare utter. She didn't bother to answer Eileen.

Jeff's voice was mocking as he watched her discomfort. "You don't really know better than the experts, Ami. Besides, where's your loyalty? These are the people you assured me I could have faith in to do the best for Amanda."

"Yes, but let her stay here. I don't want her to stay up there all the time, alone." She was aware that it wasn't what she wanted that counted here, but she couldn't keep the pleading out of her voice.

"She'll be back the first of June, but I'll visit her regularly. So can you and Rio."

"No, Jeff, don't." For a moment he remembered the turquoise eyes bright with tears that she had never explained, and he straightened away from the mantel, taking a step toward her.

"She'll be home in time for the wedding. We plan to announce our engagement on Christmas Eve." Eileen was obviously enjoying her news. "You had heard about it, hadn't you?"

Ami's eyes rested on Jeff's face an instant, then she turned to face the woman. "No, I hadn't heard," she lied. "Congratulations."

Ami went to the door, looking back at them to say quietly, "I can see why you'd want Mandy out of the way for all your preparations. A child can put a crimp in things." She caught a glimpse of Jeff's outraged expression as she closed the door and ran through the carpeted hall, outside into the early darkness. She took a deep breath, but the tears came anyway.

She couldn't remember the last time she had cried like that. When Tim accused her of lying? Their separation? The divorce? A long time ago when dreams died. She didn't try to control the tears as she ran all the way home, glad Rio was still at Sandoval's; glad she could cry all alone. Remus waited on the porch as she ran up the steps and, too late, she remembered the doggie bag Janie had made for him.

"Sorry, fella." She patted his head as he followed her inside and went to sit by the window without turning on a light. She hugged herself, feeling the pain and frustration, not knowing if she cried for Mandy or for herself. When she convinced herself that Mandy was none of her business, she'd get along much better. It served her right for daring to fall in love again, especially with her boss, who belonged to another woman. Love is a fairy tale, best left to competent storytellers.

Hours later she stumbled to her feet, stiff from sitting so long, her throat dry from crying. She ran hot water in the basin, bathing her burning, aching eyes. The rumble in Remus's throat sounded just before the knock on the door.

"Who is it?" she asked, her voice husky from the tears.

"Jeff. May I come in?"

She stood in the middle of the room, feet apart, hands clenched into fists, but she didn't answer him.

"Ami?" The knob turned on the unlocked door, and Jeff stood across the room from her. One glance told her he was furious as he pushed the door closed, looking her up and down.

"Who the hell do you think you are that you know better than anyone else what's good for Amanda? Just because I slept with you doesn't give you license to tell me what to do."

Her head jerked and her body flinched as though dodging a blow. She stared, unable to speak, seeing the sudden realization in his eyes that he had hurt her. If that was his intention, he succeeded. The pain in her chest was so sharp that her doubled-up fist went automatically there to press against it, and she stared at him through a mist.

"I don't believe I deserved that." Her voice was a whisper. "But if I did, then we're even and you can leave now. I promise no more interference with Mandy." She walked into the bedroom, closed the door, and slid the double-lock bolt.

There was a moment of complete silence, then his voice came low and demanding just the other side of the door she leaned against. "Ami, open the door." When she didn't answer him, he repeated the order, finally slamming the door behind him as he left.

The hurt that filled her was unbelievable, but what had she expected? Jeff had taken the love she gave so willingly and used it as a buffer against his worry over Mandy. Somehow she couldn't find it in her heart to blame him.

She found the pills the doctor had given her after her divorce, swallowed two from the almost-full bottle, and went to bed, sleeping the sleep of the damned, turbulent dreams that left her exhausted. At five the next morning she got up, emptied the pills into the garbage, and without making coffee, dressed, whistled for Remus, and left the house. There were no lights on in the big house, nor at Janie's. Everyone was sleeping in late for the holiday, but her heartache went along for a companion as she rode toward the mountains.

It was daylight when she reached the area where the odd patterns decorated the arid soil, and she sat studying the marks before she shook her head and gave up. Steve was probably right. The mountain passes could turn eighty-mile-an-hour winds into machines that ruffled everything, even rock-hard soil.

Between her and the designs she inspected, Jeff's face came into focus, anger shooting sparks from the gray eyes, his voice a dagger stabbing into her as he reminded her of the night they spent together in Newark. They had slept together—that was all it meant to him, and it was up to her to wipe out the memory for her own sake.

Pushing thoughts of Jeff away from her, she stood looking around the vastness of the open range sur-

rounded by distant mountain peaks. It would take
weeks to round up the Charolais she knew were in the
outlying areas, and she would need help from Carue
and his men, probably from Jasper, too, flying over the
places he could scan from the air.

She didn't return to the ranch but went on into Tucson for the Saturday night dance. It had been weeks
since she had gone, but she was certain Jeff wouldn't
be attending. With the upcoming engagement announcement, Eileen wouldn't put up with that.

She waited outside the grange hall till she saw Steve's
truck pull in. "Hi, stranger." Janie hugged her.

Ami laughed. "Yes, two whole days since I've seen
you."

Steve eyed her, wondering if she could possibly get
any thinner. "Found any more tracks?"

She shook her head. "No, I gave up. It probably
wouldn't make a very good pet anyway." At least they
laughed with her instead of at her.

When band intermission time came, she was reluctant to join Steve and Janie. Singing love songs had
been her substitute for tears more than once, her way
of giving voice to pain. But this pain was too new, too
raw. She wasn't sure she could do it right now.

Janie urged her. "Come on. We've missed you."
She gave in.

Steve asked, " 'Crying Time'?"

She was glad her face was turned from him, but she
didn't hesitate as she said, "Sure." Janie's clear so-
prano joined her in harmony, and she had to admit it
sounded good.

Someone called "Old Flames," and their voices carried the message that a long-ago love was in the past,
where it belonged, and would never hold a candle to
the current flame.

Somewhere there must be a totally enveloping old
flame to burn out the pain of the new.

Back at their table, Janie said, "Are you staying over, Ami?"

"I think I'll go straight to camp. There isn't any need for me to go all the way back to the ranch. Ask Jasper to bring Rio out to Camp Nineteen tomorrow or Monday, whenever he'll be out that way."

Janie sighed. "Why must you be so dedicated to your job? Well, okay, but we'll see you before Christmas, won't we?"

She laughed. "Yes, I guess so." As she left them, she realized it had helped a little to go to the dance. She needed all the help she could get and a little was better than none at all.

A chilly full moon hung over the mountain range to the west as she pulled up to the line shack nearest Camp 19. Smoke came from the chimney, and beside her, Remus growled low in his throat. It was then she saw the Bronco Jeep on the far side of the small building. Jeff. Had something happened to Mandy? Or Rio?

She hit the ground running, Remus beside her. The door swung open before she reached it, and Jeff stood waiting for her.

"Where have you been?" The hard voice brought her up short.

"What's wrong?" She held her breath.

"Nothing's wrong, except I've been here four hours."

"I thought Mandy—or Rio—" She stopped, weak with relief. Then, surprise in her voice, "You've been here four hours? How did you know I'd be coming here?"

"A guess. You were at the dance, weren't you? I expected you back earlier."

She was conscious of shivering, whether or not from the cold she couldn't tell. "May I come in? It's cold out here."

He stepped aside, closing the door as she and Remus passed him. She stood near the potbellied stove, hold-

ing out her hands to the warmth. "Why were you looking for me?" Their last encounter was still fresh in her
mind and the hurt just as sharp.

"To apologize. I know what I said was unforgivable,
but I hope you'll consider it anyway." His voice was
low, sending vibrations through her body.

She stiffened. "Why should you apologize? Everything you said is true."

"No, Ami, it isn't true. I wish I could take back all
the things I said, but since I can't, please let me apologize. Believe me when I tell you I'm sorry." She swallowed hard at the tenderness in his voice and stiffened.

"You've apologized; I accept." She turned her back
to him. "Please go."

"I want to stay with you, Ami," he said softly. "Let
me hold you the way I held you before."

She whirled, turquoise eyes staring in disbelief.
"You're engaged. You can't."

"The engagement isn't official." If Jeff was ever
capable of being uncertain, it was at that moment. It
showed in the total absorption of his plea for her to
listen to him, in the gentle expression in his eyes.

She shook her head. "No."

He didn't argue but watched as she stood belliger-
ently in front of him. "I see you were right. You aren't
pregnant, are you?"

Her head came up. "No, but don't push your luck."

"I came prepared this time." He reached for her.

She backed away from him, wings of fright beating
inside her. However Jeff might be prepared, she
wasn't, unprepared to give love that wasn't returned in
full.

"Are you that conscientious, Ami? You don't really
like Eileen. I thought you might welcome the chance to
take what belongs to her."

She bit hard on her lips, hurting them. "I don't want
what belongs to her. Whatever I am, I'm not a thief."

"If it were given freely?" Jeff was leaning against the rough logs of the wall, his eyes taking in the tall figure a few feet from him.

I should tell him I love him, she thought. *That would get rid of him in a hurry.* "Leave me alone, Jeff. I'll stay out of your way or, if you prefer, I'll resign."

He smiled at her. "No, don't resign, Ami. I'd have the entire cowboy population in Arizona to fight. Besides, you're a good veterinarian whom I have neither the time nor inclination to replace."

Yes, she thought, *Eileen is pretty demanding on your time.*

Dark gray eyes searched bright turquoise, taking in the withdrawn look, tilted nose, the leanness of her that he still remembered against his bare body. Long slim fingers locked together were ringless, and they had been bare long enough that the sun had erased any indication rings had ever been worn.

"What about your husband, Ami? Incompatibility meaning what? Not enough sex? Too many women? Or men?"

She hoped the pain she felt at the questions didn't show. "None of the above."

"What, then?"

"I don't want to talk about it. I promised myself I'd forget him and I have." Her eyes closed as she flinched away from remembering the price she was paying to forget him.

"If you can't bear to talk about him, you must still love him."

She got up and filled the coffeepot with water from the five-gallon jug of drinking water, placing it over the eye of the stove. She took the can of instant coffee she used when in the shack, and measured out enough for two cups. Pushing the crate around she used for a table and another crate near the stove, she sat down, drawing her knees under her chin.

"It will take a few minutes," she told him. "But if you insist, at least let's have coffee."

She took a deep breath. "Tim and I met my senior year in college. I was on my way to being a veterinarian, and he was well-established as coach and physical education instructor. His team had a couple of Olympic contenders in swimming and track. We dated a year till I graduated, got married, and I went on to graduate school."

She paused, got up to get the coffee, and brought it back, handing him an old ceramic mug. She didn't look at him.

"No children?"

Keeping her mind carefully blank, she shook her head. "No children. We had two years together, then Tim wanted out." She was beginning to have trouble with her breathing, but she went on. "I went to El Paso. Last I heard, Tim was still in Cheyenne and had remarried." She took a swallow of the coffee, grimacing at the bitterness.

"It couldn't have been so sudden that you didn't see it coming."

"Haven't you ever heard the old cliché 'love is blind'? I was."

"You didn't want any children?"

She shrugged, swallowing more of the coffee. "It just never happened."

The nightmare scene she thought left well behind her surfaced: Tim's disbelief when given the doctor's verdict that she could never have children; his final accusation that she was intentionally not getting pregnant because she didn't want to ruin her fashionably slim figure and be tied down to the house and a child; the weeks and months they lived in deadly cold silence; the divorce. Had it been another woman, she might have understood, but to condemn her for something she had no control over had been more than she could take.

"Are you all right?" Jeff was regarding her with curiosity as she sat motionless, looking into her empty coffee mug.

"Yes." She got up. "Want some more coffee?"

He handed her the mug. "There are a lot of eligible men around these parts, Ami. You don't have to be lonesome. You're a very pretty minority."

She smiled as she handed him the cup. "I'm not lonesome, Jeff. Someone else in due time, but there's no hurry." *When all my wounds heal,* she thought, *but I keep getting new ones.*

Neither of them spoke for several minutes, although she knew his eyes were on her. "Are you sure you don't want me to stay?" he asked.

She looked up at him. "I'm sure."

It was just daylight as he rose to go, and she walked outside with him into the chilly dawn. "Jasper and I are flying to Abilene to a cattle auction tomorrow. We'll be gone about a week." They stood side by side, looking toward the mountains to the east, where the sun would appear in a few more minutes.

"You spend a lot of time in these wild mountains, Ami. Seems like a pretty girl would get lonesome away from all the action." He looked down at her and smiled. "How many cowboys have asked for dates in the grange halls?"

She shrugged. "A couple."

He laughed. "I can imagine." The quiet went on until he said, "Why aren't you interested in dating, Ami, or am I wrong in thinking you don't?"

She watched the sky brighten over the mountain before she answered him. "If loneliness is what causes the need for dating, then I don't need it. I never get lonely." She wondered at his reaction if she told him of the many nights she remembered Newark and the times her body yearned for him the same as her wayward heart.

"You really love the mountains and desert that much?" He, too, watched the mountain rim. "I thought you were a little odd to want this job and figured you'd last about thirty days before you ran back to the city."

"Why did you hire me, then, if you thought I'd only be temporary?"

He turned to face her and put his hands on her arms, pulling her close before he said quietly, "I didn't hire you; Steve did."

The questions in her eyes turned the turquoise to dark shadows, but before she could ask them, he bent to place his mouth on hers, bringing her blood alive to sing through her veins and cause her heart to triple its beat. With an effort she kept her hands lightly on his waist.

He raised his head, smiling a little. "Bye, Ami. See you in about ten days."

"Good-bye, Jeff." She stood watching the Jeep bounce across the desert and said aloud, "You sometimes give a body more than it can stand, don't you, Lord?"

There was no answer that she could hear.

Chapter Eight

Work for Ami and Rio slacked as Christmas holidays drew near. They made sure the cattle were in protected areas and kept a close watch on the horses in the piñon-dotted aroyos near Camp 10.

Jasper found them one morning as they checked a herd of Charolais for injuries that might need attention. He left the truck a few yards away and strode to where they stood. Stetson pushed back on the salt-and-pepper hair, he grinned at the two. He carried two envelopes in his hand.

"I need a topographical map to find you guys," he said. "How's it going?"

Ami smiled and nodded as Rio stepped forward, hand out to Jasper, whom he hadn't seen since the Thanksgiving holidays.

"Are these the missing Charolais, Ami?" Jasper asked, glancing around at the healthy looking cattle.

She shook her head. "I'm really not sure if this is part of that herd, Jasper. I thought there were at least a hundred and fifty head. There's about a hundred here."

He laughed. "You should know now you can't account for each one every time. There are too many places to play hide-and-seek in these canyons." His dark eyes swept the expanse of desert and mountains around them. "They'll show up before spring when they get good and hungry." He handed her an envelope and one to Rio. "Jeff said to tell you the holiday officially begins the twentieth, and requests the honor of your presence at the Christmas Ball on the twenty-third."

Ami looked at the envelope in her hands to hide the tightening around her mouth and the look of dread that must be in her eyes. "Is today the eighteenth?" she asked. She knew it was—she kept a calendar in the small notebook she always carried in her truck and marked off the days, because it was easy to lose track of days and dates when you moved to your own time schedule.

"Yes, it is," Jasper said. "Late on the eighteenth, Ami. Can I help you finish up here?"

She shook her head. "We've finished, and there's only one place left to check. I can do that. Take Rio back with you so he can get a hamburger from Lily before he has to start eating all the holiday feasts. Remus, too."

Jasper laughed. "Okay, but are you sure you don't need help?"

"No, thanks, I can manage."

"I don't want to leave you alone, Ami," Rio told her.

Her eyebrows went up. "Nonsense. I've been alone before."

"But we could do the job faster if I stayed," he protested.

She smiled at him, knowing he was looking forward to seeing Nada after almost a month. "Go with Jasper and Remus, Rio," she said. "I'll bring your paint supplies from the shack."

"All right, but don't open the flat case," he said.

"Secrets from me, Rio?"

He grinned. *"Sí."*

Good-byes said, she turned back to the few remaining animals she needed to look over, her thoughts going to the party. She'd rather not go, but Janie had said Jeff almost demanded each and every hand be there, and she was one of the hands.

Hearts had to go, too, she thought, a wry grin touching her mouth as she sprayed antiseptic solution on the forelegs and hooves of a huge steer standing placidly near her. The announcement of the engagement had been moved up to the twenty-third, she guessed, to allow for separate Christmas Eve activities. It didn't matter; her heart was already looking for a place to hide, and one day would make no difference in its success or failure.

Moving quickly, she reached the last sector just at sunset and finished the spraying as darkness fell. The solution would keep away most of the biting flies that could cause an infection in the animals before she came this way again. She looked toward the dark canyons and the perimeter of mountains once more, wondering how she had missed a spot that could hide fifty or more head of cattle. She knew Jasper was right, though, the area was a vast playground for animals to wander around. She headed for the line shack.

Instead of turning the little Brat truck toward Wagner's the next morning, she went toward Tucson. The old female complaint "I have nothing to wear" certainly applied in reality to her as far as the Christmas Ball was concerned. A shop for tall women had caught her eye the last trip she made into the city, and she found it again without difficulty, examining the styles displayed in the window before stepping into the quietly elegant shop.

"May I help you?"

Ami turned to face a young lady, tall and slim in her soft silk shirtwaist dress and Gucci slippers, and almost laughed as the girl's eyes went from her sun-streaked dark hair to the flannel shirt, faded jeans, and dusty boots. Her expression indicated she thought there was little to be done for her.

"Yes," Ami told her, straight-faced, with effort. "I need a long gown suitable for the holidays if you have a size seven tall."

"This way, please," the well-modulated voice said.

Ami followed the gently swaying hips to a partially enclosed section and blinked at the dazzling array of garments.

"Do you have a color preference?"

Ami thought for a moment. Eileen would be in some one-of-a-kind sparkling red or white outfit, she decided. Janie had a light rose velveteen. She had no idea what other wives and girlfriends would wear. She watched the dresses move beneath the girl's well-manicured hands.

"May I see that one?"

The slender hand hesitated at the dress she indicated and removed the padded hanger. It was a heavy silk jersey, the top lemon yellow with a simple rounded neckline that fitted to a tight waist gathered onto a skirt with yards and yards of material that was the same pale yellow shot through with gold. The long full sleeves matched the skirt.

"I'll try that," she said.

In the dressing room she shed her work clothes and boots, slipped the dress over her head, and zipped the back as far as she could reach before stepping outside to let the saleslady finish pulling it up.

"Very nice," the young lady said in a surprised tone, adding quickly, "We have lovely gold sandals that would go well with it."

Ami nodded and stood gazing at her reflection until the woman returned with the size she requested. Fastening the sandals, Ami turned in front of the mirror,

mentally shrugged a "Who cares?" and said, "I'll take
them."

The girl hesitated. "Will this be cash or charge?"

In the process of removing the clothing, Ami
glanced at her in surprise and smiled a little as she
reached for the billfold in her back jeans pocket.

"Cash. How much?" she asked.

"Two hundred and thirty-two dollars."

She counted, handing the money to the girl, and
went on with her dressing. Her thoughts went to
Mandy. What would Hazel put on her to fit the occasion of her dad's engagement and the Christmas holidays? Mandy had plenty of clothes, but Ami had no
way of knowing if formals were included. Well, they
should be, she decided as she left the shop with her
purchases.

She stood for a moment on the street, enjoying the
colorful display of decorations. She had read about the
parade with all the stars and celebrities who had attended the start of the holiday season, and shook her
head at what the pretty baubles must have cost.

Taking her time to window-shop, stopping to gaze at
some of the elaborate displays, she came to the Tots
Thru Teens Shop and went in. The woman who approached her smiling resembled someone's pleasantly
attractive grandmother.

"Good morning. May I help you?"

Ami returned her smile and greeting. "Yes, I'm
shopping for a six-year-old who is rather small for her
age. Something for a Christmas party."

"This way, please."

They stopped at a rack of street-length dresses, a riot
of color. Ami shook her head. "Do you have any long
dresses in her size?"

"Oh, yes, over here."

The older lady stood aside as she went over the small
garments, some part wool, some polyester, and some

velveteens. A royal-blue velveteen dress with a white lace Peter Pan collar and long sleeves with matching cuffs caught her eye, and she took it from the rack. It had princess lines with a slight flair at the hem.

"If it doesn't fit her, may I return it?"

"Of course, ma'am."

Outside again, she looked for a restaurant, seeing one just down the street, and went inside, depositing her purchases on the booth seat beside her, realizing she was tired.

She was used to chasing cattle, not pounding pavement, she thought, smiling at the young girl who took her order for breakfast, which she hadn't bothered with before leaving the shack. Someone brought coffee, which she accepted gratefully, and she thought about the party, four days away.

She could break a leg and get out of going, she thought, but she had too much to do, getting Rio ready to start classes at school and, after that, getting the shipments cataloged for spring, all without Rio's help. It would be a gigantic task, but keeping busy was her aim, her only target that would keep her mind off Jeff, who would be safely married to Eileen in another six months.

Her breakfast came and she ate as her mind went on thinking of how she would get through the announcement of the engagement at the party with all the congratulations and best wishes for a boss everyone appreciated.

Just like everyone, she decided, hunching her shoulders. She would grin and bear it, not looking forward to the occasion at all.

It was late when she reached her cottage, and as she opened the truck door, was forced to greet Remus before she could take her packages inside.

"I just saw you yesterday," she scolded affectionately. "Settle down." He did, but then followed her inside to make sure she wasn't leaving him again.

The house was cold, and she turned on the furnace to take the chill off, stopping to light the kindling she had left in the fireplace to add to the warmth. She took her dress from the box and shook the folds out, placing it in her near-empty closet, and put the delicate-looking sandals on the shelf.

"Let's go and find Lily or Hazel, Remus, and see if they think Mandy's dress will fit."

She put a big log on the fire that had started and closed the screen. Picking up the box with Mandy's dress in it, she debated whether to take the Christmas presents she had wrapped to put beneath the tree, and decided to wait.

As her long legs carried her the quarter mile to the big house, she surveyed the area. Lights were already on at Janie's, and she heard doors slamming at the bunkhouse and wondered if Rio was at Sandoval's. Probably.

Heading in the direction of the kitchen, she looked up as the Bronco came around the side of the house, stopping a few yards from her. Jeff swung down and turned to lift Mandy from the seat.

Ami stopped in surprise, then knelt to meet the small figure running toward her. She put the box on the ground as she hugged Mandy. "When did you get home?" she asked.

"Sunday. I came home Sunday." In her excitement her words weren't plain and she used her hands to show her meaning.

"Super," Ami told her, taking her hand as Jeff reached to pick up the box.

"We plan to have a snack," Jeff said. "Will you join us?" His eyes went over her, unsettling all the arguments she had resolved to herself about her reaction when she saw him again after his last visit to her camp.

The resolutions dissolved, leaving her defenseless against her feelings. "Yes, thanks," she said, and added, "Hot dogs?"

He shuddered. "I hope not."

Mandy skipped beside Ami and, as they got to the porch, let go her hand to run inside. She spoke quickly to Jeff to explain about the dress and keep the subject impersonal. "I wasn't sure what Mandy had for the ball, so while I was shopping I bought her a dress, too." He stopped to look around at her, holding the door open, and she went on. "If you already have one, I can return it."

His hand on her elbow kept her from moving inside. "That was very thoughtful, Ami. I think Hazel had decided to let her wear a red skirt and blouse." He looked at the box he held and asked, "What color?"

"Royal blue."

"She likes blue." He released her arm as they entered the house and went to put the box on the dining room table away from the kitchen, where they were going to snack. Mandy skipped beside him as he returned, and Jeff detoured by the cabinet to get another plate. The three of them sat down at the small kitchen table by the window, which had been set for two. A plate of cold sliced chicken with rolls in a warmer had been left there by Lily, of course. Cheeses and tomatoes were sliced, and a dressing in a glass server was nearby.

Mandy touched Jeff's hand. "I want a Coke."

He shook his head. "Not this late, honey. Water only."

"Okay," she agreed, and waited for him to fix her plate.

Ami covered her mouth to hide the smile she couldn't resist, listening to the two of them. The smile disappeared as she wondered what Eileen would think of eating a cold snack in the kitchen with Mandy sharing her attentions from Jeff.

As they ate, Mandy talked and, occasionally, Jeff would look at Ami and wink as he answered the little girl.

Mandy pushed her plate away and turned to Ami. "Are you coming to our Christmas party?"

"Yes, I am. How about you?"

Mandy gave her a quick grin. "Of course." She sounded so grown up. "I have to be there to make sure I have enough room for all the things Santa Claus will bring."

Ami feigned surprise. "How do you know he'll visit here?"

Mandy turned to Jeff. "He always does, doesn't he, Daddy?"

Jeff nodded. "But you don't need anything this year. He may not stop."

Mandy's gray eyes widened. "All my clothes are too small, and my boots have a skinned toe."

"I could buy those for you," Jeff told her, but she shook her head.

"Santa Claus knows where to get all the things I need. You can just pay him." She yawned.

"Perhaps you're right, Amanda." He stood and reached for her. "Let's go find Hazel." He looked at Ami. "I'll be right back."

Mandy gave her a sleepy smile and waved. Ami remained at the table, chin in her hands, feeling a wave of emotion, almost feeling sorry for herself. After Christmas, Mandy would be in Tucson full time, seldom home except for holidays. She didn't see her much now, but then she wouldn't see her at all. It would be better that way; with the wedding in June, she wouldn't be seeing anyone around the big house very much. Her best bet was in the endless desert with her cattle; she knew her place, at least. She stood up and began clearing the things from the table.

"Lily will be back to do that." He looked her over again, smiling as he said, "May I see the dress?"

"Oh, yes." They walked into the dining room, and Ami picked up the box to untie the ribbon, opening the top to lift out the small dress.

Jeff took it from her, his hands going over the soft material. "It's lovely, Ami. Looks like it will fit her." He grinned. "One thing Santa won't have to worry about."

She smiled, too, relieved that he didn't think her out of place buying something for Mandy to wear.

"Let me repay you."

She shook her head. "No."

Jeff didn't argue but continued to watch her. "Do you have a date for the ball?"

She smiled at him. "Well, Jim Summers did ask me to visit his ranch for the holidays, and since I couldn't take off that much time, I invited him to your party. I hope you don't mind." Jim, a rancher from around Apache Junction, north of Tucson, was a regular at the grange dances.

Jeff frowned. "Jim Summers? He's old enough to be your father. I didn't realize you knew him that well."

"Only from the dances, but we've talked."

"Evidently," he said, his voice dry.

Ami asked quickly, sensing disapproval. "Do you mind? I can cancel without any trouble." Jim Summers had been a widower for several years, but even though he had issued invitations to her before, Ami never had considered them to be dates. She took those to be as serious as his regular offers of a job as his foreman.

Jeff looked at her curiously. "At this late date? How would you explain that?"

She shrugged. "Jim and I understand each other."

"Is Summers why you never get lonely?"

"He doesn't visit me in camp, if that's what you mean," she said sharply. "This will be the first time I've seen him other than at the dances."

"I'm sorry, Ami. I have no right to complain about who you see. I guess I was just surprised it was Summers." He glanced at the watch on his wrist, and she straightened, realizing he must have a date with Eileen.

"Perhaps you'll have Hazel try the dress on Mandy, and if it needs any adjusting, I can do it before the party."

"All right."

"Thanks for the food. It was a lifesaver, considering what I have at home." She turned to walk out the kitchen door.

"Ami."

She glanced over her shoulder to find Jeff a step behind her. He turned her around to face him. "In case I don't get a chance at the party, Merry Christmas." He bent and kissed her, his mouth lingering, caressing gently as her lips parted in surprise. He lifted her to his body for an instant and let go.

The warmth of the brief kiss sent her pulses racing, and Ami backed away, looking up at him. "Thank you, Jeff." She turned to leave the house, running across the yard to her cottage, running from the memories the kiss brought back, running from certain heartbreak that lurked around the corner. Did he ever think of Newark?

The dance was in full swing as she went into the large room where furniture had been rearranged and couples sat and talked or stood around in groups. Ami stared, surprised at the men in tuxedos, all colors, from the formal black and white to the wild paisley sported by Carue, of all people.

She blinked. *I guess I assumed they'd all wear jeans,*

she thought. She grinned as Janie and Steve joined her. "I'm not sure I'll recognize anyone in these outfits," she said.

"They'll all know you," Steve said. "Except for Janie, you're the prettiest thing around."

Janie punched him lightly in the chest. "You'd better say that."

He grinned. "I know." He turned back to Ami. "Where's Jim? I thought you invited him?"

"I did, but his favorite horse died and he had to go to the funeral," she said with a straight face.

Steve laughed. "I'm sure he'd have preferred a maiden aunt as an excuse rather than his favorite horse."

"But what really happened?" Janie asked.

"He called last night and said he had such a bad cold, he'd better not spread his germs around. He sounded awful."

Jasper came up to them, handsome as could be in a navy blue tuxedo, lighter blue shirt, and cowboy boots. Ami never failed to wonder what was wrong with the women that Jasper still ran around unattached. When she mentioned such a handsome bachelor on the loose, Janie told a story about a lost love while he was still in the military service. It was a shame Jasper and she couldn't get together and solve their heartbreak together, she had thought on several occasions. But neither had been able to break away from their personal chains, and they were good friends, nothing more.

"Merry Christmas, beautiful ladies," Jasper said. "You, too, Steve." He looked at Ami. "How come you're footloose at a shindig like this?"

"The same reason as you are," Ami teased. "I didn't get asked."

"In that case, come on and let's be lonesome together." He pulled her into his arms and waltzed her across

the open space, making their way around the other
couples trying out the small dance floor. Near a table
laden with all kinds of food and drink, Jasper stopped.

"Let's feed our sorrow."

"Okay, but not much, this dress leaves no room for
expansion."

He looked down at her. "Thank goodness it fits
where it's supposed to." He grinned. "It was made for
you."

"Must be the Christmas spirit," she said, raising her
eyebrows. "It's already loosened your tongue."

Jasper leered. "Wait till I've had a couple of these,
then watch out." He held up a small glass of pretty
liquid. "If Harris mixed this, it only takes one to liven
up the party."

They took small sandwiches and their drinks and
moved to an empty seat in a corner. Ami's gaze went
over the crowd, and she immediately wished she had
kept her eyes on her plate.

Eileen was dancing with Jeff, her blond head under
his chin. As predicted, she wore a sparkling white gown
that displayed her charms to the best advantage. Her
hair had silver and blue stars tucked into the shining
strands. She was lovely; a glamorous woman who
looked just right in Jeff's arms. Ami turned back to her
plate and ate without tasting.

*I should have had a cold, too, and stayed home, where I
belong,* she thought.

A small hand touched her arm, and she looked up
into Mandy's smiling face. The royal blue of the velveteen gown touched off a sparkle in her gray eyes, and
excitement added a hint of color on her cheeks.

"You're beautiful, Mandy," she told the little girl
and meant it.

"My dad said you picked out the dress. Thank you."
The husky voice from such a little girl, some of her
words still not spoken clearly, almost brought tears to

Ami's eyes. What a blessing that she could hear so well now, and the therapy, even as much as she hated for Mandy to be so far from home, was extending the miracle to her speech. She could only be thankful, thinking of what might have been had Linda and Dave not been able to help. She was about to say something else when Rio joined them. She looked way up, thinking in surprise he'd grown a foot since they came to Wagner's. He wasn't wearing a tux, but had on a white silk shirt with dark pants and well-polished boots.

He smiled at each of them and turned to Mandy and bowed. "May I?"

Mandy looked up at him, her mouth open, glanced back at Ami, grinned, curtsied from the waist, and went into Rio's outstretched arms. Ami watched in amazement as they circled the floor.

"They do grow up, don't they?" Jasper remarked beside her.

"Yes," she agreed, her eyes still on the couple as others, too, turned to watch. Pride was deep inside her; pride at what Rio had made of himself and at what had been done for Mandy. She tasted the drink and looked at Jasper in surprise.

"Whew! You're right. Two of these, and I could outfly your plane."

They were laughing as Jeff stopped in front of them. "I see you two are enjoying yourselves," he said, smiling. As Ami looked up at him the gray eyes met hers for a moment, then went over the room. "I haven't seen Jim," he said.

"No, he didn't make it," she told him. "Jasper rescued me."

He looked back at her. "If you're through eating, may I have this dance?"

Jasper reached for her plate and glass. "Go with the boss. It's almost payday."

With Jeff's arms around her, she lost herself to the

feeling of being held closely against him without having to make an excuse for it. The fact that it was just a dance didn't enter into her thoughts as she moved with him, her body intensely aware of his touch.

He held her a little away from him and said, "The dress you bought for Amanda is just right and very becoming." He smiled. "So is yours."

She nodded and put her cheek closer to his chest without answering him. His outfit was dark gray with a white shirt, and he could have been any business tycoon enjoying his employees' Christmas party. But seldom did business tycoons use this type of occasion to announce their engagement. She stumbled a little, and he held her tighter.

"What happened to Jim?" he asked.

Ami explained briefly and he nodded, guiding her between and around the other couples on the floor.

What in the world am I doing here? she wondered, and her eyes met the cold brown ones of Eileen McKane as she stood with Steve and Janie, her chin in the air a couple of inches higher than usual to indicate her displeasure. *That's what I'm doing here,* she decided, *aggravating one Miss McKane,* and she looked up to smile into Jeff's gray eyes, holding his glance for several seconds until she was forced to look away. She was punishing herself, not Eileen. His arms tightened just as the music ended and he led her back to where the three stood.

Ami could almost see the angry tap of Eileen's foot as the five of them talked. Actually, Steve and Jeff talked. Janie's eyes glinted with laughter as she met Ami's glance and she winked. Ami pretended not to notice. Eileen stood it as long as she could.

"May I have a drink, Jeff?" He turned away and as soon as he was out of hearing distance, Eileen looked at Ami. "Jeff tells me he's missing some cattle." The brown eyes went over Ami, dismissing the holiday clothing as chain-store variety before she went on. "If you've searched everywhere, perhaps they were just overlooked." She shrugged to show her disinterest. "Oh, well, I'm sure his hands will find them before spring." Thus having had her say about lowly ranch hands, she went to meet Jeff.

Before Janie could make the remark Ami was sure would be forthcoming, Carue touched her arm and she was back on the floor. Hours later, tired and carrying the feeling of dread she had earlier in the evening, she waited for the announcement of the engagement to be made.

Hurry it up so I can leave, she urged Jeff silently. *I don't know how much more I can stand.* Mandy had come to say good night long ago, and Rio had left with the Sandovals. The sinking feeling in her stomach couldn't be from the drinks; she had limited herself to the one she shared with Jasper. Maybe she was hungry, she decided, and said to Carue, who was standing nearby, "Is there anything left to eat? I need a midnight snack."

They went to the table, still loaded with enough food to feed another party, and she took some cheeses on a small plate and rye bread she knew Lily had baked.

"Is that all?" Carue asked, filling the plate he carried.

She laughed. "If I ate all that, I'd have nightmares and I need my sleep."

"Plenty of time to catch up on rest and sleep. You're off work till after New Year's Day, aren't you?"

"More or less. I have a few things to do and I have to take Rio into Tucson and get him into his apartment before classes start."

Carue looked at her with interest. "I heard Rio wants to be a vet. As much as he loves animals, he'll make a good one some day. He's had the right kind of teacher."

She turned to him. "Why, thank you, Carue. I remember once—"

He put his hand up in self-defense. "I know, I know." He grinned. "I'm not wrong very often, though." It was as close as he would come to apologizing for giving her a hard time when she had first come to Wagner's and he had no faith in a woman veterinarian. She laughed and went on with her snack.

The band struck up a "good night ladies" type square dance tune, and couples swung around the floor. Surprised, Ami looked up and met Jeff's glance from across the room. No engagement had been announced. She didn't see Eileen.

A moment later she saw Janie and Steve speak to Jeff, and she and Carue joined them to say good night. Over the cheerful Merry Christmases and best wishes from everyone, she said her own and moved away with Janie and Steve, recalling for an instant the kiss she had received a few days ago.

"Did you drive?" Janie asked her.

She nodded. "I couldn't see walking in these shoes." Moments later she was in the small truck, heading home alone, still puzzled that the engagement had not been mentioned.

Chapter Nine

Christmas Eve. Ami lay still without opening her eyes, her first thought that of Eileen's remark about the missing cattle. It didn't worry her that Eileen considered ranch hands lower than the desert squirrels, but what did remain was the anger at her remark that indicated Ami was somehow to blame for the missing cattle at Wagner's.

She heard from Jasper that Eileen had purchased the property across the mountain from the line shack near Camp 20, and wondered about it. Jeff talked about adding it to his but had reconsidered because the six-thousand-foot mountain would split his property, making it more difficult to feed and round up his cattle. He didn't need it, anyway, he told Steve one day when they were discussing it within her hearing. She agreed; seventy-five thousand acres of land was enough for anyone. And when the two ranches were combined, what in the world would they do with all that land?

She sighed and slid out of bed. The engagement announcement must have been postponed for tonight, so it could be a more private affair. If she were the one getting the proposal, she would want it to be just for her alone. But she wasn't Eileen.

After gathering the packages she had wrapped days ago, she placed them near the door to pick up as soon as the big house stirred. The huge Christmas tree in the wide foyer already had bundles and packages under-

neath it as it sparkled with the red and blue decorations
Lily and Harris had arranged on it. The items she had
made during long dark hours in the line camps would
be added for her favorite people at Wagner's.

Well, not all her favorite people, she admitted to herself. She had nothing for Jeff. If he didn't want her
heart, then nothing else she had would suit the occasion.

Outside, she stood in the early morning sunlight,
coat collar turned up against the chill winds off the
snow-capped mountains in the distance. There wasn't a
cloud in the sky. She loaded the packages in the small
truck, whistled for Remus, and drove near the kitchen
door of the big house.

As she opened the door she smelled the fresh coffee,
but there was no one in the kitchen. She helped herself
to a cup of coffee, placed it on the table, and went back
to lug in the packages, taking them through the hall to
the tree. She placed them around the other brightly
wrapped presents and went back to her coffee, wondering absently where everyone was. There were lots of
things to do before the big day. She rinsed her coffee
cup, let herself out the way she had come in, swung
back in the truck seat, patting Remus's head as he sat
waiting, and headed for the camps.

Most of the day was spent rambling from camp to
camp, wishing everyone happy holidays, sharing camp
coffee with them. Some of them had been at the dance;
some had not. No one mentioned the engagement of
their boss, and it was not a subject she cared to discuss.

But the thought stayed with her as she returned to
her cottage at dusk. Janie called and invited her over
for a late snack, and she accepted, walking the long
quarter mile in the dark. Lights winked from bunkhouses as well as the big house.

"Wonder what happened?" Janie asked as they went
into the living room.

"When?" Steve asked, winking at Ami.

"You know what I mean. Why didn't Eileen make her big announcement last night? I thought that was to be the big item of the party."

Ami didn't answer, but Steve, who usually smiled at women's gossip, was puzzled, too. "She must be saving it for something bigger. I don't understand how she missed such a glittering opportunity with a captive audience."

"Did you know she had bought the O'Toole property, Steve?" Ami asked.

He shook his head yes. "Jasper said it was just recently. All that land for cattle to get lost in, in addition to what she already has."

"I'd better find Wagner's cattle before they wander across that mountain and she gets me for trespassing."

Ami didn't stay late. She was restless, wanting to get back to work, where she could sort out her feelings for Jeff in an attempt to force her heart to accept the fact that he belonged to Eileen, away from watchful eyes that might see the sadness inside her. The thought of Mandy belonging to Eileen hurt almost as much as the thought of her owning Jeff. She winced at the fierce jealousy she couldn't hide from herself.

Boxes and papers scattered around her, she sat in the middle of the living room, separating things Rio would need to take with him and discarding surplus items she thought he could live without. Rio was due in from Sandoval's any minute, and she'd have to wait to ask about some of the things before getting rid of them. She smiled, thinking of the Christmas present he had given her. The flat box she had been warned not to open had contained a charcoal portrait of her and Mandy sitting on the corral fence and Remus lying nearby. It was amazing to her what he could do with a piece of charcoal and paper, and she was prouder of that picture than the generous check given her by Jeff

Harlequin reaches into the hearts and minds of women across America to bring you

Harlequin American Romance.

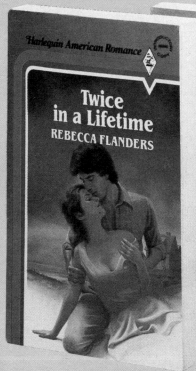

TWO FREE BOOKS!

Enter a uniquely American world of romance with

Harlequin American Romance.™

Harlequin American Romance novels are the first romances to explore today's new love relationships. These compelling romance novels reach into the hearts and minds of women across America... probing into the most intimate moments of romance, love and desire.

You'll follow romantic heroines and irresistible men as they boldly face confusing choices. Career first, love later? Love without marriage? Long-distance relationships? All the experiences that make love real are captured in the tender, loving pages of *Harlequin American Romance* novels.

What makes American women so different when it comes to love? Find out with this special *Harlequin American Romance* offer!

Send for your two free introductory books.

Get these Two Books FREE!

MAIL TO:
Harlequin Reader Service
2504 West Southern Avenue
Tempe, Arizona 85282

YES! I want to be one of the first to discover
Harlequin American Romance. Send me FREE and without
obligation my two free books. If you do not hear from me
after I have examined my two FREE books please send
me four new *Harlequin American Romance* novels each
month as soon as they come off the presses. I understand
that I will be billed only $2.25 per book (total $9.00).
There are no shipping or handling charges. There is no
minimum number of books that I have to purchase.
In fact, I may cancel this arrangement at any time…and
keep the two introductory books without any obligation.

154 CIA NATT

Name	(Please Print)	
Address		Apt. No.
City	State/Prov.	Zip/Postal Code

Signature (If under 18, parent or guardian must sign.)

This offer is limited to one order per household and not valid to current
American Romance subscribers. We reserve the right to exercise discretion
in granting membership. If price changes are necessary, you will be notified.
Offer expires December 31, 1984.   PRINTED IN U.S.A.

EXPERIENCE *Harlequin American Romance*...

with these two FREE books.

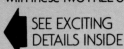 SEE EXCITING DETAILS INSIDE

Send no money. Mail this card and receive two new full-length *Harlequin American Romance* novels absolutely FREE.

for Christmas. All his employees received bonuses for Christmas, and she considered it a nice custom as well as a good tax writeoff for Jeff. She would just as soon not have had it, but it would go far toward paying for Rio's schooling, which was just what she planned to do with it. There was nothing she needed that money could buy.

When the knock sounded, she was glad. It was time Rio got in so they could plan their time to leave and what they would take. She had taken his apartment on option, and, if he liked it, they would be able to get his schedule and move into the apartment in one day or at least a day and a half. Then she could pick up a few supplies and head back, returning to a normal routine.

"Come in," she called. "Happy New Year." She looked up, smiling, to see Jeff standing in the doorway.

"Happy New Year, Ami," he said, looking around the cluttered room. "Going someplace?"

Where have you been? she wondered, but said, "Rio is. He starts college in Tucson this semester for some classes as well as preveterinary field training."

He nodded and turned a straight chair around, straddling it, to sit watching her as she went on with her work.

She smiled up at him. "Thank you for the check."

"You're welcome." He watched in silence a moment. "The quilt you gave Amanda is beautiful. She loves it and the book."

"I'm glad."

"Where did you learn your handiwork?"

"I had a roommate in college who could do anything with her hands. She taught me. I had lots of time to get the hang of it when we weren't in clases."

"Until you married?"

She glanced at him but didn't answer. He stood up. "How long do you plan to be in Tucson?"

"No more than three or four days—whatever it takes

to get Rio's schedule set up and him into the apartment. Why?''

''Curious.'' He bent to put his hands beneath her arms, lifting her to her feet, and turned her to face him. His hands slid up her arms, pulling her closer.

''Don't do this to me, Jeff, please.''

''What? I only want to wish you a Happy New Year.''

Her hands came up between them, pushing away, but he caught them in his, holding her close as he bent to find her lips. She turned her face to his shoulder. He held her, bending to slip an arm behind her knees and, lifting her, walked toward the bedroom.

''No, Jeff, I'm expecting Rio.'' She struggled to get free.

He stood her on her feet, tilted her head, and caught her mouth against his. She stood, not moving, as he took his time kissing her, his mouth quiet and warm over hers, as gentle as if she were a child. When he lifted his head, her wide eyes looked straight up into his, hurt turning them dark.

He couldn't read her expression; couldn't know the frustration deep inside as she waited for him to release her. ''Lovely, Ami, but cold,'' he said softly. He held her a moment longer, then let her go. ''I'll be taking Amanda into Tucson on the third. Can I buy you a drink while we're there?''

Bitter words came to mind that she wanted to hurl at him, wishing she had the right to accuse him of taking the easy way out with Mandy, giving in to Eileen because she didn't want to be bothered with the child. She bit back the words and told him, ''We'll be busy. I don't plan to stay any longer than it takes to get Rio into his apartment and check his schedules. The apartment is on option, and if he likes it, we'll just unload and I'll head back.''

''I see.'' He waited, and when she said nothing more, he said, ''Bye, Ami,'' and was gone.

"Damn you." Ami touched her mouth, still throbbing in response to Jeff's kiss, drew in a sobbing breath, and turned back to her packing. By the time Rio arrived from Sandoval's, where he had spent most of the holidays, she was through packing and sorting and ready for bed. Rio was ready for a big adventure, and she wished him lots of luck, knowing how much she'd miss him.

At the school in Tucson almost everyone was still on holiday, but in the Registrar's Office, they found that all his classes had been completely scheduled and set up for him, and he was ready to start the semester on Monday of the following week. They moved his things from the truck to the small efficiency apartment, which Rio was proud of, his very first place all on his own.

"There's no need for me to stay, Rio, and I have plenty of work so I'd better get on back. If you need anything, call me."

Never demonstrative, Rio hesitated, then hugged her. "Thanks, Ami. I'll try; I really will."

She smiled. "I expect you to."

Liquid brown eyes surveyed the tall figure in front of him, a woman who had taught him to be a man when he didn't think he was ready, and he grinned. "I'll miss you."

Ami lifted her hand in a salute, turned, and ran down the walk. She could be at Wagner's before dark.

As she turned the pickup onto I-10 she was suddenly too tired to face the three-hour drive home. The holidays, plus the strain of waiting for Eileen's big moment to announce her engagement to Jeff, caught up with her. She pulled into the Best Western Motel they used after the grange dances and, as soon as she checked in, headed for the bar.

She wondered how Jeff had made out with Mandy.

She hoped she'd given him a fit; he deserved it. Poor little Mandy.

I should get absolutely skunk drunk and, even if I don't forget anything, I'll be so sick, it won't bother me, she thought. The second drink in front of her looked even better than the first, and she smiled at it, turning the pretty glass around.

"Is it a private party or can anyone join?"

Ami raised disbelieving eyes as Jeff slid into the booth across from her. She didn't speak.

"What are you drinking?"

"Piña colada."

"They'll make you sick."

"Hopefully drunk first."

Jeff looked from the drink to her. "Why?"

"Why not?"

The waitress came, and he ordered bourbon and water and another drink for her. Ami smiled at him. It was good, he already looked a little fuzzy. "You're going to aid and abet?"

"Yes. Maybe it will banish all your scruples and make it easier for me."

Turquoise eyes narrowed. "I'm not staying."

"Yes, you are. You know you can't drive after drinking three of those potent things. I'll cancel your single room and get us a double one."

She shook her head. "No." His gaze held hers, and she wet her lips, trying to look away from him but failing. The look in his eyes brought a storm of feelings into her, shaking her all the way to her toes.

The waitress came. Ami took a long drink. "Have you eaten?" Jeff asked, watching her.

"Around noon."

"Let's have sandwiches sent to the room."

"No, Jeff." She shook her head, suddenly afraid of being alone with him, knowing she was defenseless.

But he was already giving an order to the waitress.

Ami heard a room number mentioned, and he was pulling her up, leading her unprotesting through the lobby, balancing both drinks. "Come on."

She couldn't drive, but she couldn't stay with him. Her blurred thoughts made no sense even to her. Inside the room, she stood near the door as he placed the drinks on the bedside table.

"How did you get away from Mandy so soon and how did you find me?"

His tan face was grave for an instant. "I left Amanda at two." He shook his head and an uncertain look touched his eyes. "It was hard to leave her, but finding you was elementary. I followed you from the school to Rio's apartment, then here."

Ami moved to the bed farthest from him. Kicking off her boots, she sighed as she lay back. Heavy gold-tipped lashes lifted as he sat beside her. "Did you come prepared this time?"

"Yes." His whisper was against her temple.

Oh, Jeff, I love you so much. Why don't you know?

The knock was soft. "Room service."

Jeff got the sandwiches and brought them to her bed. "Here."

"I don't want any."

"Eat it anyway. Otherwise, you'll be sick." He pulled her to a sitting position and propped a pillow behind her.

They ate in silence, Jeff sitting on the bed with her. Surprisingly she didn't choke and felt better as soon as she finished. He watched as she wiped the last crumbs from her face. Turquoise eyes met dark gray ones for an instant, then she pushed the pillow away, turned on her stomach, and slept, unaware that he covered her, nor that he stood a long time looking down at her still figure before he undressed and got into the other bed.

Conscious of being in bed, fully dressed, Ami lay still. The inside of her mouth tasted like burnt woolen blankets, and the room was unfamiliar. Without moving she could see Jeff's outline in the next bed. Her head detached itself from her shoulders with a white-hot pain as she sat up and holding onto it with both hands, she padded quietly to the bathroom.

Bless you, she thought as she saw her toothbrush Jeff had brought from the other room. If only she had some aspirin now. She brushed her teeth, touched the silent light switch, and made her way back to her bed, sliding out of her clothes.

"Come here."

Startled, Ami sucked in her breath, reaching for her shirt.

"Leave it and come here." She could see he had raised himself on one elbow.

She shook her head, not sure if he could see her.

"Do you want me to come after you?"

"I can't."

"Sure, you can. Turn around, one foot in front of the other, and so on."

"Jeff, this is wrong." She stopped, unsure how to go on.

"For whom?" the quiet reasonableness in Jeff's voice confused her.

"Please." She stood, waiting, but he said nothing more.

With no will of her own, Ami moved to the side of his bed. He turned the covers back and she sat down, lifting legs that weighed a ton. He reached, pulling her farther into the bed, and gathered her against him, their naked bodies touching from head to toe.

"Don't you ever sleep in anything?" he murmured.

"No."

"I'm not complaining." She felt his lips against her hair. "You smell good." His movements unhurried, Jeff started at her head, touching her dark hair, curving his fingers over her ears, his thumb pushing her chin up so he could kiss her. "It's been a long time since New Jersey, Ami," he whispered. Parted soft lips moved as he touched them with the tip of his tongue and pulsed with the fire he roused in her.

"Kiss me the way you did the first time, Ami." His voice was quietly demanding what he wanted of her.

She made a soft sound of protest, but her mouth opened to his bruising kiss, her slender legs scissored between his. He cupped her head, keeping her mouth imprisoned, one hand coming from around her to caress her breast, staying there until the brown tip swelled and hardened for him, his hand moved downward behind her hips, forcing her even closer to him. His lips kept hers, taking the sweetness she gave as his right, his body absorbing hers, possessing her, leaving none of her heart to call her own.

"Ami, sweetheart." His breath caught against the hollow of her throat. "Love me," he demanded, giving her no choice.

She could do nothing else and she answered his demand with her heart, giving herself to him, greedily taking what would never be hers to keep. He called her name sharply and, at the hard thrust of his body, she cried out.

She knew before she opened her eyes that she was alone. How else do you explain total desolation? Turning, she saw the empty bed, not so empty as her arms and heart. She stared at the ceiling for a long time before she rolled her tired body out of bed.

In the bathroom was a note on motel stationery stuck to the mirror. "Ami: Drive carefully. Jeff." The handwriting was like Jeff. Plain and straightforward. He wasn't leading her anywhere she wasn't willing to go.

Her eyes went past the note to meet the wide-spaced eyes reflected in the mirror, and she closed them to

keep from reading what was there for anyone to see.
She bit hard on her lower lip, crumpled the note, and
threw it in the wastebasket. Dressed, she sat on the side
of the bed, thinking about Jeff, about Mandy, about
Rio. Sighing, she gathered up her things, took a last
look around, and closed the door.

Riding with the windows down, seeking to clear her
muddled thoughts, Ami headed east on I-10, her beloved mountains ahead and to her right. It seemed
forever since she left Wagner's to bring Rio to Tucson.

The sign indicating the beginning of Wagner Ranch
came in sight as she topped a rise and she slowed, taking the first gravel road to her right. It ran parallel to
the line of mountains, reputedly once Cochise's strong-
hold, and on to Camp 20. She stopped the pickup, got
out, and wandered across the desert, envisoning the
wagon trains of over a century ago, making their way
across an endless sea of sand and mountains. She
thanked heaven for those sturdy people who had left
this for her.

She wished she had Remus with her. She smiled. He
was the only other being who loved the desert as much
as she did.

A few Black Angus cows chewed contentedly or
stood in the shadow of the taller saguaro cactus. Two
puffy clouds drifted toward the mountain peaks and,
after observing their certain collision course, Ami
walked back to the road. She could get lost out here and
no one would ever find her. Somehow she was certain
heartache was already there ahead of her, waiting. June
was five months away, then what? Wagner's wouldn't
be big enough for all of them after that. The whole
world would be too small.

Her thoughts returned to the night before in spite of
all her efforts not to think about what happened. If he
could love her like that, then leave her without a word
other than *drive carefully,* he wouldn't be apt to mind if

she packed up and left. She'd better get back to the vet listings. Australia would be a good location. She didn't think Apache Junction was far enough away for her to survive. Aching with every move, she climbed into the truck and drove slowly toward camp. Carue and two other cowhands were the only ones there at that hour. Ami accepted the ever-present cup of coffee and, as she left, said, "Call in for me, Carue. I'll be out here for a day and a half, at least."

But she didn't stay. An uneasiness kept her on the move, through Camps 16 and 17, till she headed toward the ranch house on Saturday morning. She avoided Steve and Janie, taking a roan from the corral to ride into the desert east of the big house with Remus romping like a young pup beside her. She circled a several mile area, checking the cattle as she went, reaching home after dark.

Hungry, Ami glanced in the near-empty refrigerator without any luck. She shrugged. Lily's Sunday morning breakfast would make up for it. Sleep came as her head touched the pillow.

Awake early, Ami headed for the back door of the kitchen. Lily was there, and she could smell the coffee.

"Ami, I declare, you're so skinny." Lily clucked her disapproval.

"I'm starved. Fill me up." She helped herself to coffee and stood looking out the back door. "Is it going to rain, Lily? My bones ache."

"Or snow."

"Come on, Lily. I've got too much work to do for that." And too much heartache to be caged in the house. The last was only a thought.

Stuffed to Lily's satisfaction, she headed toward the corral. Charlie was nuzzling any animal that would let him and generally making a pest of himself. Swinging long legs over the gate, she went to pet him.

"Do you miss Mandy, Charlie?" Ami rubbed the

white spot over his eyes. "Me, too." Her throat ached, wondering again if she hurt more for Mandy or herself.

A shout brought her attention back. It was Janie and Steve, dressed in Sunday best on their way to church at the small mission over near Tombstone.

"Where've you been?" Steve asked.

"Earning my excellent salary."

"It's darned lonesome with you, Rio, and Mandy gone. And we haven't seen Jeff except in passing in ages." Janie was pretty in a black gabardine suit with pale pink print blouse, reflecting the color in her cheeks. "Don't forget the Valentine Dance; we don't want to miss that."

"Of course, I won't. Maybe I can scrounge up a new dress."

"Yeah, no jeans," Steve said.

Back in her cottage, Ami dug through her small store of material. In the bottom of the trunk, she found the picture of her and Tim she had tucked away—how many eons ago? She sat looking at the laughing faces—so happy, so young, so long ago. Slowly she tore the picture in half, then across again. One heartache down; one to go.

She found a piece of plain red cotton, but there was only a yard and a half. That wouldn't go far on her long frame. Inspiration came and she went to her linens, found a plain white sheet, and pulled it out. Her mind envisioned the pattern and she nodded. Gathering all the items she would need to complete her outfit, she loaded them into the truck. She could finish most of the dress in the line shacks. Satisfied with her plan, she went to work on her books, brought all the ledgers up to date and, with that out of the way, showered, slid between the fresh sheets, and heard a voice so close, she turned her head.

"Don't you ever sleep in anything?" The mind can be a dangerous, lone companion.

As time neared for the Valentine Dance Ami found herself looking forward to it. The dress turned out even better than she had hoped, considering her materials and working time. It had been a long time since she had attended either of the grange dances and Cotton-Eyed Joe and Cripple Creek would be fun if all the regular gang was there.

Darkness caught her before she reached her cottage on Friday evening. The big house was full of lights, as was Janie and Steve's place, but she didn't go near either. Somewhere in the past few days she had got a cold and her head was stuffy. She took aspirin and went to bed.

Still feeling the dragging effects of the cold on Saturday morning, she dreaded the drive alone to the dance. A call to Janie got a welcome to join them. She spent the day lying around, pampering herself with aspirin and hot lemonade.

At six Janie called to alert her that they were ready to go. "It's raining. Had you noticed?"

Ami groaned. "Maybe I shouldn't go."

"Nonsense. Do you good to get out. Besides, I haven't seen your dress. You wouldn't want all that effort to go to waste."

It wasn't Steve's truck but a sleek Mercedes that stopped by her door. Jeff's car. Ami was already running before she realzied it, and there was no turning back, although her heart was choking her. She seemed always to be at the point of no return, she thought as she slid into the front seat, where the door had opened for her.

"Greetings," Steve and Janie chorused from the back.

Her eyes met Jeff's, but a general hi was all that was expected of her. Jeff smiled at her the way he would any of his hired help and said, "The car will hold the road better in the rain."

General conversation went on around her, and Ami was glad. She didn't want to think at all, much less speculate on what the evening held in store for her.

It was almost time for a band break and, since Jeff was calling the dances, she hadn't had to be too careful. He had taken the time to tell her the dress was becoming. Ami knew it was. The white showed off her smooth tan. It had a plain sweetheart neckline with tiny appliquéd red hearts down the close-fitting bodice, and full skirt with larger red hearts around the wide circle swung just above her knees. She had touched her cheeks lightly with a tint and matched her lips with the same color. The dark cap of hair was brushed up and away from her ears, just long enough to frame her face.

Ami danced with the regulars, smilingly accepting their compliments. Her throat dry and looking for a drink, Ami skirted the crowd, digging into her handbag for aspirin. She murmured an apology as, with head down, she bumped into a solid form.

"Need some help?" Jeff asked.

On a swiftly indrawn breath, Ami looked up. "No."

"Steve wants you to join them in singing."

She shook her head. "I can't. My throat's too scratchy."

"Come on. We'll find him." Jeff took her arm. "Here. Take your aspirin with this." He handed her a glass of water, and she obeyed him, then turned with him to find Steve.

Back at the table alone with Jeff, she tried not to look at him. "Haven't seen much of you lately." His voice was teasing.

Her breath caught and she turned to see his eyes moving over her body, her slim waist accented by the tight band on her dress. When she said nothing, he said, "I thought maybe I'd pushed my luck too far."

She sat silent for another moment then, in a voice matching the lightness in his, she asked, "And if you had?"

Jeff went still, the smile fading from his face. Leaning his elbows on the table, he stared at her, eyes narrowed. "Are we in trouble?"

"We?" Her eyebrows lifted.

"I was there."

"So you were."

His voice roughened. "Answer me straight, Ami."

She surveyed him, gray eyes as serious as she had ever seen them, a questioning light in them demanding an answer. "I don't believe Eileen would look too kindly on your deserting her for your veterinarian at this late date. Let's drop it."

"The truth, Ami." The anger in his voice surprised her.

She gave in after another few seconds of silence and smiled into the angry gray eyes. "You're safe, Jeff. I told you before not to worry."

It was his turn to draw a sharp breath, and the look he sent her way was one she could only describe as disturbing. "Ami—" he began when Janie and Steve appeared.

"I know we're not supposed to talk shop, but how about those Charolais that wandered off, Ami?" Steve asked.

Jeff's head swung around at the question, but he waited for her answer. She shook her head. "They aren't in the northwest corner where I thought they were. Jasper and Scully are checking the canyons beyond that. Ed and Cecil are working the other side of Camps 17 and 18."

"How many are missing?" Jeff asked.

"At least fifty," Ami said.

His eyes narrowed. "Are they the ones you marked with clips?"

"Yes." She met his glance. "I've used clips on all I've branded."

"I'm not convinced that's an effective method," he said.

"Why?" she wanted to know.

Steve was watching him, too, but said nothing. "What's to prevent the removal of the clip and the ears healing so that rustlers could cover it or recut it in another pattern?"

"Rustlers?" Steve asked.

Jeff leaned back in his chair. "Eileen is missing about fifty head of her Charolais."

"Since when?"

"Last week."

Ami stiffened, "How are hers marked?" she asked.

"Clips in the ears as you use. Her foreman was impressed by your method and had her vet change from all brands to clips in the new shipments."

Ami's gaze went from Jeff to Steve as she recalled discussing the method with Ron Steward, Eileen's foreman on the Crooked M, and the interest he had shown. Ami didn't know he had started using the clips instead of the conventional branding. Eileen was probably unhappy at the influence she had on the man who worked for her.

"I'll get Jasper to fly over some of the lower mountain ranges next week," Steve said. "There are a lot of places they could be that we haven't been in yet."

Janie broke in. "Can we talk about something besides cows? I'm beginning to think it's the only subject Wagner people can manage."

The subject changed, but Ami's mind stayed on it and, long after she was in bed, she wondered about her cattle and the odd coincidence that Eileen, too, was missing some of the valuable stock. She sighed, thinking of Jeff's serious attention when she teased him about her being pregnant, wondering what he would have said had not Janie and Steve picked that time to return to their seats.

Chapter Ten

A week later Ami went with Janie and Steve into Tucson to the monthly grange dance. She had danced with Ben Caskey, the piano player, and was waiting for them to come back to the table when someone spoke to her.

"Ami, how's business?" It was Jim Summers.

She smiled up at him. "Hello, Jim." She motioned to the chair near her, and he sat down. She hadn't seen him since before the Christmas Ball, which he hadn't been able to attend. He was probably sixty years old, slim almost to the point of being bony, with iron-gray hair beginning to thin on top.

"Still happy at Wagner's?" Jim asked, dark brown eyes studying her.

"It's a good job, Jim."

"Not ready for a change yet?" he asked.

"What opening do you have right now? I don't think I'm qualified as a foreman."

He laughed. "I can always use another vet."

Jim didn't know how much she was tempted. When those cattle were located, maybe she'd get in touch with him, Ami thought, as he said good-bye and left her. It wasn't far away from Wagner's, but she had a feeling distance would hardly count no matter where she went.

She was quiet on the ride home, listening to Steve and Janie talking in the front. They had decided to drive back to Wagner's instead of staying over, and it was early morning when they got home.

"Jeff's home," Janie said.

Ami's heart misbehaved, but she said nothing, seeing the green Porsche belonging to Eileen also parked at the back.

"Guess our lady plans to stay the night," Steve said, his voice dry. But as they got out of his truck the door to the big ranch house opened, and they could make out two figures in the light from the house. A few minutes later the Porsche roared out of the driveway.

Ami said goodnight and went inside her house, leaning against the door in the darkness. Love Jeff, she did, but he was out of her reach; to even think about him was foolish, but what do you tell a heart that refuses to listen?

I have to leave, she decided. *The next time I see Jim Summers, I'll accept whatever job he offers me.*

The next morning she was sitting on the back steps with a cup of coffee, watching the sun make a brassy rim over the mountains to the east, when Jeff strode around the corner of the house. She had no control over the quickening of her breath. He wore jeans and a lightweight denim jacket against the chill of the late winter winds.

"Good morning," he said.

"Hello, Jeff." She stood up. "Let's go inside, and I'll get you some coffee." He nodded, following her into the kitchen.

Ami poured coffee into a heavy mug, smiling as she passed it to him. "At least sit down to enjoy it," she said, wondering at the early morning visit. Jeff was an early riser; perhaps he wanted someone to share his coffee with, and she was willing. It wasn't necessary that he know what his presence did to her.

He looked about to refuse, then sat opposite her,

pulling the mug of coffee to him. "Ami?" The questioning uncertainty in his eyes, along with something else she couldn't identify, kept her attention riveted on him. The cup of coffee must have had a lot of interesting qualities to hold his gaze so long.

Finally, he took a long breath and looked up at her. "Ami, it's time we talked." She met his look, her heart beating an abnormal amount of beats per second, but she said nothing. His mouth tightened as they sat looking at each other.

"Will you marry me?"

The question simply took Ami's breath and her body went stiff. The seconds ticked by, and the silence in the room seemed to echo through her head. Of all the things he might have asked, that question was furthest from reality to her. She stared at him, lips parted and eyes wide with shock.

He leaned forward and smiled at her, reaching across the table to pick up her hand lying beside her coffee cup. "I understand if you need time to think it over, but at least say something."

She wet her lips. "I—I—" She shook her head, but that didn't clear the jumbled thoughts zinging around inside it. "What about Eileen?" she finally managed to ask.

"She knows I planned to ask you to marry me. I told her last night."

Remembering the roar of the Porsche as it left the driveway last night, Ami could well imagine the outraged anger Eileen felt at having been told he planned to ask his veterinarian—a veterinarian!—to marry him.

Slowly she turned her hand inside his until their fingers intertwined. "You didn't announce the engagement at Christmas, and I wondered why it was never mentioned around the ranch. Was that your idea?"

He nodded. "Eileen and I have been friends all our lives, and I guess we sort of drifted toward an engagement." His fingers curved around hers. "Then you came along, and I found I wasn't ready to announce our engagement as we planned and I spent a lot of time thinking about you." He shook his head this time. "You were always ready to give Amanda attention, and when I needed you..." Jeff smiled at her as she blushed and looked away from him.

"You don't have to—" she started to say.

"No, I don't have to, but I want to, Ami." He dropped her hands and pushed his chair back from the table, moving quickly to her side, and reached for her. She stood up, and he pulled her into the circle of his arms. Her body trembled as she leaned against him, standing on tiptoe to bring her face closer to his. Head tilted back to look into his shadowed gray eyes, she watched the firm mouth come closer to hers and her lips parted against the warmth of his as he folded her to him. Love for him flowed through her, and behind closed lids she saw his face again as he demanded, "Kiss me, Ami."

He lifted his mouth just enough to whisper against her lips. "Does that mean yes?"

She nodded and pulled his head down to continue the kiss as his hands moved upward, exploring her body through the robe, curving under her small breasts, thumbs caressing the firm mounds.

She gasped as their lips parted, and he smiled down at her. "Soon?"

"Oh, yes, Jeff, yes. Soon." She rubbed her head on his chest, holding tightly around his waist. He turned her around and led her into the living room to push her down on the couch and sit beside her, holding her close, whispering, his hands stroking her shoulders and arms. Finally, he said, "Would you mind if it's a small wedding right now? If you want a big one later on, we could have two ceremonies."

She gazed at him, puzzled. "A small wedding is fine. Why do you think I need a big one?"

"Most women would," Jeff answered, smiling.

She shook her head. "Would everyone here be invited?"

He studied her face before he answered. "Not for the actual ceremony. Jasper can officiate, with Janie and Steve as witnesses."

"But I'd want Mandy and Rio to be with us," Ami protested.

He smiled. "Of course." He leaned against the back of the couch, his arm across her shoulders. "Later, we can have a reception where everyone would be invited. I'd have some mad employees and friends if I tried to get away with not having one. Perhaps Linda and Dave could be persuaded to take time off and fly out, too." He cupped her chin with his hand. "Dave called last night."

Ami sat up straight. "Is anything wrong?"

"No, but he wants us to bring Amanda back to check the grafting in her ears. She'll want you to go with her, and we can be married before we go."

She wasn't sure whether to laugh or cry. Jeff had asked her to marry him, and Mandy was doing very well, and her mind lay in total confusion. Swallowing hard, she thought of Mandy going through more tests and refused to believe that they wouldn't show that she was progressing at a good pace. But now, Mandy was hers to love freely, and Jeff—Jeff would belong to her the way he did in her dreams.

"Mandy's doing so well. I hope they find everything taking as it should," she finally managed over the uneven beat of her heart.

His reply was fervent. "I'll breathe easier when they go over her again." She sensed a hesitation in him before he went on. "Ami, perhaps you should stay near the ranch this week and not go out into the camps. How much work do you have unfinished?''

"It can wait, although I had planned to drive up that north slope above the shack at Camp 20 and look around for those Charolais. They have to be somewhere in those canyons not too far away."

His hands went to her shoulders, tightening there. "Leave it alone, Ami," he said, and she looked in surprise at the anger in his eyes. "That's the one place I don't want you to go."

"Why?" she asked.

"I asked you not to, Ami, and I want your promise."

She pulled away. "I don't understand why you want me to stay away from the camps. There's no danger there."

"If we're to be married Saturday, you'd better be doing some preparation." The anger disappeared from his eyes and he teased. "Or do you plan to be married in jeans?"

Ami was puzzled at his changed expression and, suddenly, a horrible thought occurred. He didn't know why Tim had divorced her, but she would have to tell him before she could marry him.

"I didn't know we had set such an early date," she said, unable to bring herself to volunteer the information to him right then.

"Dave wants to see Amanda as soon as possible, and I promised him we'd be there Monday. I want us to be married before we go."

She drew a sharp breath, trying to visualize belonging to Jeff after loving him so long without any idea that he returned her love. Steeling herself for his reaction to what she must confess, she reached to take his hand just as a knock sounded on the front door.

"Are you expecting someone?" Jeff asked.

She shook her head, pulling away from him to

straighten her robe and stood up to move to the door. She opened it to face Steve and Jasper. Surprised at the appearance of the friends at her door on an early Sunday morning, it was a moment before she smiled and pushed the storm door open. "Come in," she invited.

They hesitated an instant. "Is Jeff here?" Steve asked.

Warm color stung her cheeks. "Yes, he's here."

They walked past her and, uneasy for some unknown reason, she pushed the door closed and leaned against it. Jeff stood up, a questioning look on his face, but he didn't seem surprised to see the two men.

"I'll get you some coffee," Ami said and went into the kitchen. Puzzled at the visit of the three men she seldom saw all at the same time, she took mugs from the top shelf of the cabinet, rinsing them because they were never used and dust collected when things were stored anywhere in the desert. She poured the coffee, standing for a moment looking out into the bright sunlight of the late February day. Soon the weather would be in the high sixties and seventies during the day, sometimes dropping to freezing at night, but not often. Spring in the high desert was her favorite time of year.

She picked up the mugs and went toward the living room, pausing as she heard voices speaking quickly, sounding angry. Jeff was saying "I want to know who found them and why they weren't spotted a few days ago."

"They were put there as late as yesterday morning, Jeff, I'm telling you," Steve said, "because we were in there two days ago. It has to be an inside job for them to know exactly where to put them. A place we had already inspected and wouldn't likely to go back to any time soon."

"What about it, Jasper?" Jeff asked.

"No doubt about it," Jasper said. "I hate to admit it,

but the way things look now, someone could think Eileen was right, even though we know better."

Ami's mind clicked with each bit of conversation and she walked back into the room, looking from one face to another as she handed the mugs of coffee to Steve and Jasper.

"You found the Charolais?" she asked and waited.

"Yes. In the blind canyon up from the shack at Camp 20, just across the ridge from Eileen's new property," Jeff told her.

"Eileen could be right about what?" She looked at Jasper this time.

He glanced at Jeff before he said bluntly, "She said you were responsible."

The dead silence that followed seemed to go on forever as the statement sunk in, and when she spoke, it was barely a whisper. "And you believe her?"

"No," Steve denied, "we don't. The evidence is only circumstantial, Ami, and we know it was planted to involve you."

Her lips were stiff. "What evidence?"

"The clips had been removed from the cattle and were found in the camp where you stayed last," Jeff said.

Her head came up. "You knew I'd be suspected," she said. Jeff started toward her, his hands outstretched, but before he could speak, she went on.

"What you're saying is that I masterminded the plan to take the cattle along with Eileen's, and when the search shifted to another part of the range, I'd be free to move them wherever I planned to sell them without fear of discovery until it was too late to stop me."

Jeff shook his head. "No, Ami, Steve told you that we know better than that."

Ami faced him, arms hugged around her trembling body as she asked, "Is that why you asked me to marry you?" When he hesitated, she looked at Jasper. "A husband can't be made to testify against his wife, isn't that right?''

Jasper nodded, his eyes turning to Jeff. Ami's voice grated. ''Thanks a lot. You've already decided I'm guilty.''

Jeff was in front of her, holding her arms. ''No, Ami, that isn't true and you know it. If Eileen goes to the Cattlemen's Association with charges against you, we'll have to answer them even though they're untrue.''

Turquoise eyes were wide with hurt as Ami stared into his face, remembering that he had not said he loved her, only that he couldn't stop thinking about her—thinking about his veterinarian turning out to be a cattle rustler. Her voice was dull as she said, ''I didn't rustle your cattle, Jeff, nor did I lend any assistance.'' She continued to look up at him. ''Your cattle can be identified easily from the others. The clips can be removed, but a flashlight with a simple infrared bulb can detect dye covering the ear. The same dye is sprayed on the hooves so when the cattle are shipped, the lights under the loading platform will show it, too. It's an antiseptic that helps keep insects off them.'' She turned away from him and walked to the window to stand looking out, and her voice was muffled. ''When I talked to Ron, I didn't mention the antiseptic dye because I assumed he knew about it, even though it's fairly new on the market. Maybe you should check some of the cattle that's supposed to belong to the Crooked M to see if they have dye on them.''

''Are you accusing Eileen of double-dealing?'' Jeff asked, watching her closely.

Ami swung around. ''Why not? She accused me. Does the difference in the name give her immunity? A pillar of the community against someone with a renegade Indian name like Whitelake that doesn't even belong to her.'' Hurt churned inside her. ''If you'll excuse me, I have work to do.'' Her eyes went again to Jeff. "The proposal wasn't necessary, Jeff, and I won't hold you to it."

Jeff looked at Steve and Jasper and nodded. The men turned and left. Jeff's arms came out to her, but she backed away, anger replacing her stunned feelings. "I'll leave as soon as I can get everything packed and send you an address when I have one, in case you decide to prosecute."

"No, Ami, you're not to leave. We're not accusing you of anything." His hands closed on her arms, pulling her to him, and he smiled down at her. "The cattle have been found, so there's no loss."

"You'll forget I'm a thief because you can recover your losses?" She shook her head, but he held her, one hand holding her head to his chest, his chin pressed to her dark head. She stayed a long time, thinking that fairy tales seldom come true in real life and her fairy-tale existence had been very short-lived.

Her hands came up, pushing him away, and she went toward her bedroom. At the door, she turned her head to look at him. "I hope Amanda will be all right." She had never called the little girl Amanda; it seemed too formal for such a tiny girl, but she'd better get used to thinking of her as a stranger. She closed the door of the bedroom behind her and stood listening, knowing that Jeff had not yet left the room.

"Ami," Jeff's quiet voice came from just beyond the door. "I know this is upsetting, but we can work it out together. We're not accusing you and surely you realize that." He waited, but she didn't answer him. "My proposal wasn't a spur-of-the-moment thing; it's permanent, and we're getting married as soon as we can." Again a moment of silence, then, "Honey?" the tenderness in that one word almost made her weaken, but she bit her lip, waiting.

Finally, she said, "It's all right, Jeff. I understand."

"I'll be back soon, Ami. Don't go out anywhere until I get back to you, okay?"

"Yes, Jeff," she told him, and she heard the outside door close as he left.

At least I didn't have to tell him why Tim divorced me, she thought and wondered why it was such a small comfort.

There was no one around to say good-bye to, and she was glad. What could she say? Janie would hear from Steve; Hammett and Lily from Janie. Ami tried to swallow the lump in her throat, but it grew larger, choking her. On the last trip to the little truck she looked toward the ranch house. The Bronco was gone, and she assumed they were checking to see if all the cattle had been recovered. Jeff would want to verify that the dye was on the cattle for identification, checking her out to see how far she'd stretch the truth.

Ami wondered for the hundreth time how all the rustling and shifting had been accomplished with the checking they had done in the past two weeks. Almost every one of Wagner's hands had, at one time, run down a trace of some kind on the missing cattle, coming up with very little in the way of evidence that would indicate what had happened to them. Inside help was needed to move so many cattle and leave nothing behind but a stray here and there. If she didn't do it, then who?

Ron Steward, Eileen's foreman, was the only person with whom she had discussed using the metal clips for cattle identification. No one had showed more than a passing interest in the method except him. She shied away from the thought that he might be involved in the missing herds, but then, she was a suspect, too. That drew her up short and she laughed aloud, a short, derisive laugh, accompanied by a shake of her head.

The boxes of books were loaded last, and the portrait

from Rio carefully placed on top. She looked around the house she had lived in for almost a year. It had been her first real home since Tim, and she refused to dwell on how much she would miss the people at Wagner's. She was a gypsy and would move her shallow roots elsewhere. Jeff could be pushed into the past the same as anyone else—if she were lucky.

One phone call was all she needed to make before her plans would be complete. She dialed long distance to Jim Summers's ranch in Apache Junction. A soft female voice inquired her business.

"This is Ami Whitelake from Wagner's Ranch. Is Mr. Summers available?"

"One moment, please."

"Hello?" The salutation was barked into the phone.

Ami identified herself, and the brusque voice changed. "Ami," he said. "Tell me you're calling about a job."

"As a matter of fact, Jim, I am looking for a job."

"Boy, do I need to hear that. Ralph Carter, my vet, broke his leg yesterday, and I'm in the middle of getting a herd ready to ship. When can you be here?" he asked.

"Wait a minute, Jim, let me tell you why I'm leaving Wagner's, then you can decide if you still want me."

"All right, Ami, tell me."

He let her talk until she faltered, and she was quiet a moment before he said, "What's wrong with Jeff, Ami? He usually has a lot more common sense than to believe that stuff." He went on slowly. "Sounds like Eileen's been using her influence to help things along."

"What do you mean?" she asked, surprise in her voice.

He laughed a little. "Well, my boys tell me she's jealous of Jeff's lady vet, and they usually carry pretty straight gossip."

She caught her breath. "Why would she be jealous of

me when they plan to marry in a few months?'' But that wasn't true anymore. Or was it? His proposal to her was a put-up job, and he actually had no intention of breaking with Eileen on a permanent basis. She cringed at how she had been taken in so easily.

Jim was laughing. "Now, Ami, I don't try to figure out lovely ladies and their peculiarities. Enough of this. When can I expect you?''

"Do you understand what I'm accused of, Jim? A quarter million dollars loss would upset anyone.'' He, of all people, should understand the seriousness of the charge Eileen had made.

"Wagner's loss is my gain, Ami, not the herd—you. Let me tell you, he'd better have some hard facts to back him or anyone else up if he comes looking for my veterinarian with that kind of talk. Back to sensible conversation, Ami. How soon can you be here?''

"Tomorrow noon. I'd like to stop by the school and see if I can make Rio understand what happened.'' It was less than a hundred miles to Apache Junction from Tucson, and the J&R Ranch was just north of there, bordering the Superstition Mountains, subject of many wild and woolly tales of disappearing prospectors hunting the rich caches of gold supposedly in the rugged mountain ranges, some forty of them.

"That's great news. Think you can find me? You turn left past the curve in the highway about ten miles north of Apache Junction. There's a big white iron gate with J&R branded into it. The house is a couple miles inside.''

"Thanks, Jim. I'll see you.'' She hung up and stared at the phone, wondering if this were truly happening or if she would wake up soon.

Locking the door behind her, something she had never done while living there, she hung the key on the nail beside the door and ran down the steps into the bright moonlit night, sneaking away like a common

thief. Well, they should expect that of her. Ami opened
the door of the truck to let Remus in the front seat with
her and bit hard into her lip, determined not to cry.

She succeeded. As she drove through the open range
country she loved and jealously considered her own,
anger spread like fire inside. How could they even be-
gin to suspect her? Jasper and Steve she had thought
were very good friends, while Jeff— Well, Jeff was a
different story. Perhaps she couldn't blame him, since
Eileen was the accuser, a life-long friend, a respected
rancher, in addition to being his fiancée, while she was
only a maverick with a name like Whitelake.

The turnoff road to Camp 20 and her favorite line
shack went off to her left, and her gaze followed the line
of mountains standing like ghostly sentinels. Across
that range was Eileen's new property, lying adjacent to
the blind canyon on Wagner property where the cattle
were discovered; cattle that hadn't been there for very
long, according to Jasper and Steve.

Ami couldn't imagine why Eileen had bought that
land. Jeff had talked about it ever since she had known
him, hesitating because his property would be divided
by the towering range of mountains, hard to keep an
eye on unless he hired a lot more people.

The little truck skidded sideways as she slammed on
her brakes and turned around in the middle of the deserted road, heading back to the turnoff to Camp 20,
turning right into the familiar gravel road. She couldn't
see Rio before morning, anyway, and she'd scare him
to death if she went there in the middle of the night.
The line shack was a good place to stop for the last time
on Wagner property.

The dark outline of the small building came into
sight, and she switched off her lights as the truck rolled
quietly to a stop. Remus jumped out as she opened the
door, walking up to the familiar building, sniffing
around the steps. He whined.

Ami was reaching for a flashlight as she got out of the truck, and the whine surprised her. She stared at the closed door, wondering if the house was occupied. The clips they were using as evidence had been found there. Suppose the rustlers had come back for those clips?

"You're imagining things, Ami," she said aloud and walked up on the narrow porch, her boots making enough noise to wake anyone who might be sleeping there. The knob turned in her hand, and she let the door swing inward, holding her breath for a moment before shining the light inside. Remus trotted in, and she followed him, trusting that he would never lead her into a room full of enemies.

The kerosene lamp was where it always was, and she lit it, standing still to look around the room she had used so many times. It looked undisturbed. She shivered, realizing the temperature had dropped several degrees since she left Wagner's. A few minutes later she had a good fire going in the heater and put some water in a small pot she took from a nail on the wall.

The tea bags she left in a can were just as she had left them, and a little later she poured hot water over a bag in an old mug. She pulled the orange crate she used as a combination table and chair near the stove and went to pull the blankets from the bunk nearest the stove, shaking them to roust out any desert creatures that might be seeking refuge in them. Two tiny desert squirrels scuttled across the room and disappeared in the corner.

"Sorry," she said, spreading the blankets over the crate to warm them before she went to bed.

From where she stood, Ami couldn't see any signs of a search being made, but there was little in the cabin to disturb. Had the clips been left in plain view? How had they known to look for evidence in the shack used only by Camp 20 hands and her?

A weariness not associated with being tired filled her body. She had gone from the heights of happiness to the dungeons of despair in a few hours. It would be easy to believe none of it had ever happened.

Ami was spreading the blankets on the bunk when she heard the noise and glanced at Remus. He sat straight, short ears pointed forward, listening. The wind had changed and was coming from the north canyons, whistling around the shack. The noise she heard was a rumble, like thunder, but the night was clear.

"Sounded odd," she told the old dog. "Guess the wind is extra noisy tonight."

With the wind's icy breath, the stove wasn't putting out much heat, and she debated whether to take her clothes off to sleep or add more, finally giving in to the elements, crawling between the blankets with her clothes on. Just before she slipped into sleep, she heard Jeff's teasing voice, *"Don't you ever sleep in anything?"*

As late as it was when she finally slept, she was awake before daylight. The stove was still slightly warm from the fire she had banked not too many hours ago, and she stirred it to life with some of the dry wood stacked in the corner of the room. It didn't take long for the one cup of water she put in the small pot to boil, and she had a cup of black coffee as she refolded the blankets on the bunk, her mind going in all directions without finding an outlet. Although Jeff suspected her of the worst, he was willing to marry her to keep the trouble from being dragged through the courts, friend against friend, neighbor against neighbor. She smiled a little to herself. Just like the western stories she read when she was growing up and thought were so romantic. What was romantic about being accused of stealing your boss's cattle? And where was her rescuer on his white stallion? Still running around in his fairy tale, she guessed. Eileen would just as soon see her hung, the law of the land back in her fiction world of the wild, wild west. A thief in those days was worse than a murderer. Maybe beliefs hadn't changed that much.

Standing by the small dust-covered window, Ami finished the cup of coffee, used a precious bit of water to rinse out the cup, and placed it back on the orange crate used as table and shelf.

Daylight was beginning as she opened the door, taking one last look around before she closed it behind her. The air was cold, although the wind had dropped to only a breeze. Remus trotted around the corner of the shack and sat near her as she gazed toward the range of mountains between Wagner's and the O'Toole property Eileen had bought.

If there was any way across that peak, she was willing to bet that was how Jeff's cattle just happened to be found with some of Eileen's from her new land, Ami thought. What was she doing? Trying to say Eileen might rustle her own cattle to get even? Even with whom? With what?

"Very unlikely," Ami said aloud and walked to the truck. She started it, sitting with her eyes still on the mountains, letting the motor warm a little before she moved away from the shack. The questions continued to move through her head without answers but, nevertheless, were not to be ignored. Regardless if everyone at Wagner's thought her guilty and would stand by her anyway, she needed information for her own peace of mind. She flinched again at the realization that Jeff thought her guilty enough that he would marry her for her own protection—and his.

Straightening over the wheel of the little truck, she sighed and pulled away from the shack. A few feet from where she started, she changed from the direction of the well-traveled road heading back toward the ranch, turning instead down the trail she had been over many times, going into the foothills of the mountains.

She drove through a dry-wash creek bed where she had first seen the odd tracks and followed her own tracks a few hundred yards, stopping where she usually did before the cattle were moved for the winter. Sitting for a moment, she got out of the truck, Remus beside her, and walked across the rough terrain, through small piñon and dried sagebrush. For several moments she stood looking at the forbidding peaks, then changed her direction slightly to the north, crossing the dry-wash again as it curved into the mountains.

It had been several weeks since she had been this far into the area, and her examination of the hard soil showed no signs of the foreign marks. She bent forward a little as the ground inclined sharply and paused at the top of the crest to look over both sides. The sun was peeking over the mountains in back of her, but there was no warmth to it and she shoved her hands into her pockets to keep them warm. The line of Wagner's property went about where she was standing, but she turned back and walked on up the mountain, angling across it to get a better footing. At this elevation the scrub piñon were only large twigs, and she used them to pull herself along as her footing became more precarious. Topping another rise, she stopped, looking to her left where the canyon ran along the mountainside and disappeared from her sight.

If you could get a truck this far and head into that canyon, she thought, and let the idea drop there. She could never get her small truck to pull itself up the steep sides to get into that canyon, much less...

A rumble sounded ahead of her, and she looked up at the clear sky, frowning. Remus, sitting nearby, growled and stiffened, short ears pointed forward as he, too, listened. She watched in astonishment as a big sixteen-wheeler lumbered around the bend in the wash, inching slowly along the base of the mountain peak, close enough for her to read the huge blue lettering on the side of the silver vehicle: INTERSTATE MOVING AND HAULING.

Curious disbelief rooted her to the spot, and, suddenly, it registered. In one of the Tucson papers not many weeks ago she had read about a gang operating out of the northwestern states, using trucks to rustle cattle. At the time she had shaken her head at the ingenious means people would go to, taking chances to get money without working for it. Her gaze rested on the giant-size tires with tractorlike treads as she stood transfixed by the sight she saw but scarcely believed. The truck stopped, and the doors on each side opened to reveal two men who were looking up at her, and she realized, too late, she was in full view of them.

"Remus," Ami commanded sharply and turned, running surefooted along the ridge until she was forced to follow the incline downward, skidding and sliding as she tried to outdistance the men she knew were following her. Her size and speed were on her side, but as she neared her truck she saw that one of the men had cut across another ridge and was between her and any avenue of escape. Ami made him work for his victory, turning away from him, back toward the small piñon trees. He made a flying tackle, and they went down together. She came up fighting, her nails reaching for his face. It wasn't skin she contacted, but a ski mask, hiding any identification of the wearer.

They were both breathing hard and, suddenly, the odor of sour sweat and tobacco was familiar. The man holding her laughed.

"Well, well. What do we have here?" He held her shoulders, her arms caught in back of her.

The other man came up to them. "I don't believe it," he said. "Our little tiger. Where's your friend?"

A chill of fear shook her as she recognized Hank and Luke, Rio's harassers from Douglas many months ago.

Remus sat in front of them, growling, showing his teeth, waiting.

"Down, Remus," she ordered, and he sat still, the growl still low in his throat.

The man standing in front of her removed his ski mask, revealing the bearded face she recalled as belonging to Hank. He grinned, showing tabacco-stained teeth.

"And what are you doing out in this deserted country, my lovely?' he asked.

Ami didn't answer him, her mind busy as things began to fall into place. All the happenings in the past several weeks began to make sense. Valuable cattle disappearing with no clues as to when or where, and everyone assuming they'd be located in the spring roundup. They wouldn't be. They had been stolen. No wonder Jasper didn't spot them from the plane; they were in a big semi, hidden from view, possibly in that blind canyon.

Luke held her in a viselike grip, and she knew better than to struggle. She kept an eye on Remus, almost reading what was going through his scarred head. If they hurt her and she made an outcry, he would attack, but she had seen the guns they carried, and she wasn't planning to tempt them to use the weapons. She shook her head, trying to wake up if it was a nightmare she was in.

"What are we gonna do with her?" Luke asked.

Hank eyed her and grinned. "We have plenty of time, since no one knows we're here." He moved toward Ami. "I suggest a little fun before we get on with the business at hand."

She cringed, realizing what was on his mind. She started talking. "We've been looking for these cattle for weeks," she said. "I didn't know you could drive a truck through here, not to the other side of that mountain."

"You just have to know how to handle a big semi, sweetie." Hank laughed. "Of course, knowing someone who owns the land and has a mind bordering on being crooked helps." He took a step nearer. "Ron mentioned Wagner's veterinarian, but he never mentioned she was a lady, a very pretty lady." He grinned into her face.

Ron, she thought. Ron Steward.

"You mean you've taken cattle from Wagner's and the Crooked M?" she asked, stalling for time.

"Well, a little here, a little there. It all adds up to a good bit of change." He was enjoying himself as he toyed with her. "Ron and Miss McKane seem to think you're overstepping your territorial rights, and they intend to put a stop to it one way or another. If you get accused of stealing your own cattle—"

"Hank, you'd better shut up," Luke told him, his arm tightening around Ami.

But he had told her more than enough. Eileen and Ron were involved. How much and how far she didn't try to guess. Jeff would never believe her, anyway, not on the say-so of two crooks.

Hank still stood in front of her, leering, his eyes going from the dark tousled hair to the tight jeans he could see beneath the jacket she wore. He reached for her. Outraged anger dictated her next move, and she suddenly kicked out, catching him in the thigh with her boot heel, and as he grunted and stumbled away from her, she went limp, sliding from Luke's surprised grasp. Ami rolled away from him, coming up to see Remus spring at Hank, who crouched a few feet away, his gun leveled at her. The shot made no sound other than a muffled thump, and she saw Remus fall. She threw herself sideways as the gun was aimed at her again, saw a flash of light, and felt the heavy shock in her side. There was no pain, but she couldn't move and lay still, waiting for whatever they planned to do.

"Damn it, Hank," Luke muttered. "We weren't supposed to use any guns. I told you to leave them in the truck. I ain't wantin' to serve no murder charge."

"We're already into it far enough for a long jail term if we're caught, so we make sure we don't get caught. Soon's Steward finds out we really took the cattle instead of just moving them like we're supposed to do, he and his boss-lady will be after us, anyway." His laugh was nasty. "Miss McKane ain't no fool and she won't stand still for a double cross, you can bet on it."

"What do we do now?" Luke asked, looking down at Ami.

"Leave her and get out of here. These cattle will keep us in beer a long time."

Their movements were blurs to Ami until she heard the truck start and move along the canyon, heading for the wash that would take them out onto the state road that intersected with Interstate 10. She lay still until the sound vanished and stillness closed in around her. Looking straight up into the clear blue sky, she guessed it was nearly noon. Jim Summers would be looking for her about now. She rolled over and grunted as she struggled to get her left arm from beneath her. It had no feeling and didn't respond to her efforts. Remus lay several feet from her, and she gazed at the still figure for a long time. Once she had given him a new lease on life, and he had tried with all he had to repay her.

If she intended to get out of this mess alive, she'd have to move and somehow get back to the truck. If she stayed here until it grew dark and much colder, she'd freeze. Ami began the struggle to make her way back to the little truck, fairly close by, but seeming miles in the distance. She looked back at Remus and saw him move, struggling to get up. Without hesitation, she turned, moving inch by painful inch toward the old dog.

Chapter Eleven

Jeff stared at the door Ami had closed behind her after giving him a look that said volumes. Indecision gnawed at him, but he finally left when she refused to answer his pleas, feeling that she needed to be alone to adjust her thinking to all that had happened in such a short time.

Outside, he turned to look back at the house, strongly tempted to go barging into her bedroom and hold her again if only to reassure her of his love. Shaking his head, he walked on to the big house, hurrying the last few steps as he heard the phone ringing. Lily turned as he went down the hallway. "It's Amanda's school, Mr. Jeff," she said, and looked worried as she handed the receiver to him.

"Yes?" Jeff asked, already apprehensive. He listened to the voice on the other end and said, "I'll be there by noon. I'd rather see her before you give her any medication." He hung up the phone and stood there. Problems never came singly. Amanda had a severe cold, and they wanted to know if they could give her medicine for it and, by his own rule, they never gave her anything without his approval.

"I'm going to see Amanda, Lily, and I'll probably be late getting back. Nothing serious, but I haven't seen her in over a week, so I'm going in."

Lily nodded, wondering what else was bothering the

boss. He was not a worrier, but something other than Amanda's cold had his attention.

On his way toward Tucson Jeff stopped by the air-strip to see Jasper, glad to see Steve's truck there, too. They came out to meet him, and he explained where he was going.

"Keep an eye on Ami and don't let her go near the camps. We still aren't sure where the rustlers are, nor if they have plans to come back for the cattle. You might make a couple of runs over that range today, Jasper, to see if anything's moving."

"I could fly you into Tucson, Jeff," Jasper offered.

He shook his head. "I'd rather you keep an eye on things here."

Jeff left them, taking an uneasy gut feeling with him, something not quite right, as though he had left out something important somewhere. When he reached the school, Amanda was fretful and feverish, and he sat with her until she went to sleep around eight thirty that night. Deciding against returning to the ranch so late, he checked into a motel and called Steve.

"Everything's quiet, Jeff. Ami hasn't left the house all day, and I've had to fight Janie to keep her away from there. Aside from the fact that I'll probably end up in a divorce court over this, I guess we can wait it out."

"I'll be home as early as I can tomorrow," Jeff promised.

He hung up the phone and dialed Ami's number. After the tenth ring, he replaced the receiver. She could be sitting outside, as he knew she loved to do, or down at the corral, walking off the worry she must be feeling. Exhausted, he went to bed to fall into a restless sleep.

Monday morning, Jeff checked on Amanda and found her in much better spirits, even though still coughing. "I'll be back Saturday and bring Ami. Would you like that?" he asked. He would have to cancel the appointment with Dave in Newark until her cold was gone.

Mandy grinned, nodding vigorously, and let him go with a big hug. Jeff's throat tightened as he left the little girl. Ami was right—she belonged at home. As soon as the rustling episode was resolved, he'd have the school locate a tutor for her, one who wouldn't mind living on an isolated ranch. Ami, he thought suddenly. Ami would be better than anyone else. What better than a combination mother and tutor? It sounded good to him and brought his thoughts back to Ami. She thought he had asked her to marry him to protect her if she was tried for rustling, and his first job was to convince her she was wrong. He had only one reason for asking her to marry him, although chances are he had gone about it in such a way that he was going to have to start over. He would have to convince her that his proposal came from his love for her; love that he had discovered many weeks ago.

It was a total shock to him to find that, after they left Newark, he was letting Ami fill his thoughts day in and day out. Even as he worried over Amanda's chances of having at least partial hearing and the fact that she would have to live away from him while attending the special school, he carried a lighthearted feeling when he saw Ami from a distance or occasionally ran into her at the grange dances.

Much to his own surprise, he balked when Eileen insisted they announce their engagement at the Christmas Ball and flinched as he remembered her accusations against Ami. They had the party, but no announcement had been made, although he knew most of his employees expected it.

Try as he would, he hadn't been able to gauge Ami's feelings for him. Even after the night in each others' arms in Newark, she had been friendly, not overly so, her turquoise eyes showing him nothing. Then, when he maneuvered her into staying with him in Tucson, he had sensed that her feelings somehow were as strong as his when she responded to him so completely. He still reeled when he thought about it. The love she gave him that night left him with a deep satisfaction, and he was biding his time before he asked her to marry him, a little sorry when she let him know she wasn't pregnant at the Valentine Dance. Mingled love and desire for the slender dark-haired girl caused him to straighten behind the wheel of the Bronco, and he pressed his foot harder on the gas pedal. She needed his assurance that he loved her and didn't believe her to be a thief, and he could give her that without any trouble at all.

The trip from Tucson had never taken so long. Not bothering to stop in the yard of the big house, Jeff drove on to Ami's and muttered an oath of disappointment when he saw the small truck was not in her yard. His stomach muscles knotted as Steve and Jasper came to meet him.

"Is Amanda all right?" Steve asked, but the expression on his face held Jeff's attention.

He nodded. "Ami?"

Jasper answered. "She's gone, Jeff. She was here when we went to bed around ten, but when we got up this morning, she was gone. She took most of her things."

He stared at them, swallowing over the uneasiness filling him. "Did she leave a note?"

Both men shook their heads. "Are you sure she took all her things? Even her books?" he asked.

"Yes. Everything."

They stood there in the bright midmorning sunlight. Jeff drew in his breath. "She'll go see Rio before she does anything else. Let's call him."

As they entered the house Jeff raged inwardly at himself for the way he handled the situation, failing to convince Ami that he believed her innocent and leaving her too soon afterward to deal with her thoughts alone.

I wouldn't much blame her if she didn't want to talk to any of us, he thought as he dialed Rio's number. He smiled as Rio answered at the other end of the line and, after pleasantries, asked, "Is Ami there, Rio?"

"No. Was she coming up here today?" he asked. "I hope so. There's some questions I need to ask her. You want her to call you if she does come by?"

Jeff thought quickly about excuses for Ami being in Tucson. "She was going for supplies, Rio, and I just thought she might stop by to see you. There was something I needed her to pick up for me and thought maybe I could catch her at your place. If she does drop by, ask her to call. She may not have time to visit you, but just in case."

"Okay, Jeff."

Jeff hung up the phone and turned, shaking his head. "Where else?"

"Jim Summers was after her to work for him," Jasper said. "He made her a great offer, I heard from some of his men." He waited, but neither of the other men commented. "I can't believe she'd go through Tucson and not stop to see Rio."

Jeff thought a moment. "If she went that way, I should have met her somewhere between here and Tucson. I stayed at the Best Western last night, the one where we usually stay, so she didn't stop there, either. Of course, we don't really know when she left here." He walked to the window. The winds from the snow-capped mountains were cold, and he thought of the cabin where Ami usually stayed, where she spent most of her time. The cold, dry air agreed with her, leaving tanned cheeks with a light tint from sun and wind, but he didn't want her there alone anymore. Nowhere alone.

He looked over his shoulder at Jasper and Steve. "I'll wait by the phone if you'll take a run over that canyon, Jasper." He grinned a little. "You'd better try to pacify Janie, Steve. All we can do is wait."

After they left him, Jeff stared out over the land he knew and loved—a vast emptiness that he knew Ami loved almost as well. He had heard her comment on the beauty around them many times in the eleven months she had been his veterinarian—and a competent one at that. It was hard to believe she had been there so long, and even harder to think of the ranch without her. It had been five months since he first made love to her in Newark, a few days after a soul-shaking kiss he had tried to ignore. It was nearly two months since they shared a night of love in Tucson. Where the hell was his mind all that time? He grimaced, remembering the look on Ami's face as he told her Eileen was planning to bring charges against her for rustling some of her cattle. He hadn't been too reassuring, only warning her they needed to hear her statement that she wasn't involved. He had never suspected her, but he hadn't said that to Ami, not in plain words. He had said— He stopped, trying to remember what he had said, but instead, remembered her soft voice, trembling as she said, "I love you, too." Had he assured her of his love? Jeff couldn't even remember and shook his head at his own ignorance. He had few occasions to mention love since he lost Myra and didn't care for the people who used the word without thinking of real emotions that should go with it. Eileen was a life-long friend, and it went without saying that he loved her, whether the all-consuming kind or not. It might have proved to be enough for an enduring marriage between them had Steve not hired a tall lady veterinarian with strange turquoise eyes.

Standing by the window, his thoughts racing like sand in the wind, he forgot Steve and Jasper. How had the cattle become mixed? How many were his and how many Crooked M stock? Ami said— What had she said? *"Has the difference in the name given her immunity?"* Eileen wouldn't deal him an underhanded blow such as rustling his cattle and some of her own to divert suspicion, he was sure.

Jeff recalled the glint in her eyes as she hurled her bomb on Friday night. "You think your veterinarian is such a treasure. I have proof that she is in with rustlers and taking stock from both of us."

"What in the world are you talking about?" he asked, not bothering to hide his disbelief.

Eileen was furious at his scoffing question. "Ron suspected Ami and went to that line shack she's always supposed to be in. There were hundreds of the clips she uses on the cattle that had been removed from my herd as well as yours." When he only stared at her, she went on. "I'm filing charges against Ami on Monday."

Eileen had the upper hand at that moment, and she knew it. Jeff had gone looking for Ami on Saturday, but she had gone into Tucson to see Rio and from there on to the grange dance. Eileen came over late Saturday night to gloat and to bargain. If he got rid of Ami, she'd drop the charges. That was when the explosion resulted as he told her he planned to marry Ami. From then on it was war between them, and his only wish was to protect the woman he'd asked to marry him.

Jeff started as the phone rang, moving toward it before the first ring was half completed. He picked up the phone to become instantly alert when he heard Jim Summers's name.

"I've been trying to call Ami, Jeff," he said. "But there's no answer at her house. Has she left to come up here?"

"Why would she be going to your place?" Jeff asked, fingers tightening around the phone.

"She finally accepted my job offer and she said she'd be here by noon today. When she didn't show, I thought maybe you'd come to your senses and talked her into staying on with you." After a moment when Jeff made no comment, he went on. "I'm prepared to offer her more money to keep her from staying with anyone who'd accuse her of stealing."

Jeff stiffened and his voice was hard with anger. "Who told you I accused her?"

"Ami. She seemed to think I ought to know what charges might be brought against her before I hired her, in case I had any doubts."

"And you didn't?"

"Never will have, Jeff, no matter who accuses her. Now, do you have any idea what time she left there?"

For a moment Jeff was tempted to hang up on him, but they had been friendly acquaintances too long to jeopardize a potential ally.

"She left here sometime during the night, Jim. She hasn't been to see Rio, and we don't know where she is." As he spoke the unease from the early morning returned. Trying not to let his fear show, he said, "To be on the safe side, I'll call Archie Denton, the sheriff in Tombstone, and have him run a check on some of the side roads. In the meantime we'll alert the camps in case she shows up there."

Jim Summers hesitated. "Do you suspect foul play?" he asked finally.

"Everything until I have her back," Jeff said.

Jim Summers grunted. "You forget, Jeff. You don't get her back."

"I haven't forgotten anything."

He heard the other man's indrawn breath. "Let me know if you hear anything, and I'll do the same."

Jeff hung up the phone and turned as Jasper and Steve came in. "Did you get through to Carue and the others?"

"Yes."

"Let's drive out to Camp 20 and go to the line shack from there."

"Why Camp 20?" Steve asked.

"It's the only one they could leave from and possibly get across that range of mountains without being seen."

"Not very likely that they could," Jasper said.

"No," Jeff admitted. "But let's check anyway." He turned to Steve. "Call Denton and tell him as much as you have to, that it's only suspicion about cattle being rustled and worry over Ami. Keep a good watch here." His smile was grim. "I imagine Janie wants to know what's going on. You may as well tell her everything, as limited as our information is." He looked at Jasper. "Let's go."

Carue's camp of hardworking cowhands was still out on the range, but the hard-bitten old trail boss came out to meet them. He looked at Jeff and Jasper and opened the door to let them walk into the cabin ahead of him.

"No word?" he asked quietly.

Jeff shook his head and gave him as many details as he could. The older man's jaw set in a hard line. "You mean to tell me you accused Ami of rustling her own stock? She's been checking for weeks, running herself ragged trying to cover seventy-five thousand acres of wilderness, and you have the nerve—" He stopped, sputtering.

Jeff listened to him then said, "We don't suspect Ami, but Eileen is bringing charges, Carue. She has more head missing than we do and the ones that have been found are on Wagner property just across from the O'Toole ranch she bought. You know when a charge like that is made by a rancher, it has to be checked out."

Carue snorted and didn't think of Jeff's feelings as

he said, "Why don't you just throttle Eileen, since she's the main source of trouble?" He looked sourly at Jeff. "I guess you assume Ami ran away?"

"No, I don't, Carue. She's either still looking to see how the cattle crossed that mountain range or—" He stopped.

Jasper spoke into the silence. "Where are a couple of your men we can take with us? We don't want to wait too long and not be able to see."

"Ed and Cecil are the closest. You can pick them up at the south end of the canyon that runs back of the Camp 20 line shack," Carue told him.

Carue walked outside with them, staring at the ground as they got into the Bronco. He looked up as Jasper started the motor. "Ami could figure she'd had enough of your accusations and just went somewhere to think it over. I wouldn't feel too friendly toward somebody who thought I'd been stealing from them. Would you?" His voice challenged his boss to answer him.

Jeff smiled a little as he agreed. "No, I probably wouldn't, Carue. But we told Ami as much as we knew and to stay put until we got some answers ourselves. We weren't trying to drive her away from Wagner's, but wanted to be sure she was protected."

"I hope you find her and aren't too late with your protection," Carue said.

Inside, Jeff cringed. Carue had put into words what he had tried to keep out of his mind. "So do I. We'll keep in touch."

At the end of the canyon they found Ed and Cecil and explained what they wanted. The two men silently unsaddled their horses, placing the equipment near a fence post and tethering the horses several yards apart. They removed rifles from their packs and carried them, barrels down, as they walked to the vehicle where Jeff and Jasper waited.

Before he climbed into the back of the Bronco, Ed asked, "Do you for one minute think Ami would be behind something like this?"

Jasper sent a long look at Jeff as he said, "No." He stopped there, figuring, rightly so, that he didn't need to say any more. The men with him had condemned Eileen before he was half through with his explanations about what had happened, and it would take a self-admission from Ami before they would believe the worst of her.

The Bronco took the hills and rough terrain easily, and they still had a good deal of daylight left when they topped the ridge above the shack. There was no sign of life from that vantage point, and Jasper drove slowly down the hill and around the building to the closed front door.

Jeff was out and moving toward it before the Bronco was fully stopped. He turned the knob slowly, letting the door swing wide before he stepped inside. He knew the men behind him had the rifles pointed at the building, just in case. He turned and motioned, and they came at a run. They stood looking around the almost bare room at the neatly folded blankets on the end of the bunk, the coffee cup turned upside down on the orange crate, and the oil lamp with the wick turned down. Jasper moved to the stove, lifting the eye to look inside and put his hand down into the ashes.

"She's been here, or someone has. The ashes aren't completely cold."

"Come on," Jeff said.

Outside again, they looked for tracks. Cecil, at the back of the shack, called. "She might have gone on down this trail. Look." He pointed to a mesquite bush that had been pushed to the side by pressure such as would come from a tire running over it. A little distance away, a small ridge of sand showed a definite tire print.

"Does that go anywhere in particular?" Jeff asked, looking to see if tracks were visible any farther from them.

"It goes into that north canyon that leads up the mountain toward the O'Toole property," Ed said. "We were in there about two weeks ago and picked up some of the strays we had been looking for. Not many. You can't go any farther that way. Turning around and going out the other side is the only way to cross over that ridge."

"Let's go," Jeff said, and they climbed into the Bronco. He pointed toward the canyon Ed had described and Jasper guided the vehicle along ridges and mounds until they came to the peak that separated Wagner's and the new Crooked M property.

Shadows were beginning to lengthen from the mountains when Jasper stopped. Ami's familiar Subaru Brat truck stood several hundred yards away from them on a slight ridge, and it took only seconds for them to pull up beside it, the men out and moving before the engine stopped.

Jeff's hand gripped the door handle of the truck and his knuckles whitened as he looked inside to see Ami crumpled on the seat with Remus on the floor, her left hand curled into the thick fur of the old dog.

The door on the opposite side opened, and Ed stared at the two still figures. 'Damn it all," he said quietly.

Jeff had opened the door he held and leaned forward to put his hand on Ami's throat. The pulse barely fluttered. He said, without turning, "Get Carue on the radio and have him contact Med-Evac out of Tucson. There isn't much time." He straightened. "Tell Carue to call Archie Denton, too, and alert all patrols state-wide."

The grimness of his voice penetrated the shock the men were feeling, and Cecil moved toward the Bronco, hoping he could raise Carue over the highest of the peaks between them and camp. Sometimes the atmosphere was too rare for them to make radio contact at this elevation.

Jasper had returned to the Bronco to pull a blanket from the back and handed it to Jeff, who spread it over Ami, letting some of it cover Remus. As he tucked the edges around her, his fingers touched the stiff shirt where blood had soaked through and dried. Carefully he unzipped her jacket and folded it back to see the dark stain beneath her left arm. He rezipped the jacket, putting her arm along the seat so that it would be covered. He touched Remus. The old dog was breathing—barely, but breathing. He couldn't see where he had been injured, but the hair on his foreleg and shoulder was matted with dark red.

After one brief glance at Ami's face, Jeff had concentrated on getting some warmth into her, but now his gaze returned to look at the dark cap of hair, full of sand. He pushed strands away from her cheek, turning her chin with his fingers. Gold-tipped dark lashes lay fanwise against the light tan of her face. The short upper lip was swollen and a reddish brown streak of blood went from the corner of her mouth over her chin.

He looked up as Cecil came back to the truck. "Carue'll get back to us as soon as he can."

Jeff nodded. "The helicopter probably won't be able to get in here after dark, Jeff," Jasper said. "We'd better try to take her back to camp."

"I told them to land in the clearing near the shack," Cecil said. "The wind's died down; they shouldn't have any problem there." He stood looking at Ami, long legs hanging partly off the seat. "How are you gonna get her out of there?"

"I won't move her. I can sit over on the side and drive the truck," Jeff said. He got in, careful to move her legs only a little, and sat on the edge of the seat.

"You follow me," he told Jasper, "in case I have trouble and have to stop."

They drove slowly back to the clearing, and Jeff looked down to see that Ami hadn't moved. Neither had Remus. Their stillness was frightening, but he turned away to step from the door of the little truck. Jasper came toward him, carrying a wide plank he had dragged from somewhere back of the cabin.

Carefully they lifted Ami from the seat of the truck onto the plank, each holding their breath as she moaned. Jeff held her so she wouldn't roll off, and they carried her inside, where Ed had relit the fire and oil lamps. Behind them, Cecil came, carrying Remus, placing him near the stove.

"Turn the lights on in the truck and the Bronco," Jeff told them. "The moon will be up enough to give them some light, but they'll need something to pinpoint the clearing."

Ed and Cecil left to figure out the angle they could aim the lights to be most effective. Jasper took one look at Jeff, sitting close to Ami, holding her hand, and turned to Remus. The old dog whimpered as Jasper straightened his bent front leg. He poured water into the small pan and put it on the stove to heat. As it simmered, he took a handkerchief from his pocket and bathed the shoulder that had been hit by the bullet.

"This is a clean wound," Jasper said. "I think he'll be all right." He was talking to hear a sound of something. He couldn't endure Ami's stillness nor Jeff's silence, wondering what was going through Jeff's mind as he sat watching Ami, unaware of anyone else in the room.

He would have been shocked at what was going through Jeff's mind. He was calmly killing the men who had done this to Ami. Jeff had never hated anyone; not even in Vietnam. Conditions, yes; people, no. Now he hated, clearly and coldly; he hated whoever was responsible. And blamed himself. He should never have left her, not even to go to Amanda. He should have taken her with him; should have made her go immediately into Tucson and marry him the first day it was possible. They could have had a big reception later at the ranch, at which everyone could have celebrated. His chance might not come again.

His hand, holding Ami's, tightened, and she moaned, turning her head restlessly. Jasper handed him a towel he found and wet it in the hot water. Jeff took it, wiping her mouth gently. The blood was dried too much to get off without force, and he stopped trying, letting the damp towel remain on her lips a moment at the time.

Jasper knelt beside them. "Her jacket is torn and full of dirt and trash." He brushed at the sleeve and turned to look at Remus. "That must be the way she got him to the truck, dragging him." Jeff stared at him with blank eyes and shook his head.

"It's hard to tell what happened," he said.

Ed came to the door. "The chopper's coming." He looked for a moment at the disquieting scene on the floor of the shack and added, "We built a fire on each side of the clearing. That should help the pilot see a little better."

Jeff nodded. "Good idea." As he spoke he heard the uneven beat of the chopper blades in the thin mountain air. "Get another blanket, Jasper, and let's make sure she stays warm."

Jasper had already moved to the bunk and was holding a blanket near the stove to warm it. He wrapped another one around Remus, who was trying to get up.

"Never mind, boy," Jasper said. "She's all right."

"If they have room, put him in there with her," Jeff said, looking up as two men entered with a stretcher between them. He stood, letting them take Ami without a word. Jasper lifted Remus and looked at the men.

"Got room for another passenger?"

The young man, looking to be in his early twenties, looked at the shaggy animal Jasper held. "I don't think we have any vets at the hospital," he said, "but we'll take him." Evidently someone had filled them in on the details of the reason for their trip, because he didn't sound surprised to find there would be an extra canine passenger.

The four men watched as the still figures were loaded into the helicopter, and as the aircraft lifted straight up from the ground, leaving a whirl of dust and sand, they turned to the fires they had started, methodically covering them to prevent any danger of spreading.

As they walked in silence to the Bronco, Jeff said, "Let's get back to the ranch and fly into Tucson."

They stopped to let Ed and Cecil off near their post, where they had picked them up many hours before. "We'll let you know whatever we find out," Jeff promised them. "I appreciate your help." He slumped against the door as Jasper headed for home.

"I don't understand, Jeff," Rio said, standing stiffly in front of him. Jasper had gone to pick him up as soon as they arrived at the hospital. The boy's eyes were dark, frightened pools as he waited for a logical explanation. That anyone would harm Ami was beyond his imagination.

Jeff tried to keep his voice even so Rio wouldn't sense the fear he felt for Ami. "We suspected some cattle had been taken and told Ami to stay away from the isolated camps, but she must have gone back there for something and ran into rustlers unexpectedly."

"But why would they shoot her?" Rio turned away and walked to the window, his shoulders hunched as if against the cold wind still whistling out of the mountains.

Jeff didn't answer. A white-coated figure came into the room, stripping a white mask from his mouth.

"I'm Dr. Barry," he said, cramming the mask in his pocket.

"Jeff Wagner, Dr. Barry. This is Rio Lawson. Miss Whitelake is his legal guardian."

The doctor grunted, but he wasted no time. "I operated to remove the bullet from her side and she's stable now. However"—here the bushy brows raised half an inch—"we have shock and pneumonia to contend with." He leaned against the wall, his eyes on Jeff. "We'll know more in about twenty-four hours. She'll be in intensive care until further notice." He straightened from the wall. "Does she have any family?"

Jeff shook his head, a cold knot choking him. He thought briefly of Tim as he faced Dr. Barry, voicing the hardest question he had ever asked. "What are her chances?"

The doctor's face was grim. "Loss of blood and shock could be fatal," he said. "She has youth and good health on her side."

Rio's swiftly indrawn breath drew Jeff's attention. The boy was deathly pale beneath the brown skin, his fists clenched at his sides.

The doctor went on. "As I said, we won't know much for a few hours. There's a coffee shop on the first floor." He started out. "Someone will call you in case of any change. Check with the nurses' station if you need anything."

Jeff glanced at the impersonal face of the standard hospital clock. It was ten thirty on Tuesday morning, and the doctor said it would be twenty-four hours before he could tell much about Ami's condition.

"Come on, Rio, let's get some coffee."

Rio's voice was muffled. "I'd rather stay here."

"They'll call us if there's any change. We need to move around."

Rio followed him, footsteps dragging. Jeff sympathized, his own heart heavy with dread of the next few hours.

It was four in the afternoon before Jeff put in a call for Steve. "Still no change. Dr. Barry was around a few minutes ago and, though he says her vital signs are stable, he's very noncommittal about her chances right now." He looked around at Rio, who leaned against the wall near the phone booth. "Rio's here, and I haven't been able to talk him into going home."

Worry edged Steve's voice. "I can't blame him, although I know he can't do any good there." He was quiet a moment. "I'd better call everybody. The guys are driving me and themselves crazy." Jeff smiled a little as he agreed and hung up.

Rio was asleep on the couch, and Jeff sat in one of the bigger chairs, his head against the back of it, when a nurse came in at six the next morning.

"Mr. Wagner, Dr. Barry is in with Miss Whitelake. She's conscious."

Rio sat up, looking from one to the other. The nurse went on. "One of you can go in for five minutes."

"You go, Jeff," Rio said.

Jeff didn't argue. He went down the long hallway and turned to the right, where the intensive care unit was. Ami's room faced the south and the blinds were open. His first thought was: She'd like the view. Her beloved mountains stood guard as far as the eye could see, the sun not yet putting in an appearance. He looked at the bed and his chest tightened. Tubes entered her body in countless places; blood dripped into one arm, clear liquid into the other. Tubes drained from her nose and mouth. The right eye was lacerated and swollen, and there were purple welts down her cheek to the cracked lips.

Jeff was glad Rio hadn't come in.

He wanted to touch her, but there didn't seem to be

anywhere to touch that wouldn't hurt. Her left hand lay palm up, and he laid his fingers across it.

"Ami?"

The purplish lid lifted, showing a hazy turquoise shadow. "Hello." It was just a whisper.

"Jeff?"

"Yes."

"I want to see Rio."

"Dr. Barry said no visitors, Ami."

"It's—it's important." The tip of her tongue touched the feverish lips. "Just one minute. I need to tell him." Her fingers closed over his hand. "Please, Jeff."

"Okay. I'll be right back."

Rio was at the window, shoulders slumped forward, staring at nothing. "Rio."

Startled, the boy straightened.

"She wants to see you."

When Rio didn't move, Jeff said impatiently, "She won't be awake long. Come on." He hesitated as the boy followed slowly. "Rio, listen. She looks bad, but she'll be all right." He pushed Rio into the room and backed away to wait outside.

I wish I could be sure she'll be all right, he thought.

A few minutes later he looked up as Rio came out of the room. Added to the shock in his face was something else. As soon as he spoke Jeff felt the anger in him. "She knows who it was."

"She knows them? How?"

Rio shook his head. "Not really. I mean, we had a run-in with them in Douglas on our way out here. Because of me."

Jeff waited, but he gave no more explanation. When Rio spoke again, he had changed subjects.

"She wants me to sketch pictures of the men and give them to you for the police."

"You mean a composite picture?"

"I can do it from memory."

"How long will it take you?"

Rio drew a deep breath. "A sketch in an hour. Probably a couple more to make it worthwhile to the police."

"By tonight?"

"Yes."

"Take a cab home and call me when you're finished."

"She went back to sleep. If she wakes up again—"

"If there's any change, I'll call you," Jeff promised.

The hours dragged on, and Ami rallied from time to time, but was never fully conscious. Every few hours Jeff was allowed in for five minutes to stand looking at her, frustration seething inside him. Her lips, cracked and dry, moved at times and once he thought she whispered his name. In memory he traced the full lower lip with his own, touching the curved upper lip, the tilted nose, and remembered the eyes with a sparkle of tears—laughing eyes as she romped with Amanda and Charlie. He looked at the slim outline under the sheets, feeling again the bare warmness of her against him, the questioning thrust of the tip of her tongue. She would hate the plain white hospital gown.

His eyes moved back to her face to find hers wide open and staring.

"Ami?" A half-smile tilted one corner of her tortured mouth, and he felt her fingers move in his hand, then they were still again and he was all alone.

Steve and Janie were in the waiting room when he went back. Steve spoke first "We couldn't wait. Jasper flew us up. How is she?"

Jeff shook his head. "Not much change. She opened her eyes, but she hasn't said anything since she talked to Rio about the pictures."

Janie's voice was teary. "What do the doctors say?"

"Nothing really. If she can weather the shock and not get pneumonia, she'll have a fighting chance. He said twenty-four hours, and it's been almost that."

A nurse interrupted them. "Mr. Wagner, you have a call at the nurses' station."

It was Rio. "I have the drawings ready."

"I'll be right there." Jeff was on the move as soon as he hung up the phone after calling a cab. He left Steve and Janie at the hospital and picked Rio up, heading straight for the police station. The investigators, already well informed in the case, examined the sketches with deep interest, comparing them to pictures of some well-known wanted criminals.

There were two pictures of obviously the same man. "That's the one Ami said had a scar when we saw them in Douglas but had grown a beard to cover it. I couldn't get it right till I drew him without the beard, then I just covered most of the scar, except about an inch she said showed on his cheek."

The man who spoke was Sergeant Scarsdale. "Remember the teletype we got from Montana about two months ago, Cal? Without that beard, it could be the same man."

"You're right. If so, it might be part of the gang operating out of Montana and North Dakota." Excitement showed as the two men looked more closely at the sketches and the book they were checking.

"These are good, Rio. We'll do our best."

They shook hands, and Jeff took Rio back to the hospital with him. Jasper had arrived, deep concern written on his face.

"Anything at all on how bad she is?" he asked.

Jeff shook his head. "Dr. Barry said twenty-four hours, and it's been that. So far as I can tell, she's the same. No worse but no better, either." He was so tired, he couldn't remember what day it was. He hadn't slept since Sunday night, and that had been restless.

It was late as they left for the motel, all but Jeff. Jasper said, "I'll stay, Jeff. You need sleep."

He wasn't interested. "I'll sleep here. If she wakes, I want to know. Take Rio home as you go."

Between catnaps, Jeff walked the floor until morning and was standing at the window, watching the sky lighten in the east, when Dr. Barry came in.

"Ami's awake. You can see her for ten minutes."

"How is she?" He held his breath.

"Out of danger, I'd say." Dr. Barry's voice was smiling.

Ami saw blurred white that moved from her vision, then returned. She blinked, and the white became a nurse with a smile on her face, looking down at her.

"Hello, Ami. Can you hear me?"

Ami's lips were stiff and sore, but she tried to move them in answer to the question. The nurse wet a cloth and gently pressed it to her mouth. The second time, Ami felt the water cooling her parched throat. The whiteness of the nurse disappeared and another masked face appeared in her place. She closed her eyes, not wanting to think.

"Now, now. You've had enough sleep. People are waiting to see you who have been here a long time." All the time he was talking, the hands of the masked figure were busy, probing. She drew in a sharp breath as the fingers touched her ribs on the left side, sending a hot shaft of pain down her leg.

"Ah," the figure said. "Ah."

When she opened her eyes again, the masked figure was gone and in his place was Jeff. Jeff with a three-day growth of beard and bloodshot eyes. She stared at him, trying to remember what it was that bothered her. Unable to think clearly, she asked, "Remus?"

Jeff grinned, his teeth showing white against the dark beard. "He's at the nurses' station down the hall, being looked after quite well. What about you?"

Ami nodded. "I was afraid. . ." Her voice trailed off.

"Don't try to talk, Ami. It'll wait," Jeff said, picking up her hand to rub gently across her fingers. "If it's any consolation, we were all scared to death."

"There's something else." She frowned at her inability to recall what it was she had to tell him.

"Rio did the sketches and the police seem to think they can identify the men, possibly wanted in connection with rustling up north."

She remembered. Everything that had happened slowly came into focus and, watching Jeff, she knew she could never tell him that Eileen was part of the deal. She withdrew her hand and slid it beneath the sheet, turning away from the surprised look on Jeff's face, closing her eyes so she wouldn't give away any of what she was thinking.

His lips brushed her temple and he said, "I know you're tired. Dr. Barry said to only stay a minute. Someone will be nearby if you need anything."

Ami didn't answer as she heard him leave the room and, minutes later, she slept. When she awoke, she lay still for a moment, then reached to her left side to the bandage there, pressing it a little and flinching when it hurt. Her mouth was sore and it hurt to touch it with her tongue. She wished for water but didn't have enough energy to reach the table by her bed, wondering instead how long it had been since Hank and Luke caught her and Remus in the canyon.

The sight of the truck had been such a shock she hadn't been able to run quickly enough to escape. She still couldn't figure out how they got the huge semi into and out of the canyon when she had never seen any place wide enough for a truck to pass. The shock was greater still as she listened to Hank and Luke discuss Eileen's part in the theft, although her plan had backfired when the rustlers double-crossed her. She had merely meant to cast suspicion on Ami and then have the cattle recovered, not counting on losing the cattle and becoming a part of attempted murder. How much of the plot would Eileen explain to Jeff?

Ami turned restlessly, flexing her legs, but she

couldn't roll over on her side because of the injured ribs. Her thoughts wandered on. Had Mandy gone to Newark? She hadn't asked Jeff and he hadn't volunteered. Anyway, there was no reason for her to worry about it anymore, in spite of Jeff's proposal. She bit into her lips and moaned as they stung, and she tasted blood where her teeth cut into the tenderness of her swollen mouth. The least she could do was put his mind at ease and let him know she realized why he thought the proposal was a good idea at the time.

A smiling nurse came through the door. "Dr. Barry says you need this." She slipped a needle beneath the skin of her right arm, and Ami felt a slight sting. "You'll feel better after you sleep some more."

Ami didn't protest, too tired to argue and unwilling to try to figure out the puzzle that faced her. Reality faded, and she slipped into sleep.

Jeff called Steve. "Ami's awake and talking a little, although she doesn't remember too much that went on back there. Dr. Barry says she'll make it, barring any unforeseen complications." He breathed deeply. "Tell Jasper to come for me." He called Rio to relay the good news and told him, "She can have regular visitors starting tomorrow morning. I'm going home, but Steve and Janie will be here, and I'll be back by tomorrow afternoon."

Rio was silent for a long time before he said, "Thanks for calling me, Jeff." Jeff hung up the phone and stared at it a moment. The special bond between the young man and the woman who had befriended him was clearly evident. The loner and the orphan who had made it in spite of the odds. He thought of the old dog and wondered what had gone on to enable both of them to reach the truck, possibly saving their lives by keeping them a little warmer until they were found. How far away had they been? Why had they been left to die? If not to die, surely whoever had done the shooting wouldn't have left them alive to testify.

Ami had been too weak for him to question, but he could guess that the rustlers thought she would be left overnight and would not survive the freezing temperatures in the mountains; that, combined with the loss of blood. They were right, not counting on her rescue. He shied away from thinking they had been lucky to find them.

Jeff talked to Dr. Barry before he left the hospital. "Steve Hilton and his wife will be in this afternoon. Whatever has to be done, let them know." He managed a grin. "I'll take Remus off your hands if you think he's able to travel."

Dr. Barry laughed. "First time I've ever treated a dog, but he probably considers himself human, anyway. Yes, he's able to travel, but I daresay the nurses will miss having him around."

Jeff took a cab to the airport to wait for Jasper, holding the old dog's head on his knees all the way, lifting him carefully as he got out. He put him down beside him, and Remus promptly sat, favoring the front paw where he had been hit. They waited only a few minutes for Jasper.

"I should see Amanda while I'm here, but I'd probably frighten her to death the way I look," Jeff told Jasper. He hesitated. "I'm not sure I should tell her about Ami, but I promised her I'd be back Saturday and bring Ami with me."

"Maybe by Saturday you can take her in to see Ami," Jasper said.

Jeff looked doubtful. "If she still has a fever, Dr. Barry won't even let us in, much less a child."

Jasper nodded, concentrating on the plane. Twenty minutes later he banked for a landing on Wagner's airstrip.

Chapter Twelve

It's Friday, Ami thought, and wondered how she had arrived at that conclusion when she hardly remembered when the nightmare had started nor the length of time it lasted. All the events came back to her as she lay awake, waiting for her breakfast. At least she was out of the intensive care unit and in a normal room. A very young nurse had come to help her get to the bathroom to wash her face and brush her hair. It was filled with sand, and she was anxious to shampoo it but found she was too weak to stand alone in the shower.

"You lost a lot of blood," the nurse told her. "It will take you a few days to get your strength back."

We were lucky, Remus, she mused. *Maybe you're a cat and have nine lives and loaned me one.* Dr. Barry told her Jeff had taken Remus home with him, but the old dog was going to be fine. *We're even,* she thought, and smiled. *I saved you once, and you returned the favor.*

She tried not to think of Jeff, but he was there without any bidding. *I hope he doesn't come to see me anymore. How can I tell him Eileen was the mastermind behind the plan? I can't,* she decided, *I can't.* He would have to find out from someone other than her and decided with certainty that she couldn't marry him even if he made the offer again. It was purely self-preservation, trying to avoid a scandal, trying to avoid

Ami's prosecution by his friend, thereby preventing an unpleasant trial.

He went pretty far at that, she thought. Not many men would be so generous as to lend their good name to a suspected crook.

She looked up as her breakfast tray was placed on the table arm and moved within her reach. She wasn't hungry and, after a moment, pushed the tray away and slid down into the bed, turning carefully on her right side. The tears ran silently down her cheeks as she recalled Jeff's proposal and the happiness she held for a few minutes, thinking she would be married to the man she loved. He hadn't really lied at any time; at no time had he mentioned love. He wanted her to go to Newark for Mandy's sake; he wanted to marry her for her own protection. *Men are a puzzle,* she thought, and went to sleep.

In her dream she ran. She couldn't see who was chasing her, but she was fast losing her breath, knowing that if she stumbled, she would be caught. The path she was on ended against the side of the mountain and she turned, pressing her back into the rock, facing her pursuer. Eileen stood in front of her, laughing, blond head lifted, black Stetson swinging down her back.

"You think you have Jeff hooked, don't you?" Eileen mocked. She flicked Ami with a slim whip she carried, "But the cattle are on Wagner property, and only you could have put them all there. Only you knew about the crevice between the peaks that came after the earthquake several years ago." Her laughter echoed through the canyon. "Jeff will never marry you... never marry you... never marry you."

She awoke, trembling and wet with perspiration. Her side ached from the exertion of running. She breathed hard. *I wasn't running,* she told herself, *I was dreaming.*

Her trembling had quieted when Jeff appeared in the doorway, but her face was still damp with perspiration or tears, or both. He stood looking down at her without speaking, seeing the exhaustion in her face and the tenseness in her body.

"What's wrong?" Jeff asked, picking up her hand.

"Nothing." Her voice was totally unconvincing.

"Why are you crying?"

"I must have turned and hurt my side," she said.

He held her gaze a moment before he looked at the still-full breakfast tray. "You need to eat."

She tried to pull her hand away, but he held on. "If there's something wrong, Ami, I want to know about it. Are you thinking about what happened and worried whether the men will be caught?"

Ami didn't answer and her eyes slid away from his face. One finger beneath her chin turned her face so she'd have to look at him. "If you don't want to talk about it yet, I can understand, but the sooner you tell us all you know, the more likely it is we'll catch them. The sketches Rio drew for the police have helped a lot." He sat on the edge of the bed. "He told me you had a run-in with the rustlers sometime ago, but you never mentioned it to us."

"I didn't know they were rustlers," she said.

"What happened?"

She smoothed the white spread with her free hand. "Nothing much. They were sort of picking on Rio because they thought he was alone."

"When was that?"

"As we came through Douglas on our way out here."

"Why didn't you say anything about it?"

"I never thought about it anymore," she said truthfully.

"Do you have any idea why they happened to be in this area and picked Wagner's and Crooked M cattle to rustle?"

She stiffened. "You still think I directed them here?"

He shook his head. "I thought you might have heard them talking."

"I wasn't close to them for long," she hedged. "I was up on that last ridge before the blind canyon when they came from behind it in a big semi. I didn't even know a truck could get in there." As she spoke Ami remembered her dream and asked, "Has there ever been an earthquake through those mountains? I mean, one that was recorded?"

"As a matter of fact, a couple of years ago, one registered four point five on the Richter scale, but aside from rumblings and shakings, it didn't do any damage." He watched her. "What made you think of that?"

She shrugged. "There may be a split in the mountains where we thought there was no passageway. An earthquake could cause something like that."

Jeff continued to watch her. "I'll get some of Carue's men to check it out."

She looked up, suddenly aware of what she had said, repeating a dream, and he took her seriously. Opening her mouth to tell him it wasn't necessary, she subsided. Let him find out for himself that Eileen was involved; she couldn't be the one to tell him.

He noticed the strain beginning to show in her face and his expression changed to gentle concern. "I'll be here a while, Ami, but you'd better rest. Dr. Barry isn't going to be happy that you aren't eating."

"Don't tattle on me," she said.

Jeff raised his eyebrows. "I'll bet he gets a report from whoever picks up this tray within five minutes of its being returned to the kitchen."

He looked back at her from the door. "I'm going over to see Amanda and have lunch with her. She doesn't know you've been hurt, and I have to figure out a way to tell her so she'll agree to go with me to Newark Monday. We changed the appointment until then." She continued to look at him without answering until he smiled and left the room.

Her eyes were still on the doorway when Dr. Barry appeared. He frowned, looking down at her as he picked up her wrist. "All right, young lady, what's wrong with the food here? We have an excellent dietician who is upset because you didn't touch your breakfast." Jeff was right; someone had reported her for not finishing the meal.

Ami was tired and couldn't think of a witty reply, so she promised, "I'll eat a big lunch."

He stuck a thermometer in her mouth, still frowning. He might be angry with her, but his hands were gentle as he took the bandage loose from her ribs to examine the area where the bullet had been removed. When he finished putting on a fresh bandage, he took the thermometer and read it before shaking it and putting it on the table.

"Are you in pain?" Dr. Barry asked.

She shook her head. "When can I go home?"

"You just got here, Ami. What's your hurry?"

"I'm taking up space needed by sick people."

He smiled. "We've lots of room." He patted her hand. "As soon as you get rid of that fever, we'll talk about your going home."

Home. Her mind searched for an answer. Perhaps she could pay room and board at Jim's ranch until she was able to start her new job. She dozed fitfully, waking to doze again, and was staring at the ceiling, her main occupation lately, when Jasper came in.

"Hello, love," he said, smiling down at her. He was holding a basket of yellow roses.

She smiled back at him. "Jasper, where did you get roses like that at this time of year?"

"Picked them myself from the master's flower garden," he told her. His smile disappeared. "Jeff said you were still running a fever."

"Where did you see Jeff?" she asked, remembering that he had gone to see Mandy.

"He called home to see if I was on my way here."

She frowned. "Did you fly up?"

"Yes." He hesitated. "We got a call from the sheriff out of Kane County in Utah. They've picked up a couple of men answering the rustlers' descriptions, and we're going up this afternoon to check it out."

"Oh."

He picked up her hand. "If we can make any kind of identification, Ami, sooner or later you'll have to identify them, too."

She nodded, wondering if the crooks were loyal or if they would turn around and implicate Ron and Eileen. Jasper didn't care for Eileen; maybe she could confide in him. But he was Jeff's friend and would feel obligated to report what she told him. She pressed her lips together. If Eileen went free because she kept her mouth shut, that's the way it would have to be. She couldn't tell Jeff. Eileen had done her part to rescue a good friend, and the man she planned to marry, from the clutches of a nameless renegade. She could get out of Jeff's way so he'd need to feel no further responsibility for her.

"Do me a favor, Jasper?" she asked.

"Anything, Ami."

"Get me a phone put in here."

He squeezed her hand. "That's easy. Maybe if you call Janie, she'll stop crying and threatening to murder all of us. She's been some upset by the whole deal. Lily, too. They'll be in to see you tomorrow."

Jasper left, promising to see about the phone, and she slept. Rio was standing by her bed when she woke. Ami smiled up into worried dark eyes. "I'm okay. Honest. Dr. Barry says all I need is a little time to recuperate."

"You're looking better, at least," he said.

Ami told him what Jasper said about the rustlers. "I understand you did a fantastic job on the sketches."

Rio grinned. "It was easy once I started." The grin faded. "Ami, all I could remember about them was how cold and mean-looking they were and the thought of them shooting you for no reason." He stopped.

She touched his hand. "It's an odd coincidence that probably would never happen again in a million years. As long as we survived, we might as well try to forget it."

But she knew she never would. When Rio left, she went back to thinking. How could Eileen even pretend to love Jeff and do what she did? Love takes strange twists and curves. Tim had loved her until he found she couldn't have the children he wanted. Jeff didn't love her but would marry her to keep her out of jail. And Ami—Ami had loved unwisely, not once, but twice. Human beings had to be the weirdest creatures of all time.

Carue, Ed, and Cecil came to see her Saturday. The Howards and Trentons she knew from the grange dances came. Her room filled to overflowing with flowers, and by early afternoon she was exhausted. She looked at the telephone someone had plugged in during all the other activities. She still hesitated about calling Jim and was putting it off again when he appeared in the doorway of her room.

She smiled as he took her hand. "Must be mental telepathy."

"You were thinking about me?" Jim asked, grinning.

"As a matter of fact, I was just getting ready to call you," she said.

"Then I'll save you some money," he told her.

She took a deep breath. "Jim, can I go to your ranch from the hospital? I have no idea how long it will be before I can ride, but I don't want to go back to Wagner's. I'm willing to pay room and board.''

He met her eyes and waited, but she couldn't say any more. "You know you're welcome, Ami. You're already on the payroll, so forget paying anything.''

She had half-decided to tell Jim about Eileen, but changed her mind, deciding that it would be her secret and telling him about it would solve nothing. Let Eileen's conscience decide for her. "It may be awhile before I can earn a salary.''

"Nonsense," he said. "Does Wagner know you don't plan to return there?''

Ami shook her head. "He and Jasper went to Utah to see some men they picked up on suspicion.''

"How does Jeff feel now about your part in all this?''

"He hasn't said.''

"And Eileen?''

She grimaced. "Well, she hasn't visited me, so I assume she hasn't forgiven me for whatever I've done.'' Her laugh was rueful.

Jim laughed out loud. "You're too pretty to be forgiven, Ami.'' He sobered. "When will you be getting out of here?''

"I don't know. Dr. Barry said he'd talk to me about leaving when all my fever is gone.'' She sighed. "Of course, I haven't seen him since early this morning. He could be avoiding me.''

Jim took his leave, promising to be back on Sunday. "Your house is ready whenever you can get there, Ami. We'll take good care of you until you can make it on your own.''

As tired as she was, Ami got out of bed and walked around the room, her legs shaky from nonuse. She walked for three minutes, back and forth, then sat down to catch her breath, repeating the process a couple of times. She started down the hall, moving like someone just learning to walk, when the elevator door slid back and Jeff walked toward her.

"Quite an improvement," he said, smiling down at her. "How are you?"

"Fine." She turned back to her room, and Jeff put his arm around her waist. She tried not to show any reaction to his nearness, but she trembled inside. "I thought you were in Utah."

He held her arm as she climbed on the bed. "We just got back. Jasper dropped me off." He kissed her cheek, his warm breath caressing her skin.

Her eyes questioned him as he took pictures from an envelope he carried and handed them to her. "Do any of these men look familiar?"

Her gaze still rested on his face, taking in the shadows under his eyes, tight lines around his mouth, wondering why all the worry even now. She looked down at the pictures she held, five men in the group, and studied if for a few seconds, finally pointing to one on the left and another in the middle.

"That's Hank and that's Luke," she said.

"Can you be positive?"

"Yes," she said firmly. "I'd know them anywhere and, if they were close enough, I could recognize their smell." She wrinkled her nose.

He took the pictures back. "They're the ones that were caught, Ami. However, they're also wanted in Montana and Wyoming on the same charges, and we may not see them for a while."

"What about the cattle?"

"Some of them were recovered. They told us the others are still on Eileen's property, unless they were moved by someone else."

"What do you mean?"

"That's what Hank said."

Ami frowned. "Who else would take them?"

"Eileen?" The question was soft, and her eyes widened as she looked at him. Anger and something else she couldn't determine darkened the gray of his eyes.

"Eileen?" She repeated the name as though it were unfamiliar to her.

"Did you know she was involved in taking the cattle?" Jeff asked quietly.

She sat silently watching him, wondering how much he knew. "I heard them say Eileen and Ron arranged for the cattle to be taken, but they weren't supposed to keep them, just move them to where I'd be suspected. She was double-crossed, I guess."

Jeff nodded and his voice hardened. "You could have been killed." When she said nothing, he asked, "Weren't you going to mention Eileen's part in this?"

"I wasn't sure you'd believe me," she said.

"You still think I asked you to marry me because I didn't want Eileen to bring charges against you?"

"Didn't you?"

"Ami—"

"I'm going to the J and R Ranch when I leave the hospital, Jeff. I won't be going back to Wagner's, so you don't have to make excuses for either of us." Jeff tried to interrupt, but she went on. "I never meant to come between you and Eileen; never meant to get so involved with Mandy that it would hurt her—or you." She withdrew her hands from his. "When I'm gone, you and Eileen can work it out, and you won't have to worry about my feelings."

After a long pause while he looked straight into her eyes, Jeff said, "You're right. It will be easier when you're gone."

Ami managed to control the gasp as the pain of his words ricocheted through her, and her chin went up as she met his gaze. It was what she asked for and he had given it to her without softening the blow.

He stood up. "If you want to press charges against Hank and Luke for attempted murder or against Eileen as an accomplice, Jasper can help you file the papers. Hank and Luke will probably waive extradition, and you'll have to go to Montana or Wyoming, whichever state has priority."

She nodded, waiting for him to go, but instead of leaving, he stepped closer to the bed and leaned over her, his arms going around her. He pushed her head back with his chin and lowered his mouth to hers. It was a hard, ruthless kiss, unlike any she could remember, and she struggled. In spite of herself her heart lifted to meet the urgency in his kiss, and she stopped struggling to hold on, letting him plunder with his tongue, answering his demand with fingers digging into his powerful arms.

His release was so sudden, she swayed sharply. One hand covered her mouth; the other pressed against her side as she watched him through a blur of pain.

"I'll be taking Amanda to Newark Monday, so I won't see you before you leave the hospital." His glance went from the dark cap of hair to the shapeless hospital robe that didn't quite reach her bare feet, and his eyes were the color of steel that had been frozen, just as expressionless. "Take care, Ami."

The silence in the room Jeff left was so complete, Ami realized she was holding her breath. Slowly she exhaled. She had accomplished what she wanted: convinced him she was not for him, that Eileen was his kind of people. The rich, the idle, the chosen. It hadn't taken much to convince him. Her eyes were so wide open, they hurt, and when she blinked, she found, to her surprise, there were no tears. There would be plenty of time later for tears for what she gave up today, she knew, and slid off the bed to walk around the room, pausing at the window to watch a cold-looking sun settle behind a distant ridge of mountains. She stared unseeingly until it grew dark outside and a million lights came on over the city.

Turning away, she climbed back into bed without turning on a light. It was Saturday night, she remembered. Everyone was probably at the grange dance. Two weeks ago she, too, was at a dance; just two weeks tomorrow since Jeff's proposal. Lying there in the dark, she could easily believe the past week had never happened. Hard to accept that, somehow, she and Remus had shared a near-miss with death; that Eileen was almost totally to blame; that, even so, Jeff had forgiven her and would eventually marry her as he had planned BA—before Ami.

There was a hesitant knock at the door. "Ami?" Janie called in a loud whisper.

"Oh, yes, I'm awake." She sat up and turned on the bed lamp. Janie and Lily stood just inside the door, Steve behind them.

Janie reached her first, holding her hands out. "Where can I hug you?"

"Anywhere but these ribs," Ami told her, indicating her left side. They hugged, then she was engulfed in Lily's arms, folded against the ample bosom like a child.

She whispered, "I'll bet you didn't bring me any coffee, Lily. They make the world's worst here."

"Bless your heart, child, I'll make sure you get some good coffee." She dabbed at her eyes.

"No coffee, but plenty of food," Steve said, holding up a carton. He put it on her table and bent to kiss her cheek.

"I was beginning to feel sorry for myself," Ami said. "I thought everyone was at the dance and had forgotten about me."

"Not likely," Janie said. "When will you be coming home?"

Steve met her questioning glance with a raised eyebrow. "Dr. Barry said I could leave two days after I stopped running a fever." At Steve's look, she wondered if he had been told she wasn't returning to Wagner's. Jeff kept his people informed, and she was almost sure Steve was aware of her decision.

Ami changed the subject. "How's Remus?"

Lily clucked. "Eating me out of the kitchen," she said. "I believe they left a hole in his stomach and he never gets full."

Janie showed her impatience to get in a question. "Are you going to sue Eileen for defamation of character?" Ami stared at her, stunned at the thought. "You have plenty of right, you know."

Ami looked at Lily, then at Steve, who said quietly. "She's right, Ami. That, plus being an accomplice to attempted murder."

She could get even, all right, Ami thought. But if she filed suit against Eileen, Jeff would be affected. Through Jeff, Mandy would be hurt and, eventually, all of Wagner's.

She shook her head. "No, I have no plans for that."

"But Ami—" Janie began, and Ami put her fingers on her lips.

"No, Janie. The answer is no," she said, her voice leaving no doubt she meant what she said.

Janie hesitated, glancing at Steve. "I guess I shouldn't wish hard luck on anyone, but I can't help it where she's concerned."

Ami smiled, understanding her friend. Steve patted his wife on her shoulder. "The corn fritters are still hot, Ami," he said.

"I'll have two," she said. Lily handed them to her with a napkin, and Ami sighed as she bit into the tasty bread. "You should give their dietician some cooking lessons, Lily."

As she ate, Janie talked about Mandy and the trip to Newark without daring to voice their hopes for her. "She wanted to wait for you, but Dave didn't want to put it off that long, so Jeff finally promised her you'd be home when they got back, and she stopped fussing.''

Ami withheld her comments and, when they had gone, lay back against her pillow, her mind on Janie's remark about Jeff's promise to Mandy that he would be forced to break.

She smiled grimly to herself. "I can't blame you for playing both ends against the middle, Jeff," she said aloud. "But I'll be glad when I'm no longer in the middle."

Chapter Thirteen

Jeff stood outside the closed door of Ami's room, clenched fists rammed into his pockets. He still tasted her kiss, smelled the light cologne he liked without knowing what it was. He could feel the print of her fingers digging into his arms and saw her hand pressed against her mouth, the expression in her eyes, and wondered if he had hurt her. At the moment he didn't care, but now he remembered her hand on her side. He had forgotten the bullet wound, had forgotten everything as he took the kiss he wanted from her. He half turned, one hand out of his pocket, reaching for the door, but stopped, staring at the thick panel separating them, and moved away. He had wanted Ami with him when he took Amanda to Newark, wanted her to go as his wife, so he would have the right to make love to her the way it should be. He had the license, and Jasper could have performed the ceremony, except for the fact that Ami wanted Rio and Amanda there. Circumstances had a way of playing havoc with what he wanted lately. Without warning, he remembered Ami's nude body blending itself with his, and he lost himself for a moment to the feeling of his own body's response as he made love to her.

He let his breath out and turned away, leaving the hospital to drive to the motel, stopping by the bar for one drink before he went on to bed. Amanda would be ready to leave by ten the next morning, and they'd be home in time for a good lunch.

Stretched out on the bed, Jeff was conscious of his tiredness. Even so, he couldn't sleep. He had promised Amanda that Ami would be at Wagner's when they returned from Newark, but Ami had other ideas. The worst idea she had was that he wanted to marry her out of pity. If he could only convince her how much he loved her. His thoughts went on to Eileen. He couldn't believe what Hank and Luke implied about her involvement in the rustling of both Wagner and Crooked M cattle, but the expression on Ami's face surprised him when he mentioned that Eileen could be involved. He knew instantly that she was aware of that possibility and that, even though she believed it, she wasn't going to accuse Eileen. That hadn't bothered Eileen, who had shown no compassion when it came to showing Ami up as a rank amateur, when it came to taking what Eileen considered to be only hers. He would never have believed she would be capable of cold-bloodedly planning to accuse Ami of rustling, of planting evidence to convict her.

It was two years after Myra's death when he and Eileen sort of drifted together. He had been to a few social gatherings, always with a group, usually Janie, Steve, and Jasper. Gradually he noticed Eileen showed up a lot, always unescorted, until it became just a twosome. The outings at the grange dances became fewer, and he was either alone with Eileen or flying to some party among all her friends. They had been ready to announce their engagement even though he didn't really remember asking her to marry him, but it didn't bother him much. His one concern was Eileen's indifference to Amanda, but he thought they would be closer after their marriage.

The turning point was Ami's arrival at Wagner's. Jeff had his reservations about her when he went to El

Paso with Steve for her interview, but when Steve wanted to hire her, he had agreed.

There were many things he noticed about Ami, some of them odd to his way of thinking, at least, for a woman. She was a loner; she didn't need people around her all the time; the Mexican-American teenager who was her legal responsibility— Now, how many young women would ask for that job? And that old dog of hers would never win any prizes, except maybe for being the clumsiest-looking critter around as he loped across the desert with her.

Sometime during that period, Jeff became reluctant to think about marriage to Eileen. He thought less and less about it as he watched Ami romping with Amanda and knew she had no trouble with sign language. It wasn't until Amanda asked for Ami to go to Newark with her that he realized how close the two of them had become. He closed his eyes, seeing Ami again as he made love to her for the first time, their experimental kisses turning to a passionate sharing so strong that the memory from months ago still aroused him.

He didn't recall exactly when he admitted to himself that he loved Ami. Perhaps at the Valentine Dance, when she teased him about being pregnant, and he smiled a little as he remembered her watery eyes and pink nose, the result of a cold, and a husky voice that kept her from singing with Steve and Janie. He loved to hear her sing, but he wanted her with him on that night, wanted her to say she was going to have his baby so he would have a logical reason to ask her to marry him. Whenever the realization finally got through to him, he had told Eileen the next Saturday night before asking Ami to marry him.

He had never known Eileen could speak in such harsh tones as she used that night. "Marry her?" She stared at him in disbelief. "What about us, Jeff?" She was speechless for a moment.

He said as gently as possible, "That's why we haven't been in any hurry to marry, Eileen. We've been friends for so long, we just drifted together. It isn't that I don't love you—"

"What is it, then? You can't mean you love that—that—" She sputtered. "That nobody. A veterinarian. Why, she's—" Her eyes narrowed. "You let her put-on with sweet-talking Amanda get to you, that's what. Can't you see that's all it is? Just making up to Amanda to get to you."

"Eileen." Jeff put his hands on her shoulders. "Admit it. We've been friends all our lives and were paired together from force of habit until we thought we should get married."

Eileen wasn't to be pacified, and he heard a lot about Ami that he'd rather forget, including the rustling hints he didn't take seriously. He knew he was right, however, when he asked Ami to marry him the next day. Her complete surprise, her hesitation for only a moment, followed by her confession that she loved him, had captivated him again and he couldn't wait to claim her as his wife. He was still waiting, all because of his own ignorance. He should have yanked her up and dragged her to Jasper for a civil ceremony with a bang-up reception for the Wagner crew afterward; should never have mentioned Eileen's accusations until she was safely his; should have taken her and Amanda and gone to Newark right then.

Restless, Jeff got out of bed and walked to the window, pushing aside the draperies to look out. Even with all the lights, the mountains stood in dark silhouette against the starlit sky. Southwesterners took their spectacular scenery for granted, but not Ami. He had seen her stand absolutely still for long minutes, staring at the endless desert bordered by ragged mountain peaks, a smile of satisfaction on her face. He recalled her description of the few storms they had as wild and beautiful compared to sad ones in the east. That thought brought to mind again the first time he made love to her, an armful of long legs and slim body curved to the shape of his; of firm, warm lips yielding to his demands. Desire for her was alive inside him, and he swore at himself for the way he had mishandled all his chances.

Because of him she was almost killed, he thought. Suddenly he made up his mind. Amanda had to go to Newark, but when they came back, things would change in his favor. His mouth set in a determined line. Eileen had several things to clarify for him, and he would take it from there.

The sun was still below the horizon Monday morning as Jeff guided the quiet-running Mercedes around the big house, heading southwest toward the Crooked M ranch. His eyes followed the familiar landscape—the landing strip on his right with the small building at the end. Jasper's truck was parked in its usual place, and he recalled Jasper's comment when the doctor said Ami would recover barring any unforeseen complications.

"I can perform that ceremony before she gets enough strength back to resist," he said and grinned. "All's fair, you know."

Jeff had been tempted. Looking down into Ami's scratched face, deathly pale except for the streaks, he almost said yes, wondering if she'd forgive him later. He'd wished a thousand times he'd given in to temptation and taken his chances on her forgiveness after she belonged to him.

He left the road on his property, turning right through a rock gate with the huge Crooked M logo on the top of it, still three miles from the main house. The sun was throwing a gold rim over the tallest mountain peak when he pulled up beside the green Porsche. He shook his head. The high winds this time of year would soon strip the paint off the valuable sports car, but Eileen couldn't be bothered with taking extra time to drive into the garage. Especially if she was mad, and by the looks of the skid marks, she was plenty angry when she drove in.

The doorknob turned easily under his hand, and he pushed the door inward to walk through the short entrance hall into the kitchen. He stopped short in surprise.

Eileen sat at the small table, and Ron Steward, her foreman, leaned against the refrigerator, a beer in his hand. Jeff had never known Eileen to get out of bed before sunup and had gone to the kitchen as he usually did, planning to make coffee before he woke her. She was downright unfriendly before her first cup of coffee.

When Jeff walked in, Eileen gasped, and the color rushed to her face as she threw a confused look at Ron. "Why, Jeff," she said, sounding breathless. She covered her confusion with concern. "I thought you were taking Amanda to Newark today. Is anything wrong?"

He glanced at Ron, who had straightened away from the refrigerator. "I need to talk to you, Eileen. Alone."

Ron finished the beer and put the bottle on the table. "I'll take care of that for you, Eileen," he said, nodding at Jeff as he went out.

"Problems?" Jeff asked.

Eileen laughed a little. "Not really. A couple of the boys got rowdy at the dance Saturday night, and Archie Denton locked them up. No problem." She stood up and moved toward him, hands outstretched. Jeff took them, holding her away from him. Rowdy cowboys on Saturday night weren't unusual, and he wondered why he didn't believe her statement.

He looked down at her pouting mouth, knowing expected him to kiss her, but he didn't. Instead, h her back to the chair and pushed her into it and sat on the edge of the table.

"The doctor says Ami will be all right," he said.

Eileen's eyes widened. "But, of course she will, Jeff. That was strictly for show anyway."

He stiffened. "What do you mean?"

She shrugged, watching to see what effect her next words would have on him. "Her partners had to make it look good so she wouldn't be blamed and whoever found her would be so busy looking after her, they wouldn't think of her rustler friends for a while." She smiled. "Rather a rough way, but effective."

He studied the confident smile, anger stirring inside him. "Where does your information come from?"

"It's common knowledge."

"I didn't know it," he told her. "Did Ron come to report on what happened?"

She looked quickly at him, then away. "I told you why Ron was here."

"And I don't believe you."

Eileen got up and leaned toward him. She was wearing a tan riding outfit that outlined her curves, a honey-beige sweater that almost matched her hair. She smelled expensive, and he thought of Ami's hair, which smelled of sunshine and the light fragrance she used.

"Jeff," Eileen said, and when he didn't move, she asked, "are you still planning to marry her after all this?" Her voice was brittle.

"All this, meaning what?"

"She hasn't explained how our herds mixed nor how they came through that canyon. It's always been blocked."

His eyes narrowed as he recalled Ami's off-the-wall question. "Do you remember the earthquake a couple of years ago?"

She looked startled. "Of course. Why?"

He decided to tell his own story. "Jasper and I went

to Utah, where they had picked up a couple of suspicious characters. Turns out they were driving the big semi Ami described with cattle from Wagner's and the Crooked M still inside.'' He watched closely, but her expression didn't change. ''One of them volunteered that there was an opening at the end of the blind canyon where the cattle were found and that's how they passed through. Probably no one has really checked all the way to the O'Toole property since that earthquake.''

''Ami must have, because she knew how to get them through there.''

''Not exactly,' he said. ''I believe Ron told you about it, and at the time, it seemed a good way to throw suspicion on Ami.'' He waited, but she didn't answer, her mouth set in a stubborn line, angry dark eyes staring at him, admitting nothing. He stood up. ''I'll forgive you for the shady deal, Eileen, but if Ami had been killed—'' He let the sentence drop and was rewarded when her eyes widened as she saw the danger she had put Ami in.

''I didn't mean—'' she began and stopped, realizing she had admitted too much. Her chin went up. ''She's not good enough for you, Jeff. I didn't want you to ruin your life tied to a nobody. She's part Indian and doesn't even know her real name.''

''Then I'll give her mine if she'll have it,'' he said quietly, moving to the door before he turned to look at her again. ''As soon as we can get to it, we'll separate the cattle and return yours.''

She laughed. ''How do you propose to tell how many are mine when the clips are gone and no brands on them? Another one of Ami's smart moves.''

''We'll manage,'' he said. ''Good-bye, Eileen.'' He closed the door behind him and ran down the steps to the Mercedes, sparing only a glance toward the corral, where he saw Ron watching him. Pulling from the well-kept yard, Jeff turned into the rising sun, knowing he had plenty of time to get to the ranch and carry out the rest of his plan before he had to get Amanda ready for their trip to Newark.

Resolutely he turned his thoughts from Eileen's betrayal. He would deal with his disappointment in her later. Right now he had some phone calls to make. At the house, he moved quickly, going by Amanda's room to see if she was still asleep. He smiled at the small figure, snuggled under the covers, only the blond hair, unbraided, visible spread over the pillow. She could sleep a little longer; their plane didn't leave Tucson till one o'clock.

The phone number of the hospital was written on a card lying near the phone. It had been used many times in the past week, and he dialed the familiar number again.

"Is Dr. Barry available?" he asked when the ring was answered. "This is Jeff Wagner."

"One moment, please."

There was a long buzz, and he heard Dr. Barry's gruff voice. Identifying himself, he asked, "Do you know how much longer you'll keep Ami?"

Dr. Barry cleared his throat. "I don't want to release her prematurely, Jeff. She's much better, but infection is still highly probable."

Jeff breathed deeply. "I understand. What I want is to ask you to keep her there till I get back from Newark. That could be as early as Wednesday or as late as Saturday."

"That can be arranged."

"Without her knowing I called?" Jeff asked.

Dr. Barry laughed. "It'll be our secret," he said and added, "I take it that I'm not to know your reasoning, besides Ami's well-being, of course."

Jeff laughed, too. "That's right, and thanks."

He called Jasper, then Steve, telling them breakfast

would be ready in thirty minutes and he wanted them to join him in the big kitchen. He stopped by to tell Lily she had five people coming for breakfast and went on to call a sleepy Amanda. He left her in Hazel's care and went to make one more phone call, this time to Jim Summers in Apache Junction.

Chapter Fourteen

Sunday passed quickly between visitors and two check-ups from Dr. Barry. "I know, I know, Ami," he said when she protested against his indefinite answer on when she could leave the hospital. "Wouldn't you rather leave permanently when you go, rather than have to come back?"

She subsided a little. "Yes, of course, but I feel good." It wasn't really true. She sneezed several times, causing a pain in her side, but she would never admit she felt more like sleeping than talking to anyone. She even dozed while Rio was with her and awakened to find him watching her with concerned dark eyes.

"Are you sure you're okay?" Rio asked.

She smiled apologetically. "Too much company maybe."

He left soon afterward, and she continued to lie there, feeling lazy. Her thoughts went to Mandy, who would be going to Newark alone with Jeff the next day. Linda had called, worried about Ami, and she had assured her she was doing great and looking forward to hearing good news about Mandy.

"I think you can be sure of it," Linda told her. "All we need to do is see that the grafts are taking from the inside out, and since she's had no pain, we feel confident everything is as it should be. However, it doesn't hurt to keep a watch for several months."

Ami wondered if Jeff had asked Eileen to go with them, almost knowing he wouldn't. Eileen didn't like to be around sick people. Mandy wasn't sick, Ami thought, smiling. There weren't many youngsters around any livelier than she. Even before Mandy could hear at all, she never considered herself sick or abnormal. It was the rest of the world that needed adjusting; and Ami conceded she was right. With nothing else to do, her thoughts wandered and she was aware that was all she did lately: lie in bed and think without solving any of her problems.

The memory of Jeff's kiss as he left her on Saturday made her want to cry, but she couldn't summon the tears she needed. He had only admitted what she had been preaching to him was right and agreed with her, so what was her problem? She turned over on her right side, noticing that it didn't pull the stitches anymore when she did so.

I'm much better, she thought. She sat up on the side of the bed and thought surely, by midweek, she could make the trip as far as Apache Junction. Jim had already told her she was looking too healthy to lie there much longer, and they were waiting for her at the J & R.

She woke early on Monday morning, wondering why she felt uneasy, and remembered it was the day for Mandy and Jeff to go to Newark. Ami didn't want to think that she should be with them and took a washcloth and towel that had been left by her bed, walking a fairly straight line into the bathroom, and bathed. She was slow, but at least she was on her own. She smiled to herself. People never thought about the small, everyday things they did until they could no longer do them automatically, then they became big things that someone else has to do for them.

She'd make a terrible patient if she had to stay in bed long, Ami knew, and along with the knowledge that she could take care of herself now, her spirits lifted. She wished for some clothing, but all she had was jeans, and she couldn't fasten a belt around her yet.

Aside from brief stops on his way down the hall, Dr. Barry avoided her as though she had the plague. When she tried to get a release date from him, he grinned and told her he needed just a little more money before he let her go. She wondered at the speculative look he gave her when she told him she was moving to Apache Junction and taking a job with Jim Summers. She hadn't meant to confide in him, but he had a way of getting information from his patients.

"It will be a few weeks before you ride another horse, Ami," Dr. Barry told her Wednesday evening as he checked the scar where stitches had just been removed. "You can drive in a week or so, but if there's any noticeable pulling, stop and call me. We don't want the cartilage under those injured ribs to get infected." He patted her arm. "Just be careful, reasonably so. I'm sure Jeff will agree with me."

It was then that she told him she wasn't returning to Wagner's, and he appeared about to say something, a frown touching his face briefly. He looked into her eyes a moment longer before he rose and gathered up his instruments.

"I don't know Jim Summers very well, but I've met him since you've been in here. He seems very concerned about you." He hesitated. "You've made lots of friends since coming to Arizona, haven't you?"

Smiling, she agreed with him. "Yes, lots of them. It was a good move for us."

"Even after the rustling?" he asked.

Ami nodded. "That was an experience I could have done without, but it's something to write home about." She looked up and grinned. "If I had a home to write."

Dr. Barry hadn't questioned her about home, but it

was obvious that he would like to have said more. He refrained from speaking, though, and that had been the last time she'd seen him. He was conspicuous by his absence.

On Thursday morning Janie brought her a pair of jeans and a red long-sleeved knit pullover. She left off the belt. She was ready; when Dr. Barry showed up, she'd tell him she wanted out of his sterile prison.

"I need a haircut," she told Janie, pushing the heavy hair off her neck. "And a good shampoo. I never did get all the sand out of my head."

"They have a beauty salon here. Want me to make an appointment for you to have it fixed?"

She turned to look at Janie. Something in her voice was different, but she couldn't decide exactly what she meant by that observation. The idea sounded pretty good, though, and she agreed. They walked together to the elevator and took it down to the basement, where a nurse's aide directed them to the shop. She made an appointment for that afternoon.

"I can't remember the last time I went to a beauty shop to have my hair fixed," she told Janie, laughing. "I feel really pampered."

After Janie left, Ami lay down a few minutes, then it was lunchtime. She dozed for a while, then at two thirty, went down to the basement to the beauty salon to keep her appointment.

"Just plain, I guess," she told the woman uncertainly after she finished trimming her thick hair. "I don't want anything fussy."

The woman nodded and proceeded to work on her. An hour later when she had finished with her, she looked at the reflection in the three-way mirror and grinned. The shining hair had been slightly curled, just enough to give it plenty of bounce, and the natural wave kept it close to her cheek. It was a great improvement.

"Looks good enough that maybe Dr. Barry will let me go home," she said, paid the woman with money Janie had left her, and went back to her room. In three minutes she was asleep.

She was eating just after five when the phone rang. It was Jim Summers. "You sound chipper, Ami," he said. "Feeling better?"

"I'm ready to leave here, Jim, as soon as I can catch Dr. Barry."

He laughed. "I know how you feel. They seem to be good at hiding, especially if you need them." He sympathized with her and, after a few minutes, said, "I won't be down tonight, Ami, since I just got in. I'm having to work for a living now that Ralph is laid up. Probably be down tomorrow sometime."

"That's okay, Jim, I understand. It takes everyone to keep up with work on a ranch."

She knew that very well. Steve told her that the school had sent two students out to help at Wagner's, and Rio had been there over the weekend to help out. The cold weather had Hammett's joints stiff, and he hadn't been doing much more than caring for the stables.

Ami sat by the window, her lights out, the city of Tucson spread out below her like a carpet of gold. It was a pretty city as cities go, but she was ready for the desert and mountains. She had never been to Apache Junction and knew only that it was a small crossroads city on U.S. 89 between Tucson and Phoenix and that the Apache Trail was the only road going up through the giant chain of the Superstition Mountains. The J & R spread lay somewhere just north of the Junction. Thinking of Jim's ranch and her new job occupied her for a few minutes, but her mind went back to Jeff and Mandy, already in Newark. She saw Jeff's eyes, anger and disappointment mixed, as he tried to reason with her about going back to Wagner's. There was no reason for her to return, back to the place she had learned to love again—someone she wasn't destined to have. Their short engagement must have set the record, with Jeff honorable to the end, still protesting they should get married.

No one had mentioned Eileen; no one had mentioned her charges against Ami nor whether they were still being considered. "I guess I should ask what's going on," she said aloud. "It must be bad if everyone avoids talking about it." She sighed and went to bed.

"Last X rays, I promise," Dr. Barry said as he turned her several different ways to see if she was completely mobile. "After we see the results of these, we'll talk about releasing you."

"About time," Ami grumbled, allowing the nurse to adjust the skimpy smock on her that was her X-ray costume. "You could have waited till I finished my breakfast."

Dr. Barry laughed. "You're the one's been rushing me."

She was back from the X-ray room in a few minutes but had lost interest in her food. Dressing in the jeans and shirt from the day before, she brushed her teeth and smoothed her hair with her fingers. It looked the same as it did when she left the beauty salon, still unruffled after she slept on it, Her watch said it was only eight thirty.

She was at the window, staring idly at Friday-morning traffic with its impatient drivers blowing horns and darting in and out of the lanes of bumper-to-bumper cars.

"Ami?"

Surprised, she turned to see Janie and Steve in the doorway. Janie walked quickly to meet her, and Ami stared. She wore a pale rose jersey dress with black suede pumps and bag to match, a fur cape slung over her arm. Behind her, Steve grinned, a wicked glint in his eyes. He was dressed in a dark blue suit, and over one arm he carried the long gown Ami had worn to the Christmas ball at Wagner's. The gold sandals dangled from his fingers.

"I thought I was well," she said, unable to keep the astonishment out of her voice. "You look like you're going to a funeral."

"Or a wedding," Steve said, spreading the dress on her unmade bed.

Ami stiffened. "Damned if I'll go to their wedding," she blurted and stopped as Jeff entered the room. Color washed into her face, but she lifted her chin and glared at him.

His hair was freshly trimmed and smoothed where usually it was rumpled. His mouth was a straight, stern line, but his eyes searched her face with a gentle look. His suit was dark gray and he wore a white shirt with maroon figures and a matching tie. He stopped a foot in front of her ramrod-straight figure.

"Janie will help you dress," Jeff said, smiling a little. He touched her hair. "It's very becoming."

Shaking her head, she stepped backward, eyes going to Janie, seeking an explanation.

Janie looked helpless and shrugged. "I was told what to do."

Her head swiveled to Jeff. "And what was that?"

"We're getting married in fifteen minutes, so don't ask questions. Go get dressed." It was an order.

"We?" She felt stupid and her questions matched her feelings.

"You, Ami; you and I," he said, pointing his fingers for emphasis. "That's what people do when they love each other—they get married."

Before she could draw her breath, Mandy and Rio came in with Jasper behind them. Mandy was wearing her Christmas dress Ami had bought for her, and Rio wore dark brown pants and a white shirt under a light brown sport coat.

Mandy walked up to her, smiling, and said, all her words plain, "I can hear you when you say I do to my daddy."

Ami stared down at her and slowly knelt, careful of her side. "No more operations?" she asked.

"No." The little girl continued to smile at her.

"Oh, Mandy," she said and gathered her into her arms, holding her until her words suddenly sunk in. "I do?" she asked and looked at Jeff as she stood up, shaking her head. "No, Jeff, I can't."

"If you want me to dress you, I will. If you want to cooperate, Janie and Amanda will help you."

Mandy giggled and caught her hand, tugging. "Come on, Ami. Hurry."

Jeff kissed her cheek and turned, motioning the others to follow him out the door.

As the door closed behind them, Ami said, "Janie, what's going on?"

Janie was all business now. "It seems Mr. Wagner has decided he needs a wife, Mandy needs a mother, and Wagner's needs a mistress. That about sums it up."

She stood still as Janie undid her jeans, pulled the shirt over her head, and held the formal gown up to slip it on her. Mandy pulled off her moccasins and reached for the gold sandals. A few minutes later Janie said, "You'll make a beautiful bride."

"Janie, I—we can't. You don't understand." Jeff didn't yet know she could never have children, and she couldn't marry him unless she told him first.

"What's there to understand? You love him, don't you?"

After a long silence, she nodded, unable to speak.

The two of them stood there until Mandy said, "It's time for us to go outside, Ami." The urgency in the low, husky voice claimed Ami's attention, and she looked down into gray eyes identical to Jeff's.

"Mandy," she began and looked up as Jeff came to the door.

"Are you ready?" he asked.

"No, Jeff, wait."

"Not any longer, Ami," he told her, gray eyes going over her slim figure, which left some room in the dress that fit so well at Christmas. He smiled. "You're beautiful, and I love you."

She was left standing alone as Jeff held the door for Mandy and Janie to go out. The door closed behind them, and Jeff turned to walk back to her. He took her cold hands, rubbing them between both of his. "Tell me, Ami, do you still love me?"

"Still?"

"You told me you loved me a few weeks ago."

"What about Eileen? What about the rustled cattle? What—?"

His mouth covered hers an instant, shutting her up effectively. "Answer my question first. It's the most important." His voice demanded but his eyes pleaded.

"I do, Jeff. Yes, I love you, but—"

Before she could finish the statement, the door opened to admit Dr. Barry. "Sorry, Jeff, but if I'm to give the bride away, I have to do it now. I'm due in surgery in half an hour."

Behind Dr. Barry came Jasper, Steve, and Janie, Mandy and Rio, and before the door could swing shut, Jim Summers came in. Jeff kissed her mouth gently before moving away to leave Dr. Barry holding her arm.

Ami didn't hear much of the words Jasper said until he said, "Who gives Ami as Jeff's bride?" and Dr. Barry released her to Jeff. She looked up at him, wondering if she was dreaming, and admitted to herself it was better than the nightmares she had been having.

He didn't smile, and she looked back at Jasper as he spoke.

"Do you, Ami, take Jeff to be your lawful wedded husband?" he asked and waited.

She stared as though hypnotized at Jasper until Jeff squeezed her hand and she transferred her gaze to him. The silence extended, and she could hear breathing around her, and still she couldn't speak.

Jeff bent his head until his lips touched her ear and he whispered softly, "Say I do, darling."

"I do," she responded automatically, her voice barely audible.

"Do you, Jeff, take Ami as your lawful wedded wife?"

Jeff's voice was firm and immediate. "I do."

There was a movement behind her, and Ami looked down as Mandy handed something to Jeff, smiling a wide smile as she did so. Jeff's hand separated her fingers and slipped a wide silver band on the third finger of her left hand. A diamond rectangle sparkled from the center of the band.

She heard the words *let no man put asunder,* followed by other sounds, but she looked straight at Jasper as he said, "I now pronounce you man and wife. You may—"

"No" she said firmly.

Jasper's head jerked upward and beside her Jeff stiffened. "No," she repeated. "If I'm his wife, then he's my husband."

Jasper's lips twitched and he inclined his head toward her. "Let me rephrase that last statement, please." He cleared his throat. "I now pronounce you husband and wife." By now, he was grinning broadly. "You may kiss your wife, Jeff."

There was movement around her, but she didn't stir until Jeff said, "Ami?"

Dark turquoise eyes met his gaze, and she tilted her

head for him to kiss her. As his mouth touched hers, warm and gentle, realization penetrated the fog she had been moving in.

"Oh," she said, and tightened her hold on him. She was married to Jeff for better or for worse.

In the confusion of congratulations, hugs and kisses, she lost track of everything except that one fact: she was married to Jeff.

Dr. Barry spoke as he hugged Ami. "My job's finished. You're in good hands now, I'm sure."

She nodded, and as he moved away, Jim Summers was in front of her. "Well, Ami, looks like my loss is Jeff's gain, and I wish the best for both of you." He turned to extend his hand to Jeff, shaking his head as their eyes met, and he grinned and moved aside as Rio came up.

Rio didn't speak but stood smiling at her. They had been the same height when they arrived at Wagner's, but now he was two inches taller, still straight and slim. He hugged Ami, holding her a long time. When he let her go, he asked, "Is Jeff my brother-in-law or my stepfather?"

She gazed in surprise at him, then turned to look up at Jeff, who had not left her since the last words of the ceremony. She blinked.

Jeff looked back at her, then at Rio. "Jasper could straighten us out, I guess, Rio. You can be either. Whatever you decide, we'll be a rather mixed family." He winked. "As long as we belong to each other, it doesn't matter, does it?"

Rio shook his head and repeated, "As long as I belong."

Mandy was standing just back of Jeff but holding on to his hand. Now she moved to look up at him. "Is Ami my mother or my sister?"

Jeff laughed. "You can choose, too, Amanda. What would you like her to be?"

"Can I have both?" she asked, and laughter swept the room.

"She's not really big enough to be two people, do you think?" Jeff asked.

Ami stooped in front of the little girl. "Friends, first, then all the others, huh?"

Mandy nodded and walked into Ami's arms. She looked over the blond head at Jeff and said, "I'm ready to go home."

He reached to help her to her feet, taking Mandy's hand as he did so. "The others are going home; you and I aren't ready to go to Wagner's just yet."

"Where?"

His eyes darkened as they went over her tall slimness standing close to him. "Somewhere you can convince me you're mine."

A few minutes later everyone was gone, leaving Ami alone in her hospital room with Jeff. He closed the door and turned to her where she still stood in the center of the room.

He smiled. "Want me to help you dress? You might not be comfortable riding in that."

She looked down at the sparkling gown she wore, then back at Jeff. "I don't have anything but jeans."

"That's fine for now. We can shop later." Reaching around her, he unzipped the dress and let it slip from her onto the floor. She wore no bra because of the tenderness in her ribs where the tight band would fit. Small, firm breasts were exposed to his view, and he brought his hands around to caress them. She stared up into half-closed gray eyes, transfixed, as she watched his mouth move closer to hers, and sighed as their lips met. His hands slid down to curve around her hips, holding her against the hardening of his thighs.

He groaned, releasing her. "Get those jeans on. I'll be outside."

She didn't move for a long moment after he left her,

then she stepped out of the gown, reached down, and picked it up to fold it. Someone had left her a big suitcase, partly filled with jeans and shirts, the pantsuit she wore on the trip to Newark with Jeff the first time with Mandy, and the old yellow terry robe. She smiled, guessing Janie was responsible.

A few minutes later, dressed in the pantsuit she chose over jeans, with a matching print blouse Janie had found somewhere, she looked around the room. She had spent almost two weeks in the white cubicle, sometimes unaware of what went on around her. Nightmares and dreams were all mixed, and there was Jeff's stubborn insistence that she marry him, his plans carried out with the precision of a battle commander, telling her he loved her. She had to believe that he meant it, because her entire being ached with love for him.

Ami caught her breath, realizing that whatever the reason, she was now his wife, too weak—or too willing—to fight his high-handed actions. Swallowing hard, she looked toward the door as a soft knock sounded and Jeff stood in the opening, smiling at her.

"I've already checked you out." He looked her over and nodded. "How do you feel?"

"Numb."

He gave her a long look and said softly, "I'll see what I can do about that." He took two steps and, without touching her with his hands, bent to kiss her cheek, turned and picked up the bag. He looked around the room and held his arm for her to take hold, leading her to the door. Down the hall past the nurses' station, where the two who had taken care of her when she was helpless stood smiling, she pulled away from him to hug them and went back to link her arm in his as they waited for the elevator. She didn't see anything as she followed Jeff out the door across the one-way street into the parking lot.

He unlocked the door of the Mercedes, helped her in, and went to put her suitcase in the trunk. Jeff slid behind the wheel and inserted the key in the ignition before he turned to look at her. "Don't look so frightened, Ami. I won't hurt you."

She looked away from him but didn't answer, never so unsure of herself as she was at that moment. Finally, as the silence went on, she said, "Who's taking care of my job if I'm off gallivanting with the boss?"

"Rio's class gets their spring break in a week, and three of the graduate students are coming with him to work. Don't worry."

"Okay," she said and meant it. Rio would see that the others did everything the way she wanted it done.

The car slowed, and she looked back at the road as they turned into the driveway of the Cameron Hotel, one of Tucson's finest, she had read. A doorman came to Jeff's side of the car, and the two of them exchanged a few words before Jeff came around to open her door and help her out.

Another tall gray-haired man opened the heavy doors leading into the lobby of the plush foyer, and Jeff guided her across the deep red carpeting to the elevator. Its door slid silently back, and they stepped into the empty car and, a moment later, stopped without seeming to have moved at all.

A few steps down the hallway Jeff's hand on her arm stopped her in front of Room 747. "Sounds like an airplane," she whispered.

Jeff looked up questioningly from the key he was fitting into the door, and she nodded toward the number above his head. He grinned as the door swung open and he went inside, reaching for her hand. It was an elegant three-room suite, consisting of a living room almost as big as the one at Wagner's and two bedrooms and two baths. They wandered through, hand in hand, without a word until they returned to the living room.

"Is this the bridal suite?" Ami asked, walking to the window to draw the draperies, looking out of glare-proof windows into the sparkling spring day.

"The nearest thing they had to it," he told her. "The man I talked to told me they don't have many requests for bridal suites these days."

She looked over her shoulder at him. "Two bedrooms?"

"I thought perhaps you might want to sleep alone for a few days."

"Why?"

"You aren't exactly in top physical condition, Ami."

She looked back out the window and knew he was right. She was already tired and hadn't been out of bed more than five hours, but a lot had happened in that time. She wondered at the preparations that had gone into the surprise wedding, where everyone but her seemed to have been informed.

"Why did you do it?" she asked finally.

"I wanted to marry you, Ami, and you're so stubborn, I decided that to do things as they should be done, I'd take a chance on your anger later." He waited. "Are you angry?"

"No, but, Jeff, there are so many things that should have been settled before we married."

He came to stand behind her, his arm encircling her. "Later," he said. "You must be tired, and I promised Dr. Barry I would take care of you, not put you back in the hospital." He turned her around to face him. "I ordered a light lunch for us, and, afterwards, you can lie down for a while and then shop, if you think it isn't too much."

She nodded and leaned against him, her hand resting on his chest. The solid thudding of his heart beneath it sent a quiet thrill through her body, and she trembled.

Jeff felt the tremor and tilted her head to look down at her. "You are tired. Come on."

As they started back toward the center of the room, there was a quiet knock. "Room service, sir."

Jeff opened the door for the man to enter, and she watched as he moved quickly and efficiently to set up their lunch. In the center of the table he placed a bottle of champagne in a silver ice bucket. He broke the seal, poured a little of the sparkling liquid into a delicate glass, and handed it to Jeff, who smelled, tasted, and returned it to him with a nod. She watched, fascinated, as the ritual went on and the man smiled, bowed, and left with a soft word to Jeff.

"Mrs. Wagner," Jeff said, indicating the chair he held for her. She stared at him and suddenly she smiled, showing the small dimple that had been missing for a long time.

"This isn't exactly what I'm accustomed to. Nothing at all like the Best Western."

"No, it isn't," he admitted, pushing her chair nearer to the table and going to the opposite side. Carefully he filled her glass to the halfway mark, set it in front of her, and filled his the same way. He straightened, lifted the glass toward her and, as she picked hers up, he touched it.

"To you, Ami; to your rapid recovery and a long, happy life."

"With you," she added, watching his eyes narrow and the gray darken. She would have given her all to know what he was thinking as he nodded and they drank.

She grimaced. "Piña coladas are better," she said and blushed, remembering the last one she had with him at the Best Western.

"Don't let the wine steward hear you say that," Jeff warned and turned his attention to serving her a portion of the cornish hens, prepared with wild rice and other condiments she didn't recognize. It was delicious, and she found her appetite had improved since

yesterday, finishing every bit he gave her even though
it was barely noon.

She leaned back in her chair and sighed, heavy-eyed,
as she met his glance across the table. He came around
to her chair, sliding it back for her to rise, and took her
arm, leading her toward the bedroom off the master
bathroom. At the door he kissed her cheek.

"A couple of hours of sleep is what you need right
now." Not waiting for her reply, he closed the door as
he left.

She undressed and, exhausted, turned back the satin
coverlet on the bed, slid between ivory satin sheets,
rolled over on her stomach, and went to sleep. She
dreamed. She ran, trying to outdistance her pursuer,
coming to the mountain where there was no way out,
and she turned to face Eileen, standing with her blond
head lifted, the black Stetson hanging down her back.
Her laughter echoed through the blind canyon. "He'll
never marry you . . . never marry you." Ami threw up
her hands and cried out as Eileen flicked her with the
riding whip she carried.

"Ami, Ami." The voice penetrated her dream, and
she opened her eyes to see Jeff sitting on the side of
her bed, holding her arms as she fought with her
dream. She drew a shuddering breath, and he gathered
her to him, holding her until she stopped shaking.

"What's wrong?" The concern in Jeff's voice brought
her back to realization, and she looked down at her
body only half-covered by the satin sheets. She gulped
and tried to pull away, but he held on to her for a moment longer, then slowly let her lie back on the pillows.
His glance went over her exposed breasts, lingering on
the purple scar just below the left one, before he pulled
the sheet up to cover them.

"What were you dreaming of?" he asked.

Ami frowned, unable to recall what she had been
running from. "It's a dream I've had before, but I can't

remember what it was." She shivered. "I don't want to remember."

He kissed her cheek. "You will, in time, then you'll stop having the dream. Does it have anything to do with your run-in with Hank and Luke?"

"I think so."

Jeff nodded. "It's natural that it will bother you, but let's try to forget them." He stood up. "You slept about two hours. Do you feel up to shopping?"

"Yes." She smiled up at him. "Our room clerk will probably be glad to see something besides jeans in such a fancy place."

He laughed. "We'll help him if you're game." From the door he blew her a kiss and went out.

Dressed in regular jeans with a pale yellow sweater over a loose-fitting shirt, she joined him a few minutes later. As they left the building the doorman brought the car to the curb, and Jeff helped her in before he went around to the driver's side, where the doorman stood ready to close the door as Jeff slid behind the wheel.

The line shack for Camp 20 was never like this, she thought, and resolutely turned her thoughts away from Wagner's to keep her mind on shopping for a trousseau. Three hours later they piled boxes into the car and went back to the Cameron. They walked sedately across the plush lobby, took the elevator to the seventh floor, and entered the suite they had been in such a short time.

Ami dropped into a chair. "Do we have to give up this place after that shopping spree?"

She watched him through half-closed eyes as he looked down at her. "Why would we do that?"

"Didn't we spend my whole month's salary just now?"

Jeff's expression was grave. "We didn't spend any of *your* money, Ami. We spent *ours*."

"Oh." Her eyes flew open. She continued to watch him as he knelt by her, long tanned fingers holding her chin as he bent to place his mouth on hers. It started as a gentle caress that lit fires in both of them, and her lips parted, giving him access to the warm moistness inside her mouth. The length of her body was alive as he proceeded to explore with the tip of his tongue, teasing along the ridge of her teeth. She put her hands on his shoulders and sat up in the chair, responding to the urgency in his kiss. His breath came quickly as he released her lips to move over her throat to the throbbing pulse at the base where the bone curved to make a hollow. His mouth rested there until he raised his head to look down at her and stood up as a knock sounded at the door. They both stared toward the sound until he said, "Must be the results of our toil," and went to answer the knock.

Still shaken by the kiss, she barely saw the young man bring in the boxes they had purchased. When he had gone, Jeff said, "Come on and let's look." He sounded normal as though he hadn't just wrenched her heart from its mooring as he had done many times before.

He's my husband, she thought. *He's supposed to affect me that way.*

Jeff opened boxes and took out garments, placing them neatly on the bed for her to see. She shook her head. "Where will I ever wear all of that?" she asked.

"It's only five outfits, Ami," he said, picking up a pale green dress. "Try this."

She took it from him and, with an effort, refrained from looking at the price tag. It was cotton gauze with a demure Peter Pan collar, the bodice smocked in darker green and stitched onto a wide band attached to a skirt of tiny unpressed pleats.

"Do these shoes match that?" Jeff asked, holding up dark green suede pumps.

"Yes." She continued to look at him, holding the dress in front of her.

"Do you want me to leave?" he asked.

She swallowed hard but shook her head, spreading the dress on the bed, standing with her back to him as she pulled off the shirt and sweater. Kicking off her slippers, she pushed the jeans over her hips and reached for the dress, hesitating.

"I need a slip," she told him.

He handed it to her, and, a moment later, she slipped the dress over her head, turning to let him zip it for her. She sat on the edge of the bed as he put the pumps on her narrow feet.

As she stood up he moved back and smiled. "Yes." He reached to smooth her hair. "We have reservations for the dinner theater at seven thirty. That is, if you feel up to it."

"We don't even have to leave the hotel? What's playing?"

"Same Time Next Year," he said. "I'd better get changed, too. Won't be a minute." He turned and left her, and she walked into the bathroom to look at herself in the new clothing.

"Funny, you don't look like a bride," she told the pale reflection in the mirror. She wrinkled her nose. "You haven't been treated like one, either." The dress was becoming. The thick smocking and blouse effect from the gathers hid the fact that she was braless, and the long full sleeves would be warm enough without worrying about a jacket, since they weren't going outside the hotel.

Her eyes returned to her reflection. The scars from the scratches on her face were covered by well-matched makeup, which hid the shadows beneath her eyes.

There was a tint of color to her cheeks, probably still from Jeff's kiss. Going back into the bedroom, she pulled the heavy drapes to look out over the city where lights were beginning to come on. Tall palms in the courtyard seven stories below her swayed gently in the spring breeze. The door opened behind her, and Jeff came toward her with his hands outstretched. He was handsome in the gray suit he had worn for the wedding ceremony. She felt a moment of pity for Eileen that was gone the next instant as Jeff kissed her cheek and turned her around to lead her back into the living room.

"We've time for a glass of champagne they were nice enough to keep chilled for us," he said, indicating the silver bucket filled with ice, where the half-finished bottle of sparkling liquid still rested.

Jeff's hands drew her attention. They were tanned strong hands with long fingers that she had seen gently dress Mandy; hands that on her body were demanding, yet tender, that could force her attention or let her go, sometimes when she wasn't quite ready to be let go.

"Ami?" he said, handing her the glass. Her eyes went back to his face to find him watching her with a slight smile, his eyes questioning. "If you don't feel up to going to the theater, we can cancel," he said. "I just thought—"

He was putting off the inevitable confrontation over who sleeps with whom as long as he could, she surmised before she answered him. "I feel fine, and I'd like to see the play. I haven't been to one since college."

Jeff was standing in front of her and smiled as he touched her glass with his and they drank. He surveyed her slim figure and said, "The color of the dress is perfect for you." He continued to look down at her. "Amanda is right; you do have funny-colored eyes." She laughed with him.

"Tell me what Linda and Dave said about her. I haven't had a chance to ask—or was too wrapped up in what was happening to think about it."

Jeff put his glass down beside hers and nodded. "They're absolutely elated about everything and plan to write her up in the journal they publish semiannually, and they'll make sure we get a copy."

Ami stared at him, feeling emotions that were all mixed up with love and gratefulness for Mandy; and love alone for Jeff. She said slowly, "A year can make a vast difference in the outlook of things, can't it?"

"Yes," he said and stepped closer to her before he stopped, shaking his head. "We'd better go if we plan to eat before the show starts."

At that moment she would have liked to have canceled the show and walked into his arms, but he was all attention as he opened the door to let her walk out ahead of him, and they were quiet going down in the elevator and following the maître d' to their reserved table.

The look of money was everywhere as Ami glanced around at the other diners, smiling as her gaze encountered Jeff, who was watching her. As he gave their order a soft blue spotlight moved around the room to settle on a lovely dark-haired woman standing at the edge of the stage. The beginning of the band playing was hardly noticeable, subdued to blend with the woman's voice as she sang a torch song, sending chills along Ami's spine.

As the music sounds faded away Ami sighed and sat back in her chair, looking up to meet Jeff's gray eyes. She smiled. "She's very good."

"Yes, she is," he agreed. "Which reminds me of the message I'd forgotten to give you from the grange clubs waiting for you to come back. They miss you."

Their dinners arrived, and conversation wasn't necessary as they ate. Tender lobster with just the right amount of melted butter sauce claimed her complete attention. She looked up at Jeff. "Beats C rations all to pieces."

"No more C rations for you until Lily puts some weight on you," he said. "That's an order, Ami."

She met his glance, and his eyes darkened as the look held. The moment was interrupted by the waiter returning with coffee, and they finished the meal in silence.

She shook her head when he asked if she'd like a drink, and they turned to the stage as the lights were lowered and the opening scene began. The players were excellent in their parts, and she wondered how two people with simple settings could hold the attention of all the diners. They had to be good.

After a brief interlude when the action scenery changed, the next scene showed the woman enter the motel room where her partner was waiting. She was very much pregnant, causing the man to gaze at her in astonishment.

Ami, too, stared at the awkward, bulging figure the woman presented and her hands tightened in her lap against her flat stomach. Envy of the girl in the play rose inside her and she looked away. It had been a long time since she allowed herself any self-indulgence in thinking about a child of her own. She was Jeff's wife; she could share Mandy and Rio. That was enough for her, but what about her new husband? She turned her head to meet his look.

Jeff smiled and leaned toward her to whisper, "Are you getting tired?"

She smiled back at him, made a negative movement of her head, and looked back at the stage. When the lights came on, she rose as Jeff moved her chair back and followed him out of the dining room theater to the hallway into the elevator. They held hands going down the hallway, and he didn't release her hand as he inserted the key into the lock and opened the door. A soft light had been left on, and she gazed around at the luxurious furnishings in the suite they had occupied for about twelve hours. It would be a wedding day to remember, whether for the conventional reasons or not.

Jeff tugged at her hand, turning her to face him. "You'd better get some rest. Did Dr. Barry give you anything to take?"

"Yes."

Leading her to the bedroom, he let go of her hands. "Turn around and I'll unzip you."

Ami did as she as told, and Jeff kissed the back of her neck. "I'll see you in the morning," he said, and she heard the door close behind him. Closing her mind to her roving thoughts, she got water from the bathroom to swallow the small green capsule Dr. Barry gave her to take as needed, turned out the lights, and slipped between the sheets. There was no sound from the other rooms. She stretched her long legs until her side pulled a little, then she lay still.

Sleep wouldn't come and, restless, she turned, waiting for the little pill to take effect. The connecting door to Jeff's bedroom was only a blur in the dim room, but her eyes stayed on the faint outline until, without thought, she slid her feet over the edge of the bed and walked across to turn the knob. The door opened quietly, and she stood just inside Jeff's room until her eyes became accustomed to the dimness and she could make out his outline on the bed.

He sat up quickly. "Are you all right?"

"Yes." She moved slowly to his side. "May I sleep with you?"

Without a word he moved over to let her get into the bed with him. She lay on her back, her head turned slightly to look at him, still propped on his elbow to watch her.

"I thought you had something to take to help you sleep."

"I'm not very sleepy yet."

He lay back on his pillow and reached for her hand.

"Try to go to sleep, Ami. It's been a long day for you."

Her fingers tightened around his. "We're married, Jeff. Why can't you tell me you love me?"

"If we're married, you should know I love you." One hand, resting below the injured ribs, slid around her, his fingers massaging her spine.

"Tell me."

"I love you, Ami. I would never have married you otherwise. If I sometimes neglect to state that fact, always remember it's true. I've loved you for a long time, but I thought you knew without my saying so." He drew her close. "Go to sleep."

Her naked body in close contact with his had a will of its own and moved gently against him. His breath caught and he pulled away from her.

"Ami, honey, you'd better—"

Her mouth reached his, cutting off the protest, and she gasped as he responded. She was clasped tightly to him and she felt the groan go through him, his lips going from hers to her throat.

"You're making it awfully hard for me to take care of you, sweetheart," he whispered.

She pulled his face up to her pillow. "Jeff." There was no space between them now and she fitted herself into his arms. "Take care of me," she told him softly. "Love me."

He caught his breath at the demand in her voice and slowly began to kiss her, their bodies blending together as he let his fingers soothe the tenseness from her. She sighed as he released her mouth and turned her on her back, moving his hands from the slightly raised skin where the scar was, down over her hipbones to the long thighs. His kisses started at her waist, drifting over the flatness of her belly to follow his hands. She murmured satisfied sounds as his lips and fingers caressed and stroked her with tenderness that brought an unbelievable emotion cascading through her body. Her fingers lay lightly on his head as he touched her, tightening to hold him closer.

"Jeff," she whispered. "Oh." A long ecstatic shiver shook her body.

He lay back on the pillow, pulling her into his arms, his breath coming harshly from deep within his chest. She moved on top of him, keeping her legs close together down the hardness of his body.

He bit into his lip. "Honey," he sighed. It took only a moment of sensuous manipulation of their bodies, her mouth moving over his, whispering words only for him, until he gave in and his convulsive response shook them both.

"Are you convinced?" she asked.

"Of what?"

"That I'm yours?"

He laughed softly, his mouth against her hair. "Yes." Close in each other arms, they slept.

Chapter Fifteen

It was bright in the room when Ami awakened, and she lay there, trying to sort out what had happened. She was Mrs. Jeff Wagner, a fact she no longer doubted as she recalled her wedding night. Having to make the first move to get Jeff to make love to her didn't bother her; at least he didn't refuse.

Turning to look at the pillow still showing the shape of Jeff's head, she smiled, remembering his arms around her, his vibrant voice telling her he loved her. With Jeff's love to back her up, she could face anything, even Eileen's accusations. She pushed the ugly thoughts away and slid out of bed, wondering where her husband was, glancing at her watch to see that it was almost ten o'clock.

Moving to the window to push the drapes aside to look out upon a sunny world, her gaze rested on the mountains and she smiled, turning after a moment to make her way to the bathroom. The reflection of her naked body was the way it had always been except for the purplish-blue flesh surrounding the small scar where Dr. Barry had removed the bullet from Hank's gun.

"You almost had it, my girl," she said aloud and thought about Remus protecting her, possibly taking the bullet that would have been fatal to her. They were both rather beat up, a little the worse for wear, but they'd make it. She went to shower.

Wrapped in a big terry towel, she went to look at some of the clothing purchased the day before. Choosing an off-white pantsuit with tan flecks through the linen material and a beige-striped long-sleeved blouse, gathered from a front yoke, she decided it would camouflage her braless figure. Absently her fingers smoothed over the ridge of the scar on her ribs, only a little tender now.

In answer to a light knock on the door she called, "Come in."

Jeff opened the door and stood looking at her, and she realized she was anything but dressed. Dark gray eyes went over her tall figure clothed only in a towel. He asked softly, "Did you sleep well?"

He's my husband, she thought, gazing at the tall man just inside the door. Her lips parted as she continued to look at him. Without answering his question, she went to stand in front of him and lifted her hands to place them on his shoulders, standing on tiptoe to bring her face nearer to his. He bent slightly to place his mouth over hers, sending a thrill racing through her.

When he lifted his head to smile down at her, she said, "Looks like I overslept."

Jeff grinned. "I was beginning to think we could order lunch instead of breakfast. I'm starved."

"I'll only be a minute," she promised as he turned to leave her.

Jeff was standing at the window, where he had drawn the draperies, and as she went into the room he turned to watch her walk to join him. The striped blouse was tucked into the pants, which fit smoothly over her hips, and she carried the matching jacket over her arm.

He nodded approvingly, and they went downstairs to join the many others of the hotel clientele enjoying a late breakfast. A giant pendulum clock silently proclaimed that it was eleven thirty as they finished eating.

He looked across at her as she sipped a last cup of coffee. "Let's check out and take a ride up through the country. Have you ever been through the Superstition Mountains?"

Startled, she replied, "No. I was planning to look them over...." She let her voice drop.

He waited, but she didn't add anything. "You mean when you went to work for Jim Summers you thought you'd have plenty of time?"

"Yes."

Jeff leaned toward her. "Since you won't be working for him, suppose we tour the area. Do you feel up to it?"

She blushed suddenly, remembering the night in Jeff's arms. "I feel good." But she added, "I'm not tired now and the food here is not exactly like what I've been served the past couple of weeks."

He laughed. "Decidedly not." His mouth curved with tenderness as he stood up to move her chair back, and she felt her doubts dissolve.

Back in their room, they packed, leaving most of her purchases in the boxes. Jeff called to have their luggage picked up and the car brought around front, and they went down to check out. Jeff's conversation with the man at the desk was low, and she found herself wondering if he was being congratulated on his marriage. Aside from the new softness about him as he took care of getting their things together, he hadn't mentioned their wedding night, and she was curious to know if he compared her boyishly straight body to Eileen's luscious curves.

"Ready?" Jeff asked at her elbow.

Ami nodded and walked with him outside, slipping into the car seat as the doorman held the car door open for her. She concentrated on the city scenery as Jeff drove through early Saturday afternoon traffic, heading almost directly into the sun, turning north as they left the interstate just outside of Tucson, taking U.S. 89. Highway signs indicated Apache Junction was eighty miles away. The landscape was her favorite; desert surrounded by mountains; mountains giving way to desert. there was no smoke or pollution from city industry, the only blot on the view an occasional mine opening.

At Apache Junction Jeff drove slowly. "When we head north, there's very little in the way of civilization. A few ranches, Jim Summers's among them. It's strictly for scenery and searchers for the Lost Dutchman's cache of gold."

"Wonder if that's a fairy tale, too?"

"Fairy tale?" he echoed.

Ami felt the blush rise in her cheeks and kept her face turned away from him. She had been thinking that love was a fairy tale, highly improbable, and they were entering country that was filled with legends and tall stories originating in the fertile imaginations of generations long gone.

"It's unlikely that all the stories are true, isn't it?"

He laughed. "I believe them, Ami," he said. "It makes for fascinating listening, not nearly as dull as some history is."

"I suppose so," she agreed, watching the spindly cactus and piñon trees that reached to the edge of the Lost Dutchman, only one of the many peaks of the Superstition Mountain chain. She could well believe that lots of gold as well as people had been lost in the vast wilderness when their only means of transportation was walking or an old mule or burro and, when extremely lucky, a good horse. Neither of them spoke as they passed the heavy gate with the J & R Ranch sign on top of it.

They began to climb at a sharp angle, turning around curves that met them coming the opposite way. She held her breath, looking down over the side of the mountain into a blue-green lake hundreds of feet below them.

"That body of water comes from Stewart Mountain Dam," Jeff said. "There's plenty of water up through here; it just happens to be hard to reach." He pointed through a range of tall peaks to a narrow road twisting out of sight. "This is the Apache Trail, which ends at Roosevelt Dam."

A sudden sharp turn in the road brought them into an area resembling a movie set. On the right was a motel, rustic logs squatting by the side of the road. Nearby was a sign proclaiming TORTILLA FLATS: POPULATION 6.

"Six people?" she asked in astonishment.

Jeff grinned as he pulled into a parking place near the motel. "That may include the dogs."

They sat a moment looking at the blue-green scenery that dominated the wide place in the road. Fifty feet past the motel was a café with a sign that said: WELCOME, RESTAURANT AND POST OFFICE, TORTILLA FLATS. A few yards farther up the narrow street was the zoo. At least there were two monkeys, according to the sign.

Jeff got out and came around to open Ami's door, holding her arm to help her step up on the bricked sidewalk. They walked around to the side where a door stood open to the late afternoon sun.

"May I help you?" a voice asked from the dim interior.

"Yes, we have reservations. Mr. and Mrs. Jeff Wagner," He turned to look back at her where she had stopped just inside the door and held out his hand.

"Sign here, Mr. Wagner," the older woman said, indicating the registry book on the counter. She smiled at Ami. "Where you folks from?" she asked without bothering to look at what Jeff had written.

"Southeastern Arizona, near Tombstone," Jeff told her.

The woman nodded. "I'm Mrs. Sandstrom. Just let me know if you need anything."

Jeff thanked her and led Ami through another door, looking at the number on the key he held. They walked down the hall to the last room, and Jeff stopped, looking down at her. "Okay?"

Ami nodded, and Jeff pushed open the heavy wooden door to reveal a big airy room, two wide windows looking out over green terrain running into the side of the mountain that reached into an incredibly blue sky. Two queen-size beds dominated the furnishings in the room.

"More like the Best Western," Jeff said, smiling at her.

Yes, she thought, even to having two beds.

"I'll get our luggage," he said and disappeared through the door.

She walked over and sat on the edge of the bed farthest from the windows, feeling tired. Or lazy. The thin air at this elevation might be a reason, or the events of the past two days could be catching up with her. She stretched out across the bed, staring at the heavy beamed ceiling. When Jeff came in, she didn't sit up but turned her head to smile at him.

He came to stand looking down at her. "As soon as we unpack, you can take a nap."

"That's all I've done lately," she protested. "I want to see the sights."

He laughed. "I think you saw them all but, okay, we can go see the two monkeys in the zoo." He placed their luggage on the racks in the area by the bathroom and came back, taking her hand to pull her up. "Let's go sight-seeing."

Outside, they walked past the restaurant and Post Office to the wired area that took in the zoo. The medium-size monkeys swung across the bars to stand regarding the strange two-legged creatures who looked curiously back at them. In the corner were two big cages holding multicolored parrots, one of whom carried on a one-way conversation of "Halt. Who goes there?" and "They went that-a-way."

"The population listed must not include the zoo," she said, turning to take his arm as they retraced their footsteps back to the motel. The sun was dropping rapidly behind the lofty mountain the historical marker named the Mazatzal Peak. The air had become chilly.

Inside the room Jeff turned her into his arms, bending to place his mouth over hers, holding her tightly for a moment. "Go lie down for a while."

"Where are you going?" Ami asked, curious as any wife whose husband would leave her alone in a strange motel so soon after marrying her, wanting him to stay with her.

"I saw some good-looking horses down below us in a corral. You need your own."

"I do?" she asked, surprised.

"You'll be back to riding in no time, Ami. You don't expect to sit around the ranch and do nothing, do you?" He smiled back at her from the door. "I won't be long. Rest," he instructed and closed the door behind him.

Slowly she undressed, hung up the neat suit she removed, and turned back the covers on the bed she had chosen, lying down to close her eyes wearily. Jeff said he loved her, but was it just assurance he thought she needed to get through what might prove to be a nasty time if Eileen really brought rustling charges against her? In the past few hours he had shown his feelings only a little, and that was after she initiated their love-making. Sighing, she slept.

Jeff stopped to look across the line of trees that marched straight up the side of the mountains. The sweater he wore felt good in the air, where the temperature had dropped over ten degrees since their arrival. His thoughts went to the woman in the room he had just left. Ami was puzzled at his actions; she wasn't sure why he had married her, and he wasn't sure if he had convinced her the way he wished he could. He smiled. There was a lifetime ahead to show his deep love for her and he meant to use it all. After confessing to loving him, she fought against marrying him after she found out about Eileen's charges, but that was settled as far as he was concerned. Eileen's conscience was her own to come to terms with, and the rustlers had been caught, the cattle returned.

According to Jasper and Steve, all Wagner cattle had been easy to identify, using the method Ami had described, that of turning a spotlight on them as they were corraled, cutting out the ones that showed no sign of the dye solution. There were less than fifty of Eileen's among the nearly one hundred and fifty in the herd. Ron Steward had signed a paper releasing Wagner's of any further responsibility for the cattle. Jeff grinned to himself, wondering how much persuasion Jasper and Steve used to get his signature. One look at Jasper when he was angry, which wasn't often, was enough to convince most people that they should follow the right course. Steve was not one to be crossed, either, as he recalled, thinking of a run-in with enemy ground forces once in Vietnam.

His thoughts returned to Ami as he strolled down the steep hillside toward the corral he had seen from the highway. He leaned on the cedar fence and watched the half dozen horses grazing. Ami rode any of the horses in the corral when she needed one, but he wanted something special for her. One, in particular, interested him as he watched the playful nudgings of the younger animals. A dark gray filly, perhaps a year old, with a white blaze down her face, stood with head lifted toward the mountains. The sleek neck was strong and she

assumed a proud stance that kept his attention, somehow reminding him of Ami, a no-nonsense independent carriage much in evidence.

"Pretty, ain't she?"

Jeff turned to see a grizzled old-timer, gnarled hands
hitched into faded, worn jeans. He nodded. "She's a
beauty. Who does she belong to?"

The old man laughed. "Since I'm about all there is
here," he said, "guess she's mine."

"Is she for sale?"

The old man looked at him with interest. "Well,
now," he said, "anybody interested in Gray Lady
would have to have a bit of money."

"How big a bit?"

The old man thought a moment, spit a well-aimed
stream of tobacco juice into a weed patch. "I been
known to bargain."

Jeff looked back at the horse, the strong neck now
arched as she bent to resume grazing. He studied the
lines of her back and hind legs and turned to grin at the
old man.

"Let's talk."

Ami opened her eyes to stare at the same log beams
she had been looking at when sleep overtook her. She
turned her head as the door to the room opened quietly
and Jeff came in.

She stretched and smiled at him. "Did you find the
horses?"

He nodded, his eyes going over the outline of her
body beneath the covers. He sat down on the edge of the
bed as Ami moved over to give him room, and touched
her cheek, pushing the thick hair away from her face,
and bent to kiss her. His lips, warm and light on hers,
parted to allow his teeth to graze her chin as he nuzzled
against her. He raised his head, half-closed eyes taking in
her sleep-flushed face and whispered, "Ami."

Desire for him enveloped her, and she wished for words to express her feelings for him, feelings that made her tremble. Her hands went to his face, cupping it, pulling him down to her. Lips parted, the tip of her tongue entered his mouth for an instant and was withdrawn as he drew a sharp breath.

Jeff started to pull away, then groaned, bringing her up into his arms, holding her close. He pushed her back on the pillow and slowly bent to her, taking her lips and caressing them with his own, letting the tip of his tongue intrude inside her mouth, withdrawing it to trail kisses over her chin to her throat, down into the cleft between the small, firm mounds. He lay beside her on top of the covers, his arm across her.

"Take off your clothes," she said suddenly.

His arm tightened and he laughed softly. "Brazen." But he did as he was told, turning the covers back to get into bed beside her.

"I want you, Ami," he said and held her without talking for a long time. He stirred. "I came so close to losing you and I can't bear having anything hurt you." He caressed the length of her body, one hand returning to explore the scar on her side. "Does it hurt?"

"No."

"Isn't it sore?"

"Tender, a little."

His hand moved from the scar across her flat stomach, up over the small breasts. "Did Dr. Barry give you any special dos and dont's?"

"He told me not to drive the truck or ride a horse for a while."

"What about sex?" Jeff's question was against her mouth. "I mean my having you completely?"

"It wasn't mentioned." Ami moved her body closer to him, her arm across his shoulder.

"Will you stop me if I hurt you?"

"No." Her lips parted against his.

"Sweetheart." Jeff held her away, but she pulled him back to her, pushing her thigh between his legs, her hand behind his head to keep his mouth on hers. Her back arched and there was no way he could withstand the pulsing desire filling them both, and he took her slowly, holding back until she cried out and he let go as the sweetness drained them both.

"Are you all right?" he asked.

"Yes." she whispered. "Jeff?"

"Hmmm?"

"I'm not numb anymore." Ami put her head back on the pillow to look at him. "Kiss me again."

He shook his head. "If I do—"

He kissed her as her hands inventoried his body from the thick chest hair across the tautness of his stomach, drifting downward slowly. He groaned without releasing her mouth, murmuring against her lips, and his hands moved down to fit behind her hips, pulling her up until he nestled inside her thighs. With gentle strokes he took possession of her, looking into wide-open turquoise depths. He whispered, "I love you, darling," as they floated in a never-never world.

Holding tightly, she cherished the sound of those words. With her face still against his throat, she said, "Jeff, we have to talk."

"All right," he agreed.

She waited, but he didn't say any more. "There's something I have to tell you, something I should have told you before you married me." She waited again. "Jeff?"

He continued to hold her close. "Does it have anything to do with your not being able to have children?"

Her body jerked and she moved her head swiftly back, eyes almost black as she stared at him in the room, which was growing dark. "How—how did you know?"

"While you were unconscious, you talked quite a bit," he told her. "Is it so important to you to be able to have a baby?"

Ami stared at him. "I always thought so." She bit her lip. "That's why Tim divorced me."

"I can't believe a man would give you up for that reason. Didn't you think about adoption?"

"Tim didn't want someone else's children; he wanted his own flesh and blood."

His long fingers caressed her cheek. "I understand that it hurts not to be able to have your own baby, Ami, but we have Amanda and Rio, and if you want more, I'm sure we can adopt a couple." His voice was quietly reassuring as he went on. "The fact that you can't get pregnant doesn't alter my feelings for you, if you're concerned about that." She lay still in his arms, their hearts beating in unison. Her heart was filled to the bursting point with love for the man who held her, overflowing when he declared his love for her.

"You really don't mind?" she asked after a long time.

"It won't matter to me as soon as you accept it, Ami."

"I love you, Jeff."

He gathered her to him for long moments, their bodies as close as they could get to each other. Slowly his hand moved over the small mound of her breast, his thumb gently massaging the brown tip until it swelled. He raised himself up on his elbow and pushed her over on her back, lowering his face until he could close his mouth over her throbbing breast. Her breathing became more rapid as he trailed a row of kisses across her to the other tip waiting for him. Their bodies moved together in a slow, sensuous rhythm, and as she fitted herself to him, he came back to kiss her, his tongue thrusting inside her mouth, demanding her complete surrender. She gave it gladly, feeling liquid fire singing through her veins, gasping as their bodies met fiercely, then were still.

As they drew near Wagner's, Ami tensed, wondering what awaited her as the new mistress of the ranch. A big hand closed over hers and she turned to look at Jeff. He had told her the rustling episode was finished as far as she was concerned, and any further negotiations or investigations would be handled by Jasper.

"Nervous?" he asked, and she nodded. He smiled but said no more. He drove past the airstrip and, a few moments later, turned into the lane leading to the big house. She stared as they pulled into the yard. Strung between the two big cottonwoods was a banner with bright red letters that read: WELCOME HOME, AMI AND JEFF.

"We're home, darling," Jeff said softly beside her.

Her eyes left the banner to swing toward him. "I believe in fairy tales," she said and leaned over for his kiss.

Chapter Sixteen

She stood behind the shack at Camp 20, where the drama of a few months ago had taken place and, even now, seemed somewhat unreal. Filling in where she was needed as veterinarian on the huge ranch, Ami didn't spend much time in the line camps anymore, leaving most of the work up to the graduate students from the college who needed on-the-job training as veterinarians. In a few years Rio would take over full-time, but in the meantime she and Hammett shared a lot of the duties around the home corral and less of the ones requiring extended stays from the big house. Jeff frowned on her being away from him even a few days.

She smiled, thinking of her husband, who had long since convinced her that even though he wasn't much on voicing his love for her, he certainly could show her in other ways. A soft whinny called her attention to the beautiful horse a few feet from her, the young filly Jeff had bargained for from the old mountain man in Tortilla Flats when they were on their honeymoon. The strong neck arched as she lifted her head into the wind blowing from the southeast, and Ami turned as she heard the sound of a motor.

It was Jeff in the Bronco. He came up to her, smiling. "Okay, lady, time to return to the home corral. You've been gone too long."

She laughed, walking into his arms. "One night.

What are you going to do when you go to that auction in Abilene?"

"Take you with me," he said, kissing her uplifted mouth.

She shook her head. "Mandy has a checkup coming."

"Mandy can do without her checkup easier than I can do without you." His arm tightened around her. "We'll take her in earlier and be back before the auction."

Ami leaned closer to his hard body. "Jeff, does it ever occur to you how much we have to be thankful for?"

"Every day," he said, turning to lead her toward the shack.

Ami matched her steps to his, musing briefly on the recent past events: Eileen's and Ron's confession to their part in the fake rustling that turned out to be real; the sizzling editorial in the *Tombstone Gazette,* condemning them; the extended legal entanglements worked out between Jasper and the state. It had ruined the friendship between the Wagners and McKanes, bringing a tight look of disappointment to Jeff when the subject came up. Jeff tried to take some of the blame for what happened on himself, but Ami didn't agree with that at all; however, she made no comment, recognizing the torment he went through because of the situation.

I won all the way around, she thought, smiling up at Jeff as he pushed the door to the shack open. Jeff was hers as well as the spunky little Mandy, who would be starting to attend a regular school in the fall. Mandy accepted Ami as naturally as though she had expected this to happen, never showing any jealousy of Ami's relationship with Jeff. As soon as Rio established the fact that he belonged in the family, his affection embraced Jeff and Mandy fully.

The interior of the shack was almost dark, but Jeff made no attempt to light the oil lamp. He pulled Ami close, brushing his lips over her face, lingering at her ear to whisper, "I miss you so much, Ami." He moved to her mouth, making soft kisses across it, and moaned.

He drew her with him to the bunk and they lay down, close together of necessity, on the narrow bed.

"I hate to be impatient, but it's been a long time," Jeff whispered.

"Mmmm," she acknowledged, searching for and finding his mouth as their hands busied themselves discarding clothing. His quickening breath matched hers as their bodies came together, the roughness of his hairy chest against her small breasts creating a fiery tumult through them.

For a moment his fingers touched the nearly-forgotten scar beneath her ribs, going downward to her waist, over her hip to separate her thighs.

"Ami, oh, Ami." He murmured her name over and over as he claimed the body eagerly surrendering to his desires. Love for each other swept them away, wiping out the world and its problems.

"I love you." The words came simultaneously from them, and Ami knew her fairy tale was no longer a tale, but true in every sense of the word.

LaVYRLE SPENCER
SWEET MEMORIES

a special woman … a special love …
a special story

Sweet Memories is the poignant tale of Theresa
Brubaker and Brian Scanlon, separated by Brian's
Air Force officer training, but united in spirit by
their burning love.

Alone and unsure, Theresa decides on a traumatic
surgical operation that proves devastating for both
her and Brian, a proud sensitive man whose feelings
of betrayal run deep. Through the tears and pain,
Theresa emerges from her inhibitions a passionate,
self-confident woman ready to express her love.